THE URBANA FREE LIBRARY
W9-BCL-446

ALSO BY
KAREN E. QUINONES MILLER

Satin Doll

I'm Telling

Using What You Got

Ida B.

A NOVEL

Karen E. Quinones Miller

SIMON & SCHUSTER
New York London Toronto Sydney

8-07

SIMON & SCHUSTER
Rockefeller Center
1230 Avenue of the Americas
New York, NY 10020

This book is a work of fiction. Names, characters, places, and incidents either are products of the author's imagination or are used fictitiously. Any resemblance to actual events or locales or persons, living or dead, is entirely coincidental.

Designed by Dana Sloan

Manufactured in the United States of America

ISBN 0-7432-6001-5

Maferefun Olodumare
Maferefun Oshun
Maferefun bobo Orisha

I lovingly dedicate this book to the family

ACKNOWLEDGMENTS

I need to start out by thanking the members of the Evening Star Writers Group in Philadelphia—Jenice Armstrong, Fiona Maughn, Theresa Brunson, Phyllis Lanser, Bahiya Cabral-Johnson, and Brenda Thomas. Without all of you I'd never have gotten this book done. I feel truly fortunate to belong to the best writing group in the country.

My family was also extremely supportive of me during the writing of *Ida B*. Especially my brother Joseph, who has always been my personal Rock of Gibraltar. Thanks, Joe T.!

Liza Dawson of Liza Dawson Associates in New York is the best damn agent a woman could have. Thanks for everything, Liza.

And Denise Roy, my editor at Simon & Schuster, well, what can I say. Thanks for your support, patience, and advice. It's such a pleasure working with you.

There are so many people who have supported me, and I'm sure I'm going to blank out on a couple of names, but let me at least mention Gloria Truss, Al Hunter Jr., Hana and Hassan Sabree, Lorraine Ballard-Morrill, Sherlane Freeman, Daaimah S. Poole, Helen Blue, Bobbi Booker, Belinda Cunningham, Estelle Cunningham, Deanna

Corbett, Harold King, Cheryl Wadlington, Adrian Thomas, Renee Thomas. I want to thank you all for believing in me.

And I'd also like to give thanks to the members of the Black United Front Formation Committee and the Black Political Study Group for Political Change for reminding me about the wonders of collective life.

Big thanks to the book clubs that have supported me and other African-American authors. Eye of Ra, For Da Sistas United Sisters, Sisters Uptown Book Club, Circle of Sisters, RAWSISTAZ Journey's End, Diva's Den, Escape Book Club, African Jewels, Sistahs On The Reading Edge, Pure Essence: Shades of Color, Sistah Time Book Club, 4 The Love of Books Book Club, Black Novel Book Club, EDM Book Club, Circle of Friends Book Club, Sisters Are Reading Book Club, Page Turners Book Club, Sistahs Book Club—you are all so wonderful and so appreciated by me.

I have to thank the bookstore owners who have been so sweet, encouraging, and supportive. Andre and Kim Kelton of Our Story, Emma Rodgers of Black Images Bazaar, Janifa Wilson of Sisters Uptown, Lloyd Hart of The Black Library, Trust Graham of Nubian Heritage, Larry Cunningham of Culture Plus, Frances Utsey of Cultural Connections, Malita McPherson of Heritage Books, Adline Clark of Black Classics Books and Gifts, Haneef and Haneefa of Haneef's Book Store, Felicia Winton of Books For Thought, Nia Damali of Medu Bookstore, Michele Lewis of the Afro-American Book Stop, Brother Simba of Karibu, Robin Green-Carey of Simbanye Book Store, Betty Liguorius of Liguorious Books, and Scott Wyth of Reprint Books.

I've met so many other authors who have been very supportive and loving, I'm glad to call you colleagues and friends, Especially Gloria Mallette, Mary Morrison, Eric Pete, Daaimah S. Poole, Brenda Thomas, and Zane. Thanks, guys!

And last, but certainly not least, I want to thank my daughter, Camille, who will always be my inspiration.

PROLOGUE

Little Brenda Ann Carver watched as her uncles carried her mattress into the brand-new building that she had watched being built from her old bedroom window just five blocks away. She looked around quickly to see if anyone would notice the yellow stains on the mattress and start calling her a "pee-pee baby" the way her cousins always did when they had to share her bed.

There were plenty of people around, excited strangers who were too busy carrying, pushing, and tugging at their own beat-up furniture to notice anyone else's. It looked to her like there were a lot of families moving into the new building that her mother called their new mansion in the sky. The building even had a name. Not like her old beat-up building a couple of blocks away. Everyone just called it 135 because that was the address, 135 East 128th Street. But this building was named Ida something. She couldn't remember exactly what. Ida B. something.

She tilted her head and put her hand over her eyes to block out the sun as she tried to count the rows of windows, but gave up when she kept losing her place. She was glad the new building had two elevators; because that way if one broke down she wouldn't have to walk up all those stairs. She was used to taking the stairs in 135 which didn't have an elevator, and it wasn't so bad because there were only five floors. But she didn't think she'd be able to walk all the way up to the tenth floor to the new apartment, and her mother kept telling her that now that she was four years old she was too big to be carried.

"Girl, if you're not going to help, at least get the hell out of the way," a rough voice behind her said.

She turned to look at her Uncle Rueben who was mopping sweat from his head with a dingy white handkerchief as he leaned on the U-Haul truck. "I wanted to help, but Mommy said no."

"That's because she spoils you, you little brat." Uncle Rueben said with a snort. "I ain't never seen a kid spoiled as you."

Brenda squinted her eyes at her uncle. "I'm not spoiled, and there's no such word as ain't!" She stamped her foot at him, but realized she'd gone to far when he snarled up his lip and looked like he was going to grab for her.

"Mommy!"

"Rueben, leave that child alone. Don't worry about what she's doing, get your ass in gear and help Victor bring up my couch." Brenda smiled at the sound of her mother's voice, but her uncle just made a face.

"I don't know why you gotta bring all this old junk anyway. You got a new apartment you shoulda got yourself some new furniture and let the store deliver it, 'steada making me break my damn back," he grumbled as he straightened himself up.

"Yeah, and you should pay for the new furniture," her mother shot back. "Now hurry up and get moving or you ain't getting none of the fried chicken and beer."

"Oh, I'ma get me some grub, you better believe that," Rueben said. "You ain't paying me, you damn well better feed me. And them beers better be cold."

"You okay, Sweets?" her mother patted her on the head. "You're sure you don't wanna go upstairs and wait in the apartment while we finish moving?"

Brenda shook her head from side to side, causing the large brightly colored knockers on the ends of her thick pigtails to clack noisily against each other. "No, Ma. I wanna stay down here so I can see everything that's going on. I'll stay outta the way. I promise."

Her mother shrugged her shoulders and picked up a beige lamp with one hand, and the lamp shade with the other. "Okay. Make sure you stay in front of the building where the security guard will see you."

Brenda nodded, then glanced through the glass doors of the lobby as her mother walked past. Just as she thought, the uniformed security guard was still busy trying to talk to a teenage girl wearing a pair of purple short shorts cut so high they showed the bottom of her butt cheeks.

She turned and looked around. Sure enough the little girl she had noticed earlier was sitting against the black iron fence that surrounded the small courtyard in front of the building, coloring in a Cinderella coloring book. Brenda took a good look at her now, wondering if the girl would consider sharing the crayons and the book. The girl, who was dressed in a yellow and white gingham sundress, seemed about Brenda's own age. Her stringy black hair hung limply down her back.

"Whatchoo looking at?" The girl looked up and squinted her eyes in her direction, obviously having felt Brenda's stare.

"Nothing."

"Yes you were. You looking at me," the girl said in a heavy Spanish accent.

"Okay." Brenda shrugged. Her nonchalant attitude seemed to puzzle the girl.

"Well," the little girl took her hand and flipped her hair back over her shoulder, "don't look at me anymore."

"Okay." Brenda nodded. She watched a few minutes, before speaking again.

"So what you coloring?"

"A fairy godmother," the girl said without looking up.

Brenda stepped a little closer to get a better look at the coloring book. "Why you making her dress yellow?"

" 'Cause I like yellow."

Brenda cocked her head and studied the girl again. "But aren't you Puerto Rican?"

The girl looked up at Brenda suspiciously. "Yeah. So?"

"So my uncle says Puerto Ricans like red," Brenda said simply.

The girl wrinkled her nose and glared at Brenda. "No they don't."

The girls fell silent again for a few minutes, as the Puerto Rican girl returned her attention to her coloring book. A few minutes more passed as Brenda shifted from one foot to another wondering what she should say to get the girl to talk again. "Well, do you like red?" she timidly asked.

"Yeah."

"And you're Puerto Rican, right?"

"I already told you I was."

"Well, then my uncle is right, right?"

"But I like other colors, too!" the girl protested. "I like blue and green and yellow."

"You like blue? I like blue," Brenda said excitedly.

"You do?" the girl said just as excitedly.

"Yeah!"

"You wanna go draw pictures in my new hallway?"

"Where's your new hallway?"

"In my new building," the girl pointed to the building Brenda's furniture had just disappeared into.

"That's my new building, too!" Brenda started jumping up and down clapping her hands.

"Mine too!" The girl stood up and started clapping along with her.

"Mine too!" Brenda repeated.

"What's your name?" the girl asked.

"Brenda. What's yours?"

"Rosa."

"What floor are you moving on?" Brenda asked.

"Twelve."

"I'm moving on ten!"

"Oh, good!" Rosa started jumping up and down again. "Let's go draw pictures on eleven."

"Okay," Brenda said as they skipped to the building. "I know how to write my name."

"Me too," Rosa said. "Let's write our name on the wall. You do yours with the red crayon and I'll do mine with the blue."

"Okay. Since I got red I'll pretend I'm Puerto Rican." Brenda giggled.

"Hey! You forgot your things!"

Brenda and Rosa turned around to see a husky little boy with cornrowed hair holding the coloring book and the stray crayons they had left on the sidewalk.

"Don't be trying to steal my stuff!" Rosa ran over and snatched the coloring book from the bewildered boy's hand.

"I wasn't stealing it. I was giving it to you," he stammered.

"Yes, you were," Rosa spat. " 'Cause you're a boy. And boys lie and steal."

"Sharif," a voice called out behind them. "Come carry these pillows for your grandma."

The boy took another look at Brenda and Rosa, then hurried off toward the gray-haired woman.

"Why you being so mean?" Brenda cupped her hand over Rosa's ear and whispered to her new best friend, even though no one was in hearing distance.

"Because he's a boy," Rosa whispered back. "And we don't like boys."

"We don't?"

"No, we don't," Rosa said forcefully.

"Okay," Brenda shrugged as they entered the building. "But he acted like he was nice."

"He was just pretending. My mama says that boys pretend to be nice so they can kiss you and make you have a baby," Rosa said emphatically. "So you gotta remember. We don't like boys."

"We don't like boys," Brenda nodded.

"And especially that boy." Rosa pointed in the stocky boy's direction.

"Okay," Brenda agreed. She looked back and saw the boy looking longingly in their direction. *He looks he could be a good friend*, she thought. *Too bad he's a boy*.

1

Dear Brenda,

How you doing, Kiddo? Sorry this letter is handwritten, but I couldn't get to the legal library to use the word processor. They've got us on lockdown again because some idiot gangsta wannabe in here shanked some white dude. The fucked up thing is he ain't even know the guy. He just did it to get some respect. Little punk. He's going to get respect all right. Soon as the guards let us all out of our cells he's going to get his ass kicked for getting us all locked up like this over some stupid shit. But don't worry, Kiddo, I'm not even thinking about getting involved in that shit. I'm a two-digit midget. Only thirty-five days and I'm out of this hell hole.

I got your letter, and I miss hearing your voice too, Kiddo. But I'm not going to make any more collect calls to you. It hurt my heart when your telephone got turned off a couple of months ago. A father is supposed to help his kids, not hurt them.

It's funny, but the closer I am to getting out, the more I reflect about what a lousy father I was to you. The feds have kept me away for twenty-five years, but I wasn't really part of your life even before they threw me in here. I didn't understand what it meant to be a father. What a gift from God children are, and how they need love and nurturing to make them whole. I've got a lot of making up to do. To you and to my grandkids. How's

Bootsy doing in summer school? Tell him he'd better get his act together, because Granddad is coming home and I'm going to keep my foot on his neck. Only twelve years old and he thinks he's a man. Harlem will do that to a boy, and don't I know it.

I'm going to sign off now because they're getting ready to collect the mail and I want to get this letter out to you today. Give the kids a hug from their old granddad, and tell your crazy ass mother I said hello. And let her know I'm going to kick her ass for letting you have all those kids. (Just kidding!)

I love you, Kiddo, and I look forward to being with you and the kids.

Love, Dad

P. S. Write me back real soon!

Brenda stood by the long triple row of steel gray mailboxes in the lobby of the Ida B. Wells-Barnett Tower, reading the letter before carefully refolding it, and replacing it in the envelope. She closed her eyes as she slowly moved her fingers over the return address: Jamison Edwards, U. S. Penitentiary, 1300 Metropolitan, Leavenworth, KS 66048. She sighed, and dismally shook her head. She knew his image from photographs she had seen, but as much as she wanted to, she could not actually remember the father she'd not seen since she was two years old. *The man who had started writing her only three years before to say that he wanted to reclaim the daughter he ignored while he was free.*

"Ooh, that's good. I'd better write that down," she said out loud as she started shuffling in her pocketbook and pulled out a pen and notepad. "The man who had started writing her only three years before to say that he wanted to reclaim the daughter he ignored while he was free." She looked at the words with a satisfied smile. *Oh, yeah. That's really deep.*

"Damn, it's not even ten o'clock and it's already hot as hell out there."

Brenda looked up to see a hefty chocolate skinned, middle-aged woman with a slightly skewed honey-blond wig enter the lobby of the Ida B. She was pulling a shopping cart piled high with white plastic bags filled with groceries with one hand, and wiping sweat off her forehead with the palm of the other.

"How are you doing, Miss Jackie?" Brenda asked as she slipped the envelope and notepad into her pocketbook.

"Girl, I ain't doing so good. I think I'm having heart palpitations again. I know I gotta bad heart, even though the doctors say there ain't nothing wrong with it. But what do they know." The woman started patting her heaving, but very deeply sagging, bosom as she leaned heavily against the yellow concrete walls of the building lobby.

"And you know my sugar's been acting up lately. I gotta talk to my doctor today 'cause I think he needs to put me back on insulin. Never should have taken me off, if you ask me. I told my daughter if I die she should sue that Asian bastard. They don't give a shit about black folks, you know. And I was feeling light-headed yesterday, so I think my blood pressure going up again. I'd be lucky if I don't die of a stroke like Mrs. Johnson did last week. I didn't see you at the funeral."

"I wasn't able to go because . . ." Brenda started.

"Child, I don't blame you. Ain't nobody here in Ida B. liked that mean old woman, anyway. Always calling the police on someone," Miss Jackie cut her off. "I wouldn't go myself if she weren't a member of my church."

"Well, I actually liked her, but—"

"Oh, please, you don't have to pretend for me. You know she tried to get my Ronald locked up, talking about he's the one what started that fire in the second-floor staircase a while back. I know he ain't do it."

Brenda winced at Miss Jackie's use of the word "what" in place of "that." She was a stickler for English herself, but there was no sense in trying to correct the woman.

"I raised my son better than that. She probably did it herself, just to cause some trouble," Miss Jackie started fanning herself with her hand. "I don't want to speak ill of the dead, but ain't no use lying either, if you ask me. But girl, you shoulda went to that funeral and seen the way her grandchildren acted out. I guess you heard about it, huh?"

"Well, no. But—"

"Mmm, mmm, mmm, let me tell you. You know that high-yaller one what moved up to Mount Vernon with that big-time drug dealer? You know, the one what thinks she's so cute. Well, she was up at the funeral wearing a black dress what was so short it was just sinful. Hmmph! Sinful, I say."

"Well, Miss Jackie, I've gotta go, so—"

"And then she had the nerve to be up in that church, crying and carrying on talking about how much she loved her grandmother," Miss Jackie continued, causing Brenda to utter an involuntary, but very audible, sigh which she ignored. "And then she threw herself on the casket and everybody could see her black lace bikini underwear. Oh, child, it was scandalous. If Mrs. Johnson wasn't already dead she would have died of shame. Them grandkids worried that poor woman so much they probably the ones what really killed her. You know that her youngest grandson is locked up for killing somebody up in the Bronx. And they wouldn't even let him come out to go to his own grandmother's funeral. Ain't that something?"

"Miss Jackie—"

"He never was no good, though, if you ask me. And then with that other grandson of hers, Sharif, liking men like that. And you know what the Good Book says about homosexuals . . ."

"Miss Jackie, I've really got to run," Brenda said with a note of finality.

"Oh, child, you go 'head. Don't let me hold you." Miss Jackie straightened herself up and grabbed the handle of her shopping cart. "I've got to go upstairs and put these groceries away. Where you going anyway, all dressed up wearing that nice suit? Peach really looks nice on you, Brenda. Brings out the highlights in your complexion. Not all girls dark as you got highlights, but you do. I be noticing things like that, you know. And I like them shoes. You looking real spiffy. What, you going out on a job interview or something? But I don't know if you should be wearing your hair like that. What they call it? Twists? Oh, don't get me wrong, I like them all right. They suit you. But, you know, a lot of white folks ain't gonna hire someone what looks like they might be some kind of radical or something."

"Hey, *chica*! How you doing, Miss Jackie?"

Brenda gave a sigh of relief as a thin but shapely young Puerto Rican woman—wearing blue flip-flops, rhinestone studded jeans, and a red halter top that barely covered her ample breasts—walked up and gave her a gentle shove on the shoulder.

"Girl, Rosa, I'm standing here having heart palpitations—" Miss Jackie started.

"Yeah, Miss Jackie, that's nice." Rosa gave the woman a quick nod, then turned her back on her to address Brenda. "Did the mailman get here yet?"

"Yeah. He's getting here earlier and earlier. I came downstairs at nine-thirty and he'd already been and gone," Brenda said as she gave the younger woman a return shove.

"Uh huh," Miss Jackie nodded. "He sure is been getting here early these days. I think it's 'cause they moved up Ida B. on his route so it's his first stop, and that way when they close the building next year the rest of his route isn't affected too much. Uh huh. That's just what I think. Ain't that something about them closing the Ida B.?"

"Yeah. That's really something, Miss Jackie," Rosa said absentmindedly.

"Those are just rumors about them closing the Ida B., Miss Jackie. Nobody's received any notices yet," Brenda said. "Come on, Rosa. Hurry up and grab your mail so you can walk me to the bus stop."

"You crazy? I ain't going out in that heat," Rosa said as she opened her mailbox and pulled out a bunch of envelopes. "Shit, ain't nothing here but bills."

"I know what you mean, Rosa, not wanting to go out in this heat," Miss Jackie said. "I was just telling Brenda it's so hot out there that—"

"Yeah, Miss Jackie, that's nice." Rosa grabbed Brenda's arm and started pulling her toward the door. "Okay, I'ma walk you, 'cause I got something to tell you anyway. Girl, I got the serious hook-up. One of my cousins started working at The Gap, and you know the gift cards they have now? Well, you give her three hundred dollars and she can hook you up with a seven hundred card. Is that the shit or what?"

"Damn, that'll come in handy for the kids' back-to-school shopping," Brenda nodded.

"I'm telling you, *chica*. But you can't wait until September and shit. You got to get the card now, because my cousin don't never stay at no job too long. You can use the card later, but I'm telling you, you'd better get that shit now while the getting's good. I'm going to get a card and do some my shopping for Eddie, even though my mother's not bringing him back from Puerto Rico for another two months. But I'm gonna get them one size big in case he does he some growing."

"Yeah, I hear that, girl. Hey, Sharif." Brenda said as a tall muscle-bound man with smooth almond skin and shoulder-length dreadlocks pulled back into a ponytail walked in the door as she and Rosa were heading out.

"Hey, hey," he answered with a broad smile that showed a gleaming set of white teeth any movie star would have died to possess.

"Ooh, give me my sugar." Rosa popped up on her tiptoes, and the man obediently bent down and gave her a quick peck on her lips.

"Uh huh. She's kissing you so you know she wants something, right?" Brenda laughed as Rosa punched her in the arm.

"Where are you two heading?" Sharif asked.

"Aw, man, Sharif, I've got a face-to-face meeting over at the welfare office," Brenda sighed, her shoulders suddenly sagging.

"Hmph. I feel for you," Sharif gave her a reassuring hug.

"I'm just walking her to the bus stop," Rosa said. "You gonna be around later? I gotta talk to you about something."

Sharif grinned. "Yeah, all right, Rosa. But I know you only want some—"

"Oh, Sharif. How you doing, baby?" Miss Jackie called out before he could finish. "Come help me with these groceries."

"No problem, Miss Jackie," Sharif said as he moved toward the woman. "Just knock on my door when you get back," he told Rosa over his shoulder.

"Thank you so much, Sharif baby," Brenda heard Miss Jackie say as she walked out the lobby door. "I'm so sorry about your grandmother. She was the salt of the earth. But God always takes the good first."

"Miss Jackie's such a hypocrite," Brenda said as she and Rosa stepped outside. "I think I'm going to make her a character in my book."

"That book you've been working on for the last ten years and ain't started writing yet," Rosa said as she put her hand above her eyes to block out the sun.

"I think I'm about ready, actually," Brenda said lightly. "I was going over all the notes in my boxes—"

"How many shoe boxes you got filled with notes? Ten?" Rosa interrupted.

"Fourteen. But I think I'm about ready to start writing." Brenda pulled Rosa by the hand and started walking toward the bus stop. "I just need to figure out what the book is about."

Brenda closed the book she'd been reading and looked at her watch. One-thirty. She'd been sitting on the hard plastic dirty orange chair in the welfare office for three hours waiting to speak to her caseworker. She knew her mother was probably having a fit, since she'd promised to pick up the kids before noon. She'd tried three times to call and let her know she was running late, but the line was continually busy. Her mother's call waiting and other optional features had been cut off because she was, once again, late paying the bill. *Thank God Mommy finally got registered with the foster care agency so she can start making some money to pay off some bills*, Brenda thought. *'Cause the little bit of money she gets from just baby-sitting sure isn't making it.*

The waiting room was crowded with other women like her, pissed at having to wait so long, and trying to find some way to pass the time. A woman in the row ahead of her was eating ketchup-soaked french fries, and gossiping on her cell phone about some woman stepping out with some other woman's man, and what the woman was going to do if she found out. The conjectured description wasn't pretty. Another woman, wearing headphones, was bopping her head to a song coming from a blue portable CD player which had transparent tape holding its batteries in place. Little children were running around, innocently playing tag and violently bumping into the chairs, much to Brenda's annoyance. And the woman seated next to her seemed to have drenched herself with Chloë perfume, causing Brenda's head to throb and her nose to run.

She sighed and bowed her head. This wasn't the life she'd expected, waiting for hours in hot, dirty welfare offices, only to be humiliated by smug caseworkers who acted like it was their own money they were giving away. And who looked down on her for having no job and four children, as if that was all she'd ever wanted to be—a welfare mother. They didn't care that she had dreams. She'd been planning on graduating high school with honors, being drafted by all the Ivy League colleges, and going on to become a famous author. But all that changed when she became pregnant at thirteen. The lines of the Langston Hughes poem flew into her mind.

What happens to a dream deferred?
Does it dry up like a raisin in the sun?

She raised her head and shook her shoulders, trying to shake off the thought. No, her dreams had to be deferred, but they were going to come to fruition. She was going to make it. And then she would be a benevolent benefactor giving money away to all single moms trying to make something of their lives.

If they don't call me in another fifteen minutes, I'm just going to leave. I don't care if they close my case, Brenda lied to herself.

"Miss Carver?"

Brenda looked up at the woman standing in front of her with a bulging file folder in her hand and clipboard tucked under her arm. "Um, yes," Brenda said as she stood up.

"I'm sorry to keep you waiting." The woman tucked the folder under her arm with the clipboard and extended her hand. "I'm Jamilah Cabral, your new caseworker."

"Hi. Nice to meet you," Brenda said as she gave the woman's hand a limp shake while trying to give her a quick, but hopefully unnoticed, look up and down. She looked about forty-five, and had brown locks that hung almost to her backside like thick ropes. Gold-rimmed glasses perched on her lightly freckled nose. A colorful loose-fitting peasant blouse topped a pair of faded black jeans. She looked more like someone Brenda would have expected to see carrying signs and shouting slogans against the war than a welfare worker. But one thing Brenda had learned during her years in the system: looks could be deceiving. No one could be trusted.

She followed her new caseworker to a set of cubicles, ignoring the envious looks of the women still waiting, some of whom were there long before she.

"Do you drink coffee?" Mrs. Cabral asked as Brenda took her seat.

Brenda shook her head, wondering why the woman was being so

nice. She'd never before been offered coffee, tea, or water by a caseworker. "What happened to Miss Newcombe?"

"She took family leave because one of her children was diagnosed with leukemia," Mrs. Cabral answered simply, as if it were really okay to divulge information that proved caseworkers were actually human beings. "Her caseload is being divided up, and I pulled your case. It's not permanent, but you'll be working with me for awhile." She opened the bulging file folder. "Now let's see, it says here that you have four children?"

Brenda nodded, her back was straight as she sat on the edge of her seat, steeling herself for the interrogation.

"Are you receiving support from any of their fathers?"

Brenda shook head.

"Are you in touch with any of the fathers?"

Brenda shook her head again.

The caseworker folded her hands on the desk and studied Brenda's face for a few moments, saying nothing. "I like your hairstyle," she said finally.

Brenda self-consciously patted her newly done shoulder length twists. "Um, my girlfriend did it for me. She works in a natural hair salon, so she really knows what she's doing, but she did it at her apartment." She cleared her throat, ashamed of the tremble that was evident in her voice. "For free," she added quickly.

"Uh huh. I see. But I was offering you a compliment, not accusing you of any wrongdoing," Mrs. Cabral said quietly. She stared at Brenda again for a few moments, then suddenly took off her glasses and rubbed the deep indentations they had left on her nose.

"Look, I'm not going to insult you by acting like I'm planning on being your best friend, but I can assure you I'm not here to be an enemy," she said as she put her glasses back on. "I'm not trying to trap you with my questions, I just have to ask because it's required. You know the drill. Every six months you have to come down here and answer the same questions you were asked six months before. It's a drag, but not much more than that. And believe me, I look at my job as an opportunity to help people, not hurt them. So I want you to relax, okay? Are you sure you don't want some coffee?"

Brenda shook her head.

"Would you do me a favor, and try to answer my questions verbally?" Mrs. Cabral smiled. "It's easier for me. And really, try to relax. Please."

Brenda started to nod her head, but caught herself and smiled. "Sure, no problem." Something told her that the woman was genuine. She leaned back in the chair.

"What's that you're reading, anyway?" Mrs. Cabral pointed to the book clutched in Brenda's hand.

"*Yo Yo Love*," Brenda answered, "by Daaimah Poole. Have you read it?"

"No, I usually read nonfiction these days. But is it good?"

"Oh, yeah," Brenda nodded enthusiastically. "All about a young girl that goes around making bad decisions about men."

"Sounds interesting. I might have to check it out."

"You should. I plan on writing a book myself one day," Brenda added. She pulled out her notebook. "I take this with me wherever I go, and whenever I see something interesting, or an idea or deep thought hits me, I write it down so I can put it in my book. I've been doing it since I was twelve."

"Really. What's your book going to be about?"

"I think about a slave owner who falls in love with a slave. Or maybe about a woman from Harlem becoming the first African-American president," Brenda grinned sheepishly. "I haven't decided yet."

"Well, whatever you decide, I'll be sure to buy the book." Mrs. Cabral smiled and tapped the papers on the desk to straighten them up. "Okay, what say we start from the top? You have four children, is that right?"

"Yes. Bentley's almost thirteen, Shaniqua just turned seven, Yusef is four, and Jumah is getting ready to turn two."

"Good," Mrs. Cabral nodded her head. "Are you receiving support from any of their fathers?

"I wish," Brenda sighed.

"Are you in touch with any of the fathers?"

"No. I haven't seen Bentley's father since he was born. Shaniqua's father's been in prison since she was a couple of months old, and I don't stay in contact with him. Yusef's father disappeared when he found out I was pregnant, and to be truthful, I don't even know his last name, so I sure can't find him. And Jumah's father was killed the same day I was taking Jumah home from the hospital."

"Ooh, that's sad," Mrs. Cabral said quietly.

"What is?"

"About Jumah's father."

Brenda nodded her head. "He and I were planning on getting married. In fact, he wanted to get married a couple of months before Jumah was born, but I wanted a big wedding, and I didn't want to be wearing a fancy wedding dress all pregnant and everything."

"Well, I guess that was one way to look—"

"OH, MY GOD! SHE'S THROWING HER KIDS OUT THE WINDOW! SOMEONE CALL THE POLICE!"

Brenda and Mrs. Cabral both quickly looked up to see people run by the cubicle, heading out to the hallway.

"What the hell is going on?" Mrs. Cabral managed to grab one of her colleagues by the arm.

"I don't know. They said some woman's throwing children out the hallway window," was the breathless answer.

Mrs. Cabral released the woman and ran out to the fourth-floor hallway, pushing through the crowd, with Brenda at her heels.

"Dem tell me come back next week, and dem know goddamn well I'm getting kicked out my apartment today. Dem know I got no damn money to feed me damn kids," a wide-eyed woman standing by the hallway window screamed. Tears were streaming down her face, and dribble spilled from her twisted lips. Her face was so distorted it took Brenda a moment to recognize that it was Diana, who lived on the eleventh floor of Ida B.—one of the women for whom her mother baby-sat.

"My kids tell me dem hungry. I can't even buy dey no hotdogs. What I gonna do? I can't take dey begging me for food I can't give. I can't take it." Before anyone could stop her, the woman jumped out the window head first, her piercing scream ending with a sickening thud as she landed on the bodies of her two children.

2

Rosa glanced at her watch, not wanting to rush her sister off the telephone, but not wanting to be late for the first rehearsal of her new play.

"Yeah, man, Brenda just told me. I can't believe that shit." Rosa peered at the black leotard as she cradled the telephone between her head and shoulder. It was getting threadbare, she decided. She flung it on the bed and rummaged through the bottom drawer of her dresser, finally pulling out a bright red leotard and throwing it over her free shoulder. "I mean, you know, I can see her killing herself, but why she gotta do her kids? *Coño.* That's some wicked shit." She wrapped her short red satin robe closer to her body, and tied the sash as she listened. "Well, I don't care what kind of demons she got, she still ain't got no right to be killing no innocent children like that . . . Yeah, it's good that the one child wasn't with her, but what kind of life do you think he's gonna have now, with his mother and brother and sister dead? *Pobrecito.* But listen, *chacha*, I gotta go. I wanna stop down and make sure Brenda's okay before I go to rehearsal—she's a basket case right about now. Hey, did I tell you I got that part in the play I auditioned for last week? . . . *Ay, mija*, no, I don't get paid, but at least I got a chance to show off my stuff. See, that's why I don't like telling you and Mama nothing, 'cause y'all just don't get it. So, look, I gotta go. *Mañana*."

The warm water beating down from the shower eased muscles tense with anticipation of her first rehearsal for the play in which she would be an Italian temptress—her first role ever in which she'd actually have spoken lines, and an onstage kiss. The reefer joint she smoked after her shower relaxed her even more. She closed her eyes, inhaling deeply, letting the smooth smoke tickle her lungs. Sharif must be copping from a new source, she thought as she finally allowed wisps of white haze to seep from her lips. Not only was she already feeling light-headed, but there was a sweet aftertaste that let her know it wasn't the usual Colombian stuff that Sharif usually kept around the house. She had to promise to go to one of his protest rallies to get him to give her the joint, but she figured she'd be able to beg off later, anyway.

Damn, it would be really weird not to be living in the same building as Sharif and Brenda, not to mention her own mother, she thought. As much as she tried to ignore the rumors about them closing the Ida B., they still worried her. She had never really thought about moving out. When she became pregnant with Eddie and she married his no-good father, they managed to get an apartment just down the hall from her mother. And it was a good thing, too. Living in federally subsidized housing meant that she could file an application to have her rent lowered when her Junior moved out on her. No, she really hoped that they didn't close Ida B. There wasn't another place in the city where she'd find a three-bedroom apartment for only $535 a month.

She took another long puff, then carefully stubbed the joint out in an ashtray, not wanting to show up at rehearsal with red eyes. She lotioned her body before slipping on her leotard and tying a sheer black wraparound skirt over her hips. Picking up her makeup bag, she moved to the mirror, trying to decide which shade of lipstick she should wear for her first onstage kiss. Ruby Red was her favorite color, and it would match her outfit, but maybe she should try something a little more subtle, at least for rehearsals. She wanted to let the director and the other actors know she was sophisticated. She finally applied a smoky amber lipstick and a chocolate-brown liner on her Cupid's-bow lips, then started snatching the jumbo pink rollers from her hair, raking her fingers through her full black mane when she was finished. Yes, she decided, she certainly looked like an Italian temptress. Maybe even a little like a young Sophia Loren, but with better hair. She was going to have to do a little more work to make her Puerto Rican accent seem Italian, but she figured she could pull it off.

An old Jay-Z and Angie Martinez song came on the radio, and Rosa started swaying her ample salsa hips to the hip-hop beat as she sang along.

How you say my love in Spanish?
Mi amor. How you say my love in thug?

She danced over to the window, peeked out through the Venetian blinds, and grinned when she saw a sizable number of people standing in front of the building. She hoped someone would ask where she was going as she left the building, so she could proudly announce that she was going to a rehearsal in the Village. Remind people she was not just a part-time waitress, but an *artista*. An *actriz*.

She was about to step away from the window when she noticed a flashily dressed, caramel complected man with short wavy hair, leaning against a gold Toyota Camry. A sallow-skinned but heavily made up young woman, with thin blonde cornrows hanging down to her mid-back, leaned against him in an embrace.

"That *hijo de puta*," Rosa hissed as she watched the couple kiss. She grabbed her keys and large red pocketbook and stormed out the door.

"Yo, Junior. Why you got to bring your bitches up here on my block?" she said when she reached the couple. The man looked at her, trying—unsuccessfully—to hide a grin.

"Hey, Rosa. How you doing?" he said as he pulled the sallow-skinned woman closer to him.

"Who you calling a bitch?" the woman said as she twisted in his arms to face Rosa.

"Excuse me. I wasn't addressing you, okay?" Rosa held her index finger in front of the woman's face. "I was talking to my son's father so step off before you get hurt and shit." She gave the woman a wicked look. "Or didn't he tell you he was a no-good motherfucking deadbeat dad who can't give a dime to support his only child but can manage to buy a new car every other year?"

"Oh, Rosa, calm down." Junior waved his hand at her dismissively.

Rosa snorted and planted her hands on her hips. "How you going to tell me to calm down, Junior? If you wanted me to be calm you wouldn't be out kissing on this little hootchie mama. You live on 115th Street. Why don't you take your skanky bitch down there?" Rosa shook off Brenda, who had suddenly attached herself to her arm, and continued talking to Junior. "You come up here in front of my building disrespecting me like this and then you going to tell me to calm down and shit? *Besa mi cula.*"

"Man, Rosa, why you care who I'm with—" Junior started.

"Forget her," the woman sucked her teeth. "She's just mad because you quit her stink ass. And now that I've met her I can see why."

Rosa jerked her head back in surprise. "Quit me? I'm the one that quit him." She turned and addressed the crowd who had started to gather to witness a possible fight. "Someone tell me what I would want with a thirty-two-year-old man who parks cars for a living and still lives with his mama."

"Man, Rosa, shut up." Junior growled. "You ain't no prize, you know. Thinking you some kind of actress and shit. You couldn't act your way out of a paper bag. You can't do nothing but give a good time on the casting couch."

"You come down here acting like a little bitch 'cause you mad that I got your man," the woman with Junior pushed him aside to face Rosa.

"*Besa mi cula, puta,*" Rosa hunched her shoulders back. "And in case you don't know, that means kiss my ass, you whore. Wasn't nobody talking to you."

"Well, if you're talking to my man, then you talking to me. Bitch! So why don't you just shut the fuck up and carry your ass back to whatever hole you crawled out of before I kick your ass." The woman started jabbing her finger in the air in front of Rosa's chest.

"Oh? You think you going to come up here to my block and call me out like that? I don't think so." Rosa stepped back, a smile on her lips as she threw her pocketbook at Brenda and quickly pulled off her gold hoop earrings. "That shit just ain't gonna fly."

Rosa stepped back further, her fist balled, and ready to throw a punch, when someone grabbed her from behind, pinning her arms to her sides. Before she could react she was suddenly lifted off her feet and swung around, away from Junior and the woman.

"Sharif, let me go!" Rosa howled as she tried to twist out of his arms. "I'm going to kick that bitch's ass."

"Damn, Sharif. Let her go. Why you always gotta be the peacemaker, yo?" a teenager from the crowd yelled. "We wanna see a fight."

"Man, shut up, Ricky." Sharif told the youngster who scowled back at him with disgust.

"Girl, you don't have any business out here fighting over a man," Sharif said gently as he released Rosa but used his huge body to block her from lunging at the girl. "Don't give him that kind of satisfaction."

"Yeah, you'd better be glad someone stepped in," the girl taunted.

"Sharif, what you expect me to do?" Rosa stopped struggling and closed her eyes, shaking her head and sniffing a couple of times as if to fight tears. "She's up here kissing on my man in front of all my friends and shit."

"He ain't your man," the girl snapped.

"Oh, yes, he is my man," Rosa said as she tried unsuccessfully to sidestep Sharif. "I've got his child, and I've got his love, too. Just like I love him, he loves me." She turned to face Junior. "Don't you, *papi*?" she asked in a gentle tone.

"I thought you didn't want me," Junior said cautiously.

"I just wanted you to straighten up," Rosa said as she pushed past a less resistant Sharif and walked up close to Junior. "But I always thought it was going to be me and you for the long haul. And Eddie, he called me all the way from Puerto Rico last night and told me how much he wanted his mommy and daddy to get back together, and he almost made me cry. He wants us to be a family again, and so do I. And I thought maybe you did, too."

"Come on, Rosa, don't play yourself like this." Brenda tried to pull her friend away, but Rosa shook her off, her eyes never leaving Junior's face.

"No, Brenda, just go away, 'cause this ain't got nothing to do with you. And this ain't got nothing to do with you either, Sharif. This ain't got nothing to do with no one but me and Junior." She wiped at the tears that were trickling down her face. "Ain't that right, Junior?"

"Junior, kick that bitch to the curb and let's go." The girl said as she rolled her eyes.

"So you saying you wanna get back together, Rosita?" Junior asked, ignoring the dagger looks his former companion was throwing his way.

"I've always wanted to be with you, *papi*. Don't you know anything?" Rosa sighed. "But then you gotta come up here with Miss Thang here, letting me know you've moved on and shit. I ain't gonna fight no losing battle here. You know I want you, so if you want me you gotta let me know."

"Aw, man, this shit is whack. There ain't gonna be no fight," Ricky grumbled.

"Yeah, I want you, *mami*." Junior stroked Rosa's damp face.

"What about her?" Rosa sniffed again and pointed to the girl who was standing with a dumbfounded look on her face.

"She don't mean shit to me. I was using her to make you jealous."

"What? You ain't say that shit when you was licking my pussy last night," the girl screamed, to appreciative howls from the crowd.

"Bitch, shut up before I put my foot in your ass," Junior told her as his arm encircled Rosa's waist.

"So you don't want her?" Rosa asked.

"Naw, I don't want that *puta*. I got my woman right here." Junior bent down and kissed Rosa on the cheek.

"Fuck you, you stupid motherfucker. I'm outta here," the woman stomped off.

"Hold up, hold up," Rosa pulled away from Junior as she shouted after the woman. "Come back and take this little piece of shit with you."

The woman stopped and turned to give Rosa an incredulous look.

Junior's mouth dropped open. "What?" he finally sputtered.

"I can't act, huh? I acted good enough to fool your stupid ass, now didn't I?" Rosa sneered. "And now that it's established that you still want me, and . . ." she turned to the girl, ". . . and that you can't pull any man that was ever with me, both of y'all can kiss my ass. Now if you'll excuse me, I'm late for a rehearsal for a real role in a real play."

She grabbed her pocketbook from a grinning Brenda and stepped off the curb and onto the street. "Taxi," she yelled waving her hand in the air.

"You little bitch!" Junior went to grab her, but Sharif stepped in front of him.

"Why don't you just go head home, brother? You can call her later if you want," Sharif said kindly.

"Get the fuck out of my way, you *maricón*."

"Yo dawg, he called you a faggot!" Ricky hooted. "I know you ain't gonna let him get away with that shit. Kick his ass, Sharif! Kick his ass!"

Junior looked up at Sharif, as if suddenly realizing that the man had six inches and at least fifty pounds on him. "I ain't scared of you," he said in a shaky voice.

"Good. I don't want you to be," Sharif said reassuringly. "But just understand I'm not afraid of you either, and I'm not going to let you lay a hand on my friend Rosa. So why don't you just get in your car and drive off, and maybe call her later when everyone's calmed down?"

Junior glared at him and the crowd, then jumped in the gold Camry and started the engine. He rolled down the window and shouted to the woman. "Come on, Lucy."

"Fuck you," the woman shouted back and stomped off.

Rosa laughed as she climbed into the taxi that had just pulled up. She rolled down the window. "Thanks, Sharif. I'll call you when I get back, Brenda," she called out. "And Junior? Just like the bitch just said . . ." she stuck out her hand out the window, her middle finger pointed to the sky. "Fuck you!" she shouted as the cab pulled off.

"Mmm, mmm, mmm," Brenda said as she watched the taxi disappear down the street. "That's our girl."

"Yeah, I guess we gotta claim her," Sharif said with a chuckle and a shake of the head. He put his arm around Brenda's shoulder. "So how you doing, Miss Lady? I heard about what happened with Diana. Damn shame, because she was really a nice woman. I guess the system must have made her crack. You were there, huh?"

Brenda shuddered. "Yeah, it was awful. Social services came over and picked up her youngest son from Mommy this afternoon. Thank

God Diana left him with her because of his cold. Mommy said she's going to go down tomorrow to see if she can take him in as a foster kid, though."

"That poor little guy is going to be messed up for life." Sharif said as he and Brenda walked back towards the Ida B. "Tell your mother to let me know if there's anything I can do to help her out with him. What is he? About four?"

"Yeah, I think Jimmy's four," Brenda nodded, "or almost four."

"Damn shame," Sharif said. "Damn shame."

"Hey, Brenda. Waddup, Yo? You looking good."

"Oh, hey, Ricky," Brenda turned and gave a half-smile at the teenager who had been urging Sharif to fight. "How you doing? Look at you, getting all muscle-bound. You been working out?"

"Yeah, I been making out to the gym every now and then," the boy gave a slight nod. "I be trying to keep myself in shape. You know, gotta stay buff." He nodded his head a few more times as he looked at her, then stuck his hands into his pockets, appearing to struggle for something else to say. "You looking good,' he said finally.

"Yo, dawg, you already said that." Sharif chuckled.

"Yeah, well," Ricky shrugged. "She's really looking good, so I like said it twice and shit. Ain't nothing wrong with that. Why you gotta try and bust on a brother like that, yo?"

"Aw, man, Don't even try it. You know I'm just messing with you." Sharif gave Ricky a soft punch on the shoulder.

"Yeah, I know, it ain't nuttin' and all," Ricky said sullenly. "I'ma catch up with you guys later, yo." He stuck his hands in his pockets and walked away, but turned back after a few steps. "I'll talk to you later, Brenda."

Brenda smiled and waved.

"You've got that young boy's nose wide open," Sharif chuckled as they walked into the building.

"At least he's got good taste," Brenda smiled up at her friend.

"Yeah, good taste and bad judgment." Sharif ducked as Brenda tried to slap him on the head, and in doing so, noticed a large woman carrying two plastic shopping bags heading toward the building. "Uh huh, that's why Ricky made such a quick exit. Here comes his aunt."

"Mmm, mmm, mmm. There's always some drama going on out here," Miss Marcie said as she wearily trudged over to Brenda and Sharif. "If it ain't someone fighting and cursing and carrying on outside it's someone getting someone so high that they fall asleep and leaving the water running in the bathroom so that they flood other people's apartments."

"Ooh, Miss Marcie. I heard about that." Brenda started rubbing the woman's shoulder. "Did your furniture get ruined?"

"My furniture and my carpet," Miss Marcie said as she leaned on Sharif and slipped off first one of her shoes, and then the other. "Damn these shoes hurt."

"Don't worry. Sharif will carry you upstairs. Piggyback. Won't you, Sharif?" Brenda poked her friend.

"Don't be funny." Miss Marcie shot Brenda an annoyed look. "He may be strong, but you know damn well he can't carry me on his back, fat as I am."

"I'm sorry, Miss Marcie. I was only playing," Brenda said quickly. "And you know you're not really fat . . ."

"Chile, please. Don't insult me and then try to act like I'm stupid. I'm almost six feet and almost three hundred pounds." Miss Marcie rolled her eyes and refocused her attention on Sharif.

"We gotta get that security guard . . . what's his name, again . . . oh, yeah, Walter." Miss Marcie leaned on Sharif again and started rubbing her left foot on her right leg. "You know he's been letting crackheads come in here and turn tricks in the laundry room. Umph. Damn this corn is killing me. I'm have to cut it off when I get upstairs."

"Yeah," Sharif nodded. "He's got a few complaints against him."

"Well, you need to call a special tenants' meeting so we can get him fired." Miss Marcie slipped back into her shoes, grimacing as she did so. "I remember when we first moved in here, the Ida B. was the place to live. Now it's just as bad as living in the projects with all this stuff going on. I'm glad my sister moved out. The Ida B. ain't no place to be trying to raise a young boy. Especially one as bright as Ricky." She picked up her shopping bags, and looked at Sharif. "Well, aren't you going to offer to help me upstairs?"

"Of course I am, Miss Marcie." Sharif reached for the two bags.

"No," Miss Marcie held one of the bags out of Sharif's reach. "Here," she said shoving it at Brenda. "You can help, too, since you have such a smart mouth."

3

Sharif carefully studied the India rubber tree which stood in the corner of the tiny living room. The edges of the leaves were turning yellow, a sure sign of overwatering, although how that could be he didn't understand. He barely watered the thing once a week. But then, it had probably been Gran, he thought. Her motto had been: If it had a mouth—feed it. If it was in soil—water it. No one, and no thing, would go without nourishment in Gran's house.

He stuck a couple of fingers into the potted soil. It was barely moist. He wondered if the problem was too much sunlight, and made a mental note to move it to a corner away from the window. He'd switch it with the snake plant which thrived wherever it was placed, he decided. Or maybe the monstera plant. He gave a look around the room, deciding where to put the new "Free Mumia" poster he'd just bought. Fidel Castro and Che Guevara were already on one wall, and George Jackson and Geronimo Pratt on the other. But the Mumia poster would probably fit, he decided.

"Sharif! You're not even listening to me, are you?"

Sharif gave a low chuckle as he turned to Brenda, who was slouched on the brown corduroy couch, filing her nails while looking at him through narrowed eyes.

"I heard every word you said. You were talking about your father coming home."

"Well," Brenda huffed. "I wish you'd at least look at me when I'm talking to you. That's one of the things I hate about you."

"Fair enough." Sharif nodded, and then pulled his shoulder-length locks into a ponytail before moving over to the couch to sit down next to Brenda. He slipped his feet out of his brown leather sandals and propped them up on the wooden bench coffee table. "Okay, you have my undivided attention."

"Well," Brenda shrugged, "I'm just saying that it's going to be funny having him around. I mean, he didn't spend too much time with me when he was out . . ."

"He didn't spend *any* time with you when he was out," Sharif corrected her.

"Well, you know what I mean," Brenda shrugged again. "But he says he's planning to make up for lost time. I'm kinda nervous, because I don't really know him, but at the same time, I think this might just be what I need to get my life in order."

"How so?" Sharif said slowly. He chewed on the inside of his lip, already anticipating the answer. As long as he'd known her she'd always depended on someone to be her savior. He'd gladly fulfilled the role when they were youngsters. As they got older, it was the many young men who were enamored with her frail-like beauty who stepped into the role. Brenda, more than anyone he knew, had a Blanche DuBois quality about her. The "I've always depended on the kindness of strangers," kind of woman. Independent, intelligent, and yet appealingly needy. A Blanche DuBois with chocolate mocha skin, short twisted hair, and a small diamond nose ring which she wore for fashion rather than as a political or cultural statement. Unfortunately, like Tennessee Williams's pathetic heroine, she often ended up abused by her would-be saviors.

"Well," Brenda said, "it will be nice to have someone out here looking out for me and the kids. And I know he wasn't around before, but I think he really cares about me now. Maybe he can help me get focused on writing my book."

"Your book about a plantation owner falling in love with one of his slaves?"

"Yeah, that one, I think. Or I was kind of thinking of doing one on a Japanese woman who falls in love with an American serviceman." Brenda pursed her in lips as in thought. "I don't know yet."

"Brenda, why don't you just write about something you actually know?"

"Hmph. What the hell do I know about?" Brenda shrugged. "All I know about is life in Ida B., and now they're talking about closing it down." She turned to look at Sharif. "Do you really think they're going to do it? I mean, can they?"

Sharif folded his arms across his chest and shook his head slowly. "I don't know. Those shits at management aren't giving up any info. And you know I've been on them. But from what little I have gathered, the city wants to sell the land to a developer for a luxury apartment building."

"What?" Brenda stopped filing her nails and looked at Sharif.

"Yeah, well, you know with the *gentrification* of Harlem and all, they figure they can get six or seven times the rent they're getting from us. I mean, come on. You have a four bedroom apartment and you pay what? About six hundred dollars, right? And even with the federal subsidies that you and everyone else in Ida B. gets, your rent only comes up to something like sixteen hundred. Well, they could get a good three or four thousand dollars from some of these rich white folks looking for a place in Harlem. So from a dollar-and-cents perspective it makes sense. And that's the only perspective they're looking at."

"Uh huh. And what's supposed to happen to us?"

"They'll come up with some kind of program to find us housing elsewhere, you know like Staten Island or the Bronx. What the hell do they care if they displace a community? We'll just be another displaced community," Sharif sighed.

"Well, I've never set foot in Staten Island, and I'm not moving to the Bronx." Brenda sucked her teeth. "Boogie down, my butt."

"Well, hopefully it won't get to that. I'm doing research on the whole thing, and I've got a couple of grassroots housing organizations that I've done work for that I know will raise hell when I tell them what's going on."

"Yeah, you get them, Sharif." Brenda picked up the nail file and started peering at her fingers. "But anyway, like I was saying about my father coming home, you know Bootsy really needs a man in his life. I don't want him ending up on the corner like the rest of these kids, standing out in the rain and snow, twenty-four/seven, selling crack."

"Yeah," Sharif nodded. "I know what you mean."

"You know," Brenda continued, "I saw Scotty out there the other day, and he isn't but ten years old. Younger than Bootsy."

"Scotty was out there scrambling?"

Brenda shook her head. "No, but I think he was holding product for one them guys. I told him if he didn't take his narrow butt up in the house I was going to tell his mother."

"You should have told her anyway!"

Brenda shrugged, and went back to filing her nails. "Nah. I didn't want to get him in trouble."

"Jesus Christ," Sharif said in a disgusted voice, withdrawing his arm from Brenda's shoulders.

"What?" She looked up at him with her large almond eyes, as if surprised by his reaction.

"Brenda, wouldn't you want someone to tell you if Bootsy was out there like that?"

"Bootsy isn't out there like that, so I'm not worried about it,"

Brenda said with a slight shrug. "And when my father comes home, he'll make sure that he never gets out there."

"Okay, whatever." Sharif gave a sigh of resignation. There was seldom use in arguing with Brenda, he knew, because she just never seemed to get it. And it wasn't that she wasn't intelligent enough to get it, she just had this habit of choosing what she would get, and what she wouldn't. It wasn't a habit he would tolerate with others, but Brenda's good habits outweighed her bad, in his opinion. It was just that she could be so infuriating.

He turned when he realized she was scribbling something down in her notebook. "What are you writing?"

"Both a prison and a sanctuary," she said as she continued to write. "A place where everybody was trying to break out, and nobody wanted to leave." She looked up at Sharif. "Isn't that deep? That's the thought that came to me when we were talking about them closing the Ida B."

"A deep contradiction, and very apt." Sharif nodded. "So you're going to write about life in the Ida B.?"

Brenda shook her head. "No, that wouldn't work. Nobody would want to read about people living in a building in Harlem." She cocked her head, as if in thought. "Maybe, I could make it an island . . ." She snapped her newly manicured fingers. "I could make it like Pompeii. Where they get swallowed up in the ocean because they didn't want to leave the only land they've ever known."

"Still sounds like you might be talking about the Ida B." Sharif guffawed. "Hey, you do remember that you promised to come to the protest rally Tuesday, right?" he said in an attempt to lighten the mood.

"What are we protesting now?"

"Police brutality," Sharif said with a small laugh. "I've reminded you at least a dozen times, and I've got flyers posted all over the building, and all up and down the street."

"Yeah, I'll be there, I guess." Brenda sighed. "You're always dragging me somewhere to protest something or the other. I can't believe I let you talk me into taking that bus with you to D.C. last year to protest the war."

"Well," Sharif said as he got up from the couch, "I want to keep you involved in what's going on in the world. There *is* life beyond Ida B., you know."

"So you say," Brenda said with a snort. "Do you think this shade of pink looks good on me," she wiggled her fingers in the air.

"I don't know, I guess so. Yeah, it looks okay." Sharif said absentmindedly.

"Yeah, it looks okay," Brenda mimicked him with a giggle as she playfully tapped him on the shoulder. "Sharif, I thought homosexuals were supposed to be into fashion and style, and stuff. When I ask Andre for fashion advice he gets all into it, telling me what color looks good on me, how I should wear my hair, and what kind of shoes to buy."

"Andre's a drag queen. Just because I like men, doesn't mean that I want to be a woman," Sharif yawned and stretched, his gray tee shirt lifting up just enough to show his chiseled stomach. "You want something to drink? Iced tea?"

"Lipton or that herbal junk you like?"

Sharif grinned. "Herbal."

Brenda shook her head. "Forget it. I hate the little leaves at the bottom of the glass."

"Well, I'm going to get a glass." Sharif headed to the kitchen but stopped when someone started pounding on the apartment door.

"Hey, hey, don't bang down the damn door," Sharif swung the door open without bothering to look through the peep hole. "I knew that was you making all that noise, Vincent," he said to the short thin copper-skinned man standing in the doorway. "Peace, bro. Get your ass in here."

Vincent grinned and made a fist and pounded himself across the chest, then touched shoulders with Sharif who had done the same. "Peace, bro," Vincent said as he walked in. "I'm just getting back in the city."

"I figured you were out on one of your sprees," Sharif nodded. "I've been trying to get in touch you with for weeks."

Vincent bit his lips and shook his head. "Yeah, man, I heard about your grandma. I'm sorry man. I wish I coulda been here. Gran was like my own grandmother. She was a damn good woman."

"I appreciate that, man. I appreciate it." The two men fell into an awkward silence.

"Come on in and take a load off," Sharif said finally. Vincent followed him into the living room.

"Waddup, Miss Brenda, you fine thing," Vincent said as he sat in an armchair. He lightly smoothed his hand over his closely cropped wavy hair to make sure each strand was in place, then straightened the Chinese collar of his tan silk shirt. "You looking good, as usual."

"I'm doing all right. Hanging in there," Brenda replied.

"Yo, man," Vincent looked up at Sharif. "How is it that you always have the fine shorties hanging out at your crib?"

" 'Cause he knows how to treat a lady," Brenda said as she gathered her things and stood up.

"Oh, I know how to treat a lady, and I sure would know how to treat you, with your big round fine ass," Vincent grinned up at her.

"Oh, is that right?" Brenda said as she strode over and stood in front of him, putting her hands on her hips.

"Yeah, that's right." Vincent licked his lips. "So when you gonna let me hit that?"

Sharif snorted and shook his head, but Brenda just giggled at Vincent.

"You don't want none of this," she teased him.

"Says who?" he asked.

"Says me," Brenda crossed her arms in front of her chest, and fixed her plump lips into a pretty pout. "You keep talking all that stuff, but you're not serious."

"And what makes you think that?"

"Well, if you're serious, then, why don't we get together, for real then?" Brenda put her hand on her breast, and let it very slowly slide down to just below her waist.

"You name the time, and I'm all there," Vincent licked his lips.

"Okay, how about tonight?" Brenda said in a husky voice.

"Can't tonight. I'm busy."

"Oh," Brenda jerked her head back. "Well," she started tapping her foot. "What about tomorrow, then?"

"Busy then, too." Vincent grinned.

"You ain't shit," Brenda playfully slapped him on the side of his head. "You were supposed to say yes so I could tell you I didn't want your ass."

"Well, then you shoulda called me *papi*." Vincent started laughing. "Ricky told me about that shit when I was on my way up here."

"Yeah, did Rosa play my man, or what?" Sharif extended a sideways fist toward Vincent.

"Yeah, and I heard you were about to fuck my man up," Vincent said as he gave Sharif a pound.

"Naw, man," Sharif shook his head. "I wasn't going to let it get to that point. He tried to call me out, but I cooled him down."

"Hmph. Good thing, too," Vincent snorted. "I'd hate to have to go down to Rikers Island to bail you out again. Shit, they probably wouldn't have even given you bail with you being on probation and all."

"Yeah," Sharif nodded his head slowly as the ugly memories flooded over him.

It had been just two years before. A new kid, Brad, had just started hanging out on the corner. A brash young kid, who was having trouble unloading enough product to justify getting more crack from his dealer. After two weeks of dismal sales, he knocked on Sharif's door at three-thirty one morning.

"Yeah, waddup?" Sharif said after looking through the peep hole.

"Hey man, how you doing?" Brad answered, shifting from one foot to the other.

"I'm doing okay. Waddup?" Sharif repeated as he tightened the drawstring to his pajama bottoms, wishing he had put on a top before coming to the door. Goose bumps were already forming on his huge forearms.

"Nothing man. I was just, uh, wondering if I could use your bathroom."

"Naw, man, I'm sorry, but my grandmother's asleep. She's not been feeling well, and I don't want to chance you waking her up."

"I'll be quiet," Brad said insistently.

"Naw, man. I'm sorry."

"Look," Brad glanced up and down the hallway then leaned lightly against the door. "I just gotta talk to you for a minute about a business proposition. Open the door so we can talk."

Sharif put the chain on the door before unlocking it and pulling it ajar. "Yo, man, you know I don't do that shit. I don't have any business with you."

"Yeah, yeah, I know," Brad said hurriedly. "Just let me in so we can talk."

Alarm bells went off in Sharif's head as he eyed the man up and down. "If you wanna talk, go ahead and talk."

"Man," Brad whined, "Why don't you just . . ." He suddenly moved closer to the door. "Look," he began again in a low voice. "I'm a little short on cash. I was wondering if . . ."

"Man, I feel for you, but I'm not your bank."

"Yeah, yeah man, I know that, but," Brad was now whispering, "I just, you know, wanted you to know that I'm, like, you know, a man of the world and shit. You know, like you."

"Uh huh," Sharif said slowly. "Whatever that's supposed to mean."

"I'm just saying that I'm not like some of these cats out here," Brad said urgently. "I'm not like, you know, homophobic and shit."

Sharif stared but said nothing.

"So, I mean, like I was thinking," Brad continued, "we could kinda, you know, help each other out. Like I said, I'm kinda short on cash, and I know a dude like you got your needs."

"Man—" Sharif started.

"So here's my proposition," Brad glanced up and down the hallway again before moving even closer to the door and continuing his whisper. "You give me fifty bucks, and I'll let you suck my dick."

Sharif breathed in sharply as a dark gray cloud rapidly formed in front of his eyes almost, but not quite, blocking his view of Brad, who stood tapping his foot expectantly. Everyone in Ida B. knew he was homosexual—he'd not hidden it since he realized it himself—but although there may have some whispers and maybe even a few snickers behind his back from people like Miss Jackie, no one had ever confronted him like this. Even the young guys scrambling on the corner had always given him respect, largely because he'd grown up with their older brothers, and had a reputation as a stand-up guy, as well being good with his fists.

"You'll let me do what?" he said slowly through the mental fog.

"I'll let you suck my . . . I'll let you give me a blow job," Brad whispered urgently. "Come on man. Let's do this."

"Man, get the fuck outta my face," Sharif shouted as the dark cloud thickened and began swirl in front of him, making it difficult for him to think clearly.

"What? What?" Brad backed away from the door.

"Fuck you." Sharif tried to close the door, but Brad put his weight against it.

"Okay, then listen, you freak motherfucker," Brad said through clenched teeth. "You give me hundred bucks right now, or I'll tell everybody how you propositioned me just now."

"Sharif, honey, is something wrong?" Sharif heard his grandmother call out from her bedroom.

Sharif gave the door a forceful shove, pushing Brad back, and then twisted the lock. "Nothing, Gran," Sharif called out softly as he tried to control his breathing and make the dark cloud recede. "Go back to sleep."

"Yo, Sissy," Brad taunted from the other side of the door. "Your granny know you like to take it up the ass?"

Without another word, Sharif undid the chain, unlocked the door, and pounced on Brad before the youngster could scramble out of the way. The rest was a black tornado-like blur, although he later remembered being hustled into a police squad car, his bloody arms handcuffed behind his back. He received three years probation for the assault, but only Brenda, Rosa, and Vincent knew why he had broken Brad's nose, knocked out two of his teeth, and fractured his skull, along with three of his ribs.

Sharif shuddered, and blinked his eyes a few times to rid himself of the memory. "Yeah, well, like I said, I wasn't going to let it get to that point with Rosa's ex. You want some iced tea?"

"He got that herbal stuff," Brenda warned as she walked over to Sharif and stood on tiptoe to give him a kiss on the cheek. "And I gotta run."

"Hey, Brenda. Why don't you give that young boy some play?"

"What young boy?"

"Ricky. The kid practically drools every time someone even mentions your name," Vincent chuckled. "He's funny as shit."

"Yeah, she got his nose wide open," Sharif said as he handed Vincent a glass.

Brenda gave a light laugh as she moved toward the door. "He's a boy. I need me a man. I don't have time to be teaching anybody how to do it."

"Yeah, well, baby, I'll pay you to give me lessons." Vincent grinned.

"Boy, be quiet," Brenda said over her shoulder. "I'll see you guys later."

"Damn, that's a fine ass woman," Vincent said as took a sip of the ice tea after Brenda left. "If she wasn't such a good friend of yours I'd be all over her for real."

"Yeah, Brenda's good people."

Vincent nodded. "Too bad she's such an airhead. Always writing in that damn notebook."

Sharif chuckled. "She's not as dumb as people think. Don't sleep on her."

"Shit, sleep on her? I want to sleep with her."

"Her and every other woman you lay your eyes on." Sharif sat down on the couch. "Hey, you busy on Tuesday?"

"Yeah, I gotta catch up on some business. Why?"

"What about Thursday?"

"Thursday, should be cool? Why?"

"Well, if you were available on Tuesday you could have come down to the rally against police brutality, but I'll settle for you making the protest rally we're having at City Hall on Thursday. We gotta let the powers that be know we don't want to send our young boys to die out there in the Middle East."

"What's the difference if they die in the Middle East or out here on the streets," Vincent shrugged. "But yeah, I'll try to make it, you fucking Commie. What time?"

"Eleven-thirty. We're hoping to make the twelve o'clock news. And I'm a Socialist, not a Communist."

"Same difference. You're a pinko. But you know I got your back, bro." Vincent leaned back in the armchair, kicked off his brown Italian leather loafers and wiggled his toes through his beige silk socks. "Oh, hey, I saw Miss Jackie in the hall. She told me about that woman on the eleventh floor throwing her kids out the window."

Sharif snorted. "News gets around fast here in Ida B., doesn't it?"

Vincent nodded. "Between Miss Jackie holding down the building, and Ricky holding down the street, ain't no need for nobody to read a newspaper to find out what's going on." Vincent took another short sip of his iced tea. "She also told me you hit up the boys on the corner for donations for that woman's funeral. True?"

"Yeah. I guess Ricky told her."

"Man, you got some shit with you," Vincent shook his head. "I gotta give it to you, though. You got some balls."

Sharif shrugged. "Why shouldn't I hit them up? They're making money off the community, they should be expected to give at least a little something something back. Some of those cats are pulling in a thousand dollars a night. They can throw forty or fifty bucks for a good cause."

"I ain't arguing the shit. I'm just saying you got balls, is all."

Riiiing.

Sharif leaned over to the end table and picked up the telephone receiver. "Peace, this is Sharif." He listened for a few minutes then nodded his head. "Yeah, okay, I'll tell him . . . All right . . . I'll catch you later."

He hung up the telephone and looked over at Vincent. "That was Brenda. She said she wants you to come over Friday for Jumah's birthday party."

"Who's Jumah?"

"Her youngest. He's turning two."

Vincent laughed. "What the fuck I look like, going to some two-year-old's birthday party?"

"Man, you know the deal," Sharif shrugged. "The little kid's party will start about three, and by seven it's an adult thing. Free fried chicken and liquor. The place will be packed, watch. There'll be plenty of fine girls there for you try and pull."

"Well, in that case," Vincent grinned. "I just might stop by, at that."

Sharif got up and turned on the stereo, and soon the sounds of Jill Scott's latest CD filled the room, causing Vincent to grimace. "Man, why don't you turn off that shit? Put on some Snoop Dogg or something."

"I don't have anything by Snoop," Sharif chuckled. "How about some Bob Dylan?" Sharif pulled a CD from a stack by the stereo. "I just got the *Desire* album on CD."

"Man," Vincent gripped the side of the chair as if he was going to jump up. "Why you trying to fuck with me?"

"All right, all right," Sharif put the CD back and grabbed another one. "How about Nas, then?"

"Well, yeah, shit, play him then," Vincent grumbled as he settled back down. "You know you just saying that other shit on to piss me off."

"Naw, man," Sharif said as he changed the CD. "I suggested it because I like it. It's soothing."

"Fucking Bob Dylan," Vincent snorted. "We've been friends for what? Twenty-five years? And we ain't got shit in common." He paused for a moment, then chuckled. "In fact, we're just about complete opposites, aren't we? You're a homo, and I can't get me enough pussy. You like that smooth shit, and I like hip-hop. You're—"

"Big, burly, and built, and you're a scrawny little chicken," Sharif cut in.

"Watch that shit." Vincent cut his eyes at his friend. "I dress like a—"

"Pimp," Sharif finished for him.

"—And you dress like you pulled the discards from the Salvation Army's trash cans," Vincent said without missing a beat. "You go around trying to save the world—"

"And you're always trying to find ways to rip the world off." Sharif put his feet up on the coffee table. "So what's your latest scam, bro?"

"Yeah, well, I got a little something going on," Vincent started bopping his head to the music. "Sweet thing, too. I got this hook-up for Social Security checks. I pay twenty-five cents on the dollar. Take two hundred checks, nothing big, about three hundred dollars each, and I take a trip down south and get them cashed."

"And how exactly do you do that?" Sharif cocked his head.

"I take five or six bitches with me on each trip," Vincent said. "But you know, chicks that look kinda clean cut. I hook them up with fake IDs and send them into check-cashing places, sometimes supermarkets, and have them cash them. I pay each of 'em two thousand dollars for the trip and feed them, so they're happy, and I make about seventy thousand in profit, each trip. So I'm happy as shit."

"Damn!" Sharif's head jerked back.

"Yeah, not bad for about two weeks' work," Vincent grinned. "And not as dangerous as sticking up banks."

"Yeah," Sharif agreed. "I'm glad you gave that shit up."

"It was a way to make a living. And, you know, a man's gotta do what a man's gotta do." Vincent shrugged. "But that's all in the past. Like I said, this new scam's sweet. I done made five trips already this year, and I got a new Jag parked downstairs to prove it."

"Word?" It wasn't like Vincent to buy anything as ostentatious as a Jag—this was a man who made a habit of stashing fifty percent of everything he made and saving it for a rainy day. And he bought a Jag? Sharif jumped up and strode over to the window. He whistled as he peeked through the blinds. "That's your ride? The Kelly Green joint? Oh, yeah, it's sweet," Sharif leaned further out the window. "Damn, man! Someone busted in your driver's side window."

"Get the fuck outta here!" Vincent jumped out the chair and ran toward the door, forgetting about his shoes.

"Yo! Yo . . . I was only playing!" Sharif yelled as Vincent grabbed the doorknob.

"What?" Vincent spun around.

"I was just fucking with you man," Sharif grinned sheepishly. "Sorry. Bad joke."

"You ain't shit. I shoulda known it was bullshit anyway. I woulda heard the security alarm on that baby all the way up here," Vincent grumbled as he sat back in the chair and slipped on his shoes. "I gotta blow outta here anyway. I got business to take care of." He stood up and adjusted his shirt, so that the gun holstered in the small of his back wasn't visible, then pulled out a gold money clip, bulging with one hundred dollar bills. He peeled five off and threw them on the coffee table. "Here's my contribution to that girl's funeral."

"Okay, man. Thanks," Sharif said as he walked Vincent to the door. "You gonna make that rally Thursday?"

"Yeah, yeah, just leave me a voice mail with the info." Vincent opened the door then turned and gave Sharif a not-too-light punch right above the solar plexus. "And don't be fucking with a man about his ride."

"Yeah, you got that," Sharif rubbed his chest. "Peace out, bro."

"Peace out."

4

It was getting dark, and normally Brenda would have made sure all of her children were inside watching Nickelodeon or playing video games until their nine-thirty bedtime, but the old bulky air conditioner in the living room, which she used to cool the entire apartment, had broken, and the window fans she had borrowed from her mother and neighbors were simply circulating hot air. *And God knows when I can afford to buy another air conditioner. I gotta pay for Jumah's party.*

It wasn't too much cooler sitting outside the building, but just being out in the open made the heat more tolerable, though barely. She sighed as she leaned back in the plastic green-and-white striped beach chair, her head almost touching the post of the black fence surrounding Ida B. Without looking, she reached into the blue diaper bag that sat on the sidewalk beside her chair and took out the small orange plastic water gun she had borrowed from her four-year-old son, Yusef. Spraying her shoulder length twists, she shivered gratefully as the cold water dripped onto smooth ebony shoulders. She sprayed her hand and wiped it over the face of the cream-skinned, red-haired toddler who was sitting in her lap contently sucking a bottle of strawberry Kool-Aid.

"Doesn't that feel good, Jumah?" she cooed as she chucked him under his damp chin. "Yes it does, doesn't it? Mommy's little baby loves the water, doesn't he?"

Jumah looked up at her and gave a small nod. She kissed him on the top of his head, then looked up to see what her other children were doing. She frowned when she saw her daughter dodging behind a beat-up red Chevy Malibu parked in front of the building.

"Shaniqua, I told you to play on the sidewalk!" she shouted to the girl.

"But Mommy, I ain't in the street." the little girl protested, shaking her head so vigorously that the wooden beads on the ends of her shoulder length braids clacked against each other. "And we're playing tag."

"Well, play tag on the sidewalk," Brenda said. "And didn't I tell you there's no such word as ain't?"

"Yes, Mommy," the girl scampered back on the sidewalk, just in time to be thumped on the arm by a small boy wearing a white tee shirt and jeans.

"Tag, you're it!" he shouted as he quickly dodged out of her reach.

"Dag, Yusef. You don't have to hit so hard. That's why nobody ever wants to play with you!" she shouted after him. "Mommy, why do we have to let Yusef play?"

"Because he's your little brother," Brenda said under her breath, knowing her daughter already knew the answer.

She watched as the children flew past her, and nodded approvingly to herself as she noted they were sticking to the confines she had set for them—four car lengths to the left of the building, and four to the right—well within her eyesight. She took a quick look at her watch. Nine-fifteen. She had told Bootsy she wanted him in front of the building by nine. She slid Jumah off her lap, and propped him on her hip as she stood up and walked outside the little courtyard so she could get a good view of the street corner. Five or six teenagers—all wearing knee-length New York Knicks basketball jerseys and oversized jeans, with ball caps pulled low on their heads—were hanging out in front of the bodega. She knew that only one, maybe two, were actually working—selling crack to the pipers desperate for a hit. The others were just wannabes, who thought it was cool for people to think they had poison to sell.

Across the street another group of teenagers were hunched down, shouting that their mother needed a new pair of shoes and shooting craps against the graffitied wall of an abandoned building.

Satisfied that Bootsy was not among either of the groups, she picked Jumah up, and went back to sit on the beach chair.

She closed her eyes and sprayed herself with the water gun again, wondering if she should try to talk her mother into loaning her one of the three air conditioners she had in her own small apartment. She knew the odds of her getting it were against her, but she decided it was worth a try.

"God, I wish we lived in an air-conditioned building," she said out loud to no one. She took a look at the tall brick building that had been her home for over twenty years and shook her head. "Man, I gotta get out of Ida B." She gave an audible sigh as she remembered her conversation with Sharif. It might be that she and everyone else would have to leave Ida B. Damn those politicians wanting to throw us out of our homes to make room for white folks, she thought. Don't they care that she'd lived here all her life and didn't even want to think about living anywhere else? *Okay, well, yeah, I do want to move somewhere else. But I don't want to anyone to be telling me I have to move before I'm good and ready.* Maybe after she wrote her book. It was going to be a bestseller, she knew, even though she still didn't know what it was going to be about. The island where everybody dies sounded like a good idea, or maybe they don't die, but they're forever confined because . . . because what? she pondered. Because they're all blind. No, because even though they're wise and farsighted when it comes to making the world a better place, they're all so nearsighted physically they can't see anything besides what's right in front of them. *Oh, yeah, that's good.* Brenda reached down in Jumah's diaper bag and pulled out her notebook and started writing furiously.

Yeah. They had had big dreams but because of their shortsightedness they weren't able to go anywhere. Or maybe that wasn't the book. She sighed and returned the notebook to the diaper bag. Maybe it would be something entirely different. But she knew it would make her rich. Maybe she'd even be able to buy one of the brownstones in Harlem that were running about $800,000. It would probably be a drop in the bucket, as rich as she'd be after winning the Nobel Prize for literature. And the Pulitzer, too.

"I don't know why the hell people gotta feel like they gotta pee in the goddamned elevator."

Brenda looked up. "Hey, Chante. You look nice."

"I should." Chante patted her weave ponytail to make sure it was in place, then pushed up her red leather bustier to make sure her cleavage was at its best. "This suit cost Big Buddha a cool fifteen hundred bucks. He'd kill me if he knew I was wearing it out with Vance."

"So where's Buddha?" Brenda asked as she admired the way the leather pants hugged Chante's butt. Tight as hell, but the seams weren't pulling. Perfect fit.

"Who the fuck knows? Probably sniffing up Rosa's skeezy ass." Chante looked at Brenda, and then gave a weak smile. "Sorry. I forgot that's your girl."

Brenda waved her hand. "You don't have to worry about Rosa. She only messes with Puerto Rican guys."

"What? She prejudiced or some shit?" Chante said as she craned her neck to look down the street. "That damn Vance better hurry up before I dump his ass and go to the club. Oh, there he is," she said as a white Bentley parked on the corner. "I'll see you later." She patted her hair again and strutted off on her red stiletto heels.

"Mommy, Mommy, Bootsy's fighting," Shaniqua started tapping Brenda on the shoulder.

"What?" Brenda jumped up so quickly that Jumah almost tumbled to the sidewalk. "Where is he?"

"In the back, in the playground," Shaniqua said in a sing-song tattletale voice. "Jessie just told me," she added, pointing to a seven-year-old boy who stood close by, nodding his head in confirmation.

"Shit! Go get Yusef, and y'all come on." Brenda picked up the whining Jumah and marched into the lobby of the Ida B. "You know the kids are fighting in the playground?" she breathlessly demanded of the security guard who was sitting behind the desk. He looked up and shrugged, then went back to reading his Donald Goines book.

"You know they don't care," a voice said behind her.

Brenda quickly turned and looked at the almond-skinned middle-aged woman with a flaming red Jheri Curl hairdo. "Oh, good. Mom. Watch the kids for me while I go get Bootsy," she said as she pushed Jumah into her mother's arms.

She ran to the back of the lobby, and out the small door which led to the tiny playground that connected the Ida B. Wells-Barnett Tower to the Fannie Lou Hamer Tower.

"Bootsy!" she yelled as she pushed through a crowd of kids gathered around two youngsters rolling around on the blacktop. She waited until Bootsy was at the bottom, then reached down and grabbed his opponent by the neck and pulled him backward and off her son, ignoring the groaning protests of the kids who had been watching the fight.

"Stop it," she yelled when Bootsy scrambled up from the ground and tried to go after the boy.

"Ma, that little faggot started it," Bootsy yelled.

"You're the faggot," the boy said as he violently yanked himself from Brenda's grasp. "Your fucking mother had to come save your ass, you little bitch."

"Both of you stop all that cursing," Brenda grabbed Bootsy by the arm and started pulling him toward the Ida B.

"Fuck you, you stupid bitch," the boy yelled after them.

"Fuck you!" Bootsy yelled back as he tried to escape Brenda's grasp, but she tightened her grip.

"Don't let these idiots down here get to you," Brenda whispered to him as she continued to steer him to the building.

"But, Ma," Bootsy started.

"Ma, nothing. I didn't raise you to be out here clambering on the ground like a street rat," Brenda said as she opened the door to the Ida B. and prepared to shove Bootsy inside.

"And your mother ain't nothing but a fucking ho," the boy suddenly shouted out.

"Yaw, G, you ain't gotta be wolfing on Miss Brenda like that." Brenda recognized the voice as that of one of Bootsy's friends.

"Yeah?" The other youngster taunted. "I hear the bitch got four kids by four different men. Yo, Bootsy! I bet you don't even know who your father is, you fucking trick baby."

Brenda slowly turned and looked at the boy who stared back defiantly. He seemed about sixteen, which would make him about three years older than Bootsy, and he looked a few inches taller than her son. Never taking her eyes off the sneering kid, Brenda leaned back toward Booty's ear. "He's a little bigger than you, Baby, but I think you can take him."

Bootsy grinned. He hunched his shoulders a few times and jerked his head to the side a couple of times, like a boxer impatiently waiting in the corner for the bell to ring. "Yeah, Ma. Don't worry, I got this."

"Okay," Brenda let go of Bootsy's arm and gave him a quick pat on the back. "Go kick his ass, son."

"Lord, I don't know why you boys always gotta be out there fighting." Brenda's mother shook her head sadly as they waited for the elevator ten minutes later.

"That guy started it, Nana." Bootsy winced as Brenda dabbed at his bloody upper lip with a wet paper napkin.

"Yeah, Mrs. Carver," one of the youngsters who had been outside agreed. "Those Fannie kids are always starting with us. Bootsy was just defending himself."

"Y'all need to stop calling them children the Fannie kids," Mrs. Carver chuckled.

"Well, it is kind of funny since they live at the Fannie Lou Hamer," Brenda grinned.

"And they be calling us names and stuff," the youngster piped up. "They always be trying to pick at us."

The other kids crowding around their champion nodded and mumbled their agreement.

"They even be messing with me, Nana," Shaniqua piped up.

"Yeah, me too, Nana." Yusef tapped his grandmother on the hip to get her attention.

"Hmmph! Well, it don't make no sense. Y'all are damn near neighbors," Mrs. Carver said with a frown. "But I hope you beat him good, Bootsy." She patted her grandson on the shoulder.

"Oh, yeah, Mrs. Carver! He really kicked his a—" the youngster caught himself. "Um. He really beat him good."

"Well, good, but I don't want you out there fighting anymore," Mrs. Carver said. "You going to cause your poor mother to have a heart attack at her young age. You know she don't like no fighting."

Brenda winked her eye at Bootsy, but said nothing.

"And you setting a bad example for your sister and brothers," Mrs. Carver continued as the elevator finally arrived. "And for this little one over here." She held up the hand of a small boy with black curly hair and smooth skin that looked the perfect blend of brown and red. The boy, who was sucking two fingers of his right hand, raised his large limpid brown eyes to look at Bootsy, then ducked behind Mrs. Carver's ample hips.

"Come on, Jimmy. It's all right," Mrs. Carver said soothingly as she patted him on the head. "Don't you remember Bootsy?"

Jimmy peeked from behind Mrs. Carver then ducked back quickly, nodding.

"He never was too much of a talker, poor boy," Mrs. Carver clucked. She leaned close to Brenda. "And you know he's been even worse since they put him in that foster home. You shoulda seen that place I had to pick him up from. The woman had a whole buncha little hooligans running around tearing up the house and her not caring, and poor Jimmy sitting by himself in a corner sucking his fingers all terrified."

"Aw, the poor thing," Brenda whispered back. She reached over and softly stroked the little boy's face, causing him to give a small grateful smile. "How about you being one of the guests of honor at the party tomorrow, Sweetie. It can be a birthday party for Jumah, and a welcome home party for you, okay? You don't mind sharing, do you, Jumah?" She jiggled the toddler, not realizing he had drifted off to sleep until he gave an angry whine at the disturbance.

"Isn't that nice, Jimmy?" Mrs. Carver bent down and pulled the little boy into her arms. "You're going to have a party. Isn't that nice of Miss Brenda to do that for you?"

"Mom," Brenda said as the elevator reached the tenth floor and the two women and five children got out. "Can I borrow the air conditioner from your spare bedroom? My apartment is as hot as a sauna."

"I'm sorry, Sweets, but Jimmy is going to be sleeping in there tonight, and I want him to be comfortable."

"Yeah, okay." Brenda poked her mouth out, and still cradling Jumah over her shoulder, she grabbed Yusef's hand and started walking down the hall, Shaniqua and Bootsy trailing behind her.

"Now see, you done went and got an attitude," Mrs. Carver shouted after her.

"I don't have an attitude, Ma," Brenda said without turning

around. "I'm just tired, and I want to put some ice on Bootsy's face and then get these kids to bed."

"Well, okay, then." Mrs. Carver said in a softer tone. She waited until Brenda put her key in her apartment door before finally saying. "Hey, Sweets, call Sharif and see if he can come upstairs and carry this air conditioner for you. It's too heavy for Bootsy."

Brenda turned and bestowed a huge grin upon her mother. "You sure, Ma?"

"Oh, sure," Mrs. Carver nodded her head rapidly. "I'll put one of the little cots in my bedroom and Jimmy can sleep in there with me." She turned and started down the other end of the hallway. "Tell Sharif to call me to let me know he's on his way up, 'cause you know I don't be usually answering my door this time of night."

"Okay, thanks, Ma."

5

"Ay, *coño*. Why would anyone in their right mind be cooking chitlins in this heat?"

Brenda glanced over at Rosa who wrinkled her nose, her body involuntarily shuddering as they marched down the long second-floor hallway Friday evening. Brenda's yellow flip-flops slapped against her heels and the dirty tile floor, making almost as much noise as the taps on Rosa's three-inch black high heels. She wanted to hurry to get back to the party that had started earlier that afternoon before her mother started complaining about her sneaking away to try and help Rosa out.

She frowned as she noticed the words 'D. J. Pimpmaster B' scrawled in green marker on the yellow concrete walls.

"I'm going to kick Bootsy's butt, tagging all over the place all the time." She tapped Rosa on the shoulder and pointed to the writing. "He better scrub this wall down before the maintenance people see it and tell the building manager. I already got a warning. They said they're going to charge me fifty dollars next time they have to—"

"Brenda? I thought I heard your voice."

Brenda turned to look at the woman who had stuck her head out of an apartment door. "Hi, Miss Theresa. I hope I wasn't making too much noise."

"No, no, no." The woman shook her head. "I was just sitting down by the door. Look. Do me a favor and tell your mother I got a pair of shoes that Jimmy can have. My Ernie grew out of them.

"Okay, I'll do that," Brenda nodded.

"I'd give them to you now, but I don't feel going in his room looking for them. The place is a pigsty." The woman shook her head and put her hand over her face. "And this hallway smell like shit. Pig shit." She waved at Brenda and quickly closed the door.

"God, this shit stinks!" Rosa cut her off. "I don't see how you black people can be eating something that smells like that. Pig intestines. Ugh!"

"Yeah, well. Puerto Ricans be eating blood sausage, so I wouldn't talk about chitlins if I were you," Brenda gave Rosa a small push on the shoulder.

"Yeah, but still it don't stink like this when you cook it, and shit." Rosa waved her hand in front of her nose. "Who the hell is cooking this shit in this heat, though?"

"Probably Mrs. Gray," Brenda shrugged without slowing her pace. "Tomorrow's the first Saturday of the month, so she's probably cooking for her son's poker party. He lets her sell dinners to make some extra money."

"Hmph, I can understand her wanting to make some extra money, but does she gotta stink up the whole goddamned building?" Rosa put her hand over her face and continued in a muffled voice. "I'm about to fucking gag and shit."

The smell grew stronger the further down the hallway they walked, and reached a peak as they neared Apartment 2F.

"Yeah, I knew it was Mrs. Gray," Brenda chuckled.

Rosa snorted when she saw that the door was slightly ajar. She reached out and quickly, but quietly, pulled the door closed as she passed by.

"Ooh, Rosa!" Brenda giggled. "You know she probably had the door cracked to let some of the smell out."

"So we gotta suffer, and shit? Huh! I don't think so," Rosa huffed.

A few seconds later they stopped in front of Apartment 2P. Rosa took a quick look at her watch and turned to Brenda. "I'm telling you, *chica*, she's not going to go for it. You know how she is." She shook her head derisively.

"She might," Brenda said reassuringly. "It's worth a try."

"*Coño*, of all days for rehearsals to run late. I thought I'da been back by four and been able to stop by 125th Street and pick up something. And I still have to change my clothes before I go to the party," Rosa paused when she saw the look on Brenda's face. "I promise it won't take me but a minute."

"I hope not. You're supposed to be helping with all the kids, you know. You promised." Brenda huffed.

"It won't take me but a minute to change, I swear. Soon as we finish here I'll run upstairs and be at your place in five minutes. Watch." Rosa screwed up her face. "But I still think we're not going to be able to do this. I'm telling you she's not going to go for it."

Brenda put her finger against her mouth to signal Rosa to lower her voice. "It's worth a try. And she likes me, so she might give us a break," she whispered as she gave a couple of quick taps of the metal knocker.

"Who is it?"

"It's me, Mrs. Harris. Brenda." Brenda spoke loudly, to be heard over the din of barking dogs, and took a few steps back from the door so she'd be more visible through the peephole. "I'm sorry to bother you, but Rosa and I were wondering if we could look around for something real quick?"

"Well, how are you, dear?" A grandmotherly voice answered back. "And who's that you say you have with you? The Puerto Rican girl Rosa?"

"Yeah, Mrs. Harris," Rosa piped up. "Me. The Puerto Rican girl."

"Well, now isn't that nice." Mrs. Harris said through the door.

"We just need to come in for a minute, Mrs. Harris," Brenda said.

"Well, you know it's little late, Brenda, dear. I close up at six PM. Every night. Six PM sharp, dear." the woman's shrill voice rattled back from behind the closed door. "I'm about to sit down to my dinner. I always eat at six-fifteen sharp."

"Come on, Mrs. Harris. Please?" Rosa strained to speak loud enough to be heard over the snarling and barking dogs, and yet still have a friendly tone apparent in her voice. She flashed a smile at the peephole and crossed her fingers behind her back. "I meant to get here earlier, but rehearsal ended late. I promise we'll be in and out before you know it."

"Fifi and Pinky, will you two please be quiet. I can barely hear the poor girls out there with all your fuss."

"Mrs. Harris, please!" Brenda said urgently, glancing at her watch. She really wanted to get back to the party.

"Well . . ." There was a short pause. "Well, all right, dearie. I'll do this for you just this once, because you've always been such a sweet little girl. And I like the Puerto Rican girl, too. But don't tell anybody now, because I don't want people to take advantage of my kindness."

Brenda and Rosa both breathed a sigh of relief as Mrs. Harris began to noisily undo the five locks on the apartment door. "Now I'm not trying to be nasty or pushy, dears, but you really have to be quick about it. I do have to eat at six-fifteen sharp, you know. If I eat any later than that I can't sleep," she said when she finally opened the door a crack.

Brenda smiled and was about to step inside, but quickly jumped back, almost knocking Rosa down, as a large snarling brown-and-white pit bull shoved his massive head through the slight opening.

"Pinky, get back." Mrs. Harris's heavy brown cane came down sharply on the dog's pink speckled brown nose. The dog gave a light yelp, and backed away, finally sitting next to a huge black and tan Rottweiler which was standing at full alert and staring at the young women.

"Come on in, Brenda dear," Mrs. Harris said with a toothless smile. Her thin steel-gray hair was short and pulled back into a skinny braid. Her maroon cotton housedress, which was covered with enormous yellow daisies, hung loosely on her small slightly stooped frame, and dark brown liver spots covered the hand she used to lean on her cane for support.

"Um, Mrs. Harris, don't you think you should put the dogs in the back or something?" Rosa glanced nervously at Pinky who seemed to be trying to convey through his mean expression that he blamed them for the stinging rap that had rendered his speckled nose tender.

"Now, dear, you know I can't do that. It is after hours after all," Mrs. Harris said as she opened the door wider. "But don't you worry. Fifi and Pinky will be on their best behavior while you nice young ladies look around. Won't you, sweeties?" Mrs. Harris bent down and patted Fifi on the head, and the dog gave her hand a quick lick in acknowledgment. Pinky, for his part, gave a large grunt, and Brenda could swear the dog cut his eyes at her.

"So what is it that you two dears are looking for this evening?" Mrs. Harris asked as Brenda and Rosa cautiously entered the apartment, keeping their eyes on the Fifi and Pinky.

"Well, I just need a gift for a four-year-old and a two-year-old." Rosa said.

"Boys or girls?" Mrs. Harris said as she hobbled down the dimly interior hall toward the back of the apartment, shooing the dogs in front of her, with Brenda and Rosa following.

"Both boys."

Mrs. Harris nodded and opened the second door on her right. Rows of shiny shellacked brown wooden shelves lined all four walls of the room. On the right were VCRs, CD players, DVD players, small televisions, and cable boxes. On the wall across from them were cameras, boom boxes, car stereos, and various types of audio gear. Straight ahead were computers, modems, printers, scanners, and fax machines.

Some were obviously used equipment, but some looked almost brand new. One computer system—complete with monitor, keyboard, and speakers—was still wrapped in the manufacturer's plastic, although the box was nowhere in sight. In the middle of the room were a few pieces of exercise equipment, including a full-size treadmill and a weight bench.

To the right of the door were electronic game systems like Sega and PlayStation, and the game cartridges that went with them. Mrs. Harris walked over and slid open a closet door revealing dozens of toys for various age groups, some still in boxes. It was an array that would have made Santa Claus envious. But then Old St. Nick didn't have an army of dope fiends, crackheads, and professional burglars supplying him with stolen goods at wholesale prices.

"This is all I've got right now, as far as toys, but if you'd like clothes I just got some real nice little suits in the wardrobe room down the hall." Mrs. Harris leaned heavily on her cane as she watched Brenda and Rosa poke through the closet. The dogs sat at her feet, their ears standing at alert, and their eyes fixed on the younger women.

"What about this for Jumah?" Rosa held up a brand new Chicken Dance Elmo.

"Oh, yeah, I think he'd like that," Brenda nodded.

"How much?" Rosa turned to the older woman.

"Good choice. The Elmo toys are always one of my popular sellers. And as you can see that one's in mint condition, the box has never been opened. I can let you have it for just ten dollars," Mrs. Harris said in a voice that Brenda noted had suddenly changed from grandmotherly to professional businesswoman "Goes for twenty in the store."

"Does it need batteries?" Rosa peered at the back of the brightly colored box.

"It takes four double-A batteries, and they're included."

"Good, I'll take it." Rosa tucked the box under her arm. "Now what do I get for Little Jimmy?"

"How much would you like to spend?" Mrs. Harris asked.

"Well, if I'm only paying ten dollars for Jumah's gift, and he's my godson, I don't think I should pay more than that for Jimmy. Right?" Rosa turned to Brenda for confirmation before turning back to Mrs. Harris. "I would say about six or seven dollars."

"What about a video game? I just had a couple of the new war game videos come in. Kids are crazy about those."

"Sounds good. How much?" Rosa asked as she walked over to look at the video games, all lined up on the shelves in alphabetical order.

"Yeah, well, you know, he's only four years old," Brenda interjected.

"Of course, dear, but not to worry, I've got a couple of Super Mario Brothers Deluxe videos right over there," Mrs. Harris pointed to the far right corner of the second shelf. "It goes for thirty in the stores, and I usually sell it for fifteen, but I'll let it go for eight dollars because you two are such sweet young ladies."

"Sold!" Rosa grabbed the video game off the shelf, and then pulled a twenty dollar bill out of her wallet and handed it to Mrs. Harris.

"Thank you so much, dear." Mrs. Harris sat down on a small folding chair near the dog, and then reached into her housedress and pulled a huge wad of bills from her bosom. "Let's see, I owe you two dollars, right?" She unwrapped the two pink rubber bands that were holding the bills in place, flipped the wad open, and pulled two singles from the top of bunch. "There you go," she said as she placed the bills in Rosa's outstretched hand. "Do you need a bag, dear?"

6

The air conditioner was going full blast, but the temperature in Brenda's apartment stayed at a steady eighty degrees. Brenda sighed her deep appreciation at the cool air from the freezer rushing forward to greet her as she went to refill the blue plastic ice bowl. She glanced at the green duck-shaped clock on the yellow kitchen wall as she turned to bang the ice tray against the edge of the sink to loosen the cubes. It was eight o'clock, almost two hours since she had gone down to Mrs. Harris's apartment with Rosa. *Yeah, I knew she was lying when she said she just wanted to run upstairs and change her clothes real quick. That's why she gave me the kids' presents to give them*, she thought as she dropped ice into two glasses, while bopping her shoulders to the 50 Cent CD someone had put on the stereo in the living room. She knew Rosa was trying to wait until she was sure most of the kids had left. And most of them already had. Most of the people still at Jumah and Jimmy's party were adults. Of the fifteen kids who had attended only four remained.

She rubbed her hands over her face as she thought about the cost of the party. Between the paper goods, liquor, and presents, more than three hundred dollars had been gobbled up from her measly six hundred dollar welfare check. Not to mention the two hundred dollars in food stamps that she had to use to for the potato salad, fried chicken, and collard greens. But her mother was right. It was important for a child to have a party to celebrate his birthday. Of course her mother only had one child, she had four. And Shaniqua's birthday was only six weeks away.

"Mmm, mmm . . ."

Brenda looked down to see Jimmy standing next to her, making the little puppy dog noise he made whenever he wanted something. He held his head low, but looked up at her through his dark lashes, holding a little blue plastic straw cup in front of him.

"Hey there, Party Boy! You want some more chocolate milk?" Her heart melted as it did whenever he made any attempt to communicate with her. The boy had been almost completely nonverbal since his return to Ida B., and he clung tightly to Mrs. Carver whenever someone came too near him. He had always been an especially shy child, even before the tragedy which had left him an orphan, but now he was almost neurotic. And even the word "almost" was questionable. Brenda made a mental note to suggest to her mother that she send the boy to get some kind of counseling. The City would probably pay for it, she figured.

"Let me get that for you, baby, okay?" She gently took the cup from the boy's hand and quickly poured in the chocolate milk, then handed it back to him. "You want anything else, baby?" She knelt down next to him, causing him to stumble slightly in his hurry to back away from her.

"Hey Ma! I'm going to go shoot some hoop!"

Brenda looked up to see Bootsy enter the kitchen, trying to balance a twirling basketball on his index finger.

"Bootsy, don't—" Before she could finish, the basketball went spinning off her son's finger and onto the stove, almost toppling a pot of spaghetti onto the floor, before bouncing off and hitting Brenda in the head.

"Damn it, Bootsy! Didn't I tell you about playing with that damn ball in the house!" Brenda stood up and tried to slap her son on the side of the head, but he ducked quickly out of her reach.

"Ma! Ma! I'm sorry, Ma," he said quickly.

"Oh, you're going to be sorry!" Brenda started toward her retreating son, but stopped when she heard soft laughter coming from behind her. She turned to see Jimmy, laughing so hard his little face was red.

"Ooh, Booty. You hit Miss Brenda in the head," he said pointing to the older boy.

"Oh, now you can talk, huh?" she said with a chuckle.

"Look at you trying to get me in trouble," Bootsy said. "I thought you was my man."

"Were my man," Brenda corrected him.

"I'm your man! I'm your man!" Jimmy started violently nodding his head.

"Okay, if you my man, give me a pound." Bootsy reached out his fist and Jimmy obediently pounded his own fist against it. "All right, you my man," Bootsy said with a grin.

"You my man, too!" Jimmy said excitedly.

Bootsy retrieved the basketball from the floor and turned to his mother. "Ma, can I go out and shoot some hoops for a little while?"

"Can I go with you, Booty? I wanna go!" Jimmy started jumping up and down, causing little drops of chocolate milk to drop from his straw cup onto the floor. "Please, Booty? Please can I go?"

"Yeah, you can go, little man, but you better stop calling me Booty. My name is Bootsy." Bootsy feinted a couple of punches to Jimmy's face, causing the boy to double up with laughter.

Brenda smiled as she watched the horseplay. "When did you two become so tight?"

"I don't know," Bootsy shrugged as he bounced the basketball. "I was showing him how to play some video games this afternoon and he got pretty good at 'em. I told him I'd let him hang out with me sometime. So I'ma take him down to the park. He can be my mascot." He turned to Jimmy. "You wanna be my mascot?"

"Yeah, Booty, I do." Jimmy nodded his head vigorously, his face as serious as if he were on a witness stand.

"How's he going to go out with you when he's having a party?" Brenda demanded.

"Aw, Ma. Ain't nothing going on up in here for him anyway," Bootsy protested. "All your friends are in the living room just getting drunk. Won't nobody even miss him."

"Stop saying ain't."

"Yeah, a'ight. So can he come?"

Brenda looked at Jimmy's expectant face, and chuckled. "Yeah, okay. But bring him back upstairs before dark," she said finally.

"Come on, Ma. It's going to be dark in like an hour," Bootsy protested.

"I don't want him out too late, Bootsy." Brenda said firmly as she took the plastic straw cup from Jimmy's hands. "Bring him upstairs and you can go back down for a little bit."

"All right," Bootsy agreed. "Come on, Little Man. Let's go rock the court."

"All right. You my man, Booty!" Jimmy said excitedly as he followed Bootsy out into the hallway.

"And stop calling me Booty!"

Brenda shook her head as she watched them leave. That was certainly an odd couple, she thought. But maybe Bootsy's outgoing nature would rub off on the boy, and maybe having Jimmy around would slow Bootsy down a bit. She grabbed a paper towel and bent down to wipe the sprinkling of chocolate milk Jimmy had dribbled onto the floor.

"Oh, damn! Brenda, you'd better get the mop. Nancy's spilled her Kool-Aid again!" a woman's voice rang out from the living room.

Brenda rolled her eyes, snatched a yellow sponge mop from the corner, and turned toward the doorway.

"Girl, don't worry about it. Just pass me a couple of paper towels and I'll wipe it up." A short tan-skinned young woman with long black hair pulled back into a single plait appeared in the kitchen, jiggling a whining three-year-old girl on her skinny hips, and blocking Brenda's path.

"Nancy only spilled a couple of drops of Kool-Aid out her cup, and only because she's sleepy," the woman said as she grabbed the paper towels from Brenda. "That damn Tisha's just trying to make a big deal about it to get on my nerves. I'm going to go ahead and clean this up then I'm going to take Nancy home and put her to bed. Thanks for inviting us."

"Oh, Lucia, please," Brenda gave a quick wave of her hand. "You don't have to pay Tisha any mind. Stay and enjoy yourself."

"No, I'm going to go on home, 'cause I don't want no trouble. 'Cause I'm going to hurt Tisha if she keeps messing with me. She just don't like Puerto Ricans, is all it is." Lucia stomped out of the kitchen before Brenda could respond.

Brenda simply shrugged her shoulders, grabbed the ice bowl, and headed into the living room after her.

Two men and three women were squeezed onto the green leather sofa on one side of the room, and two other women were sitting on each arm. Three people were sitting on the love seat which was meant to hold two. Vincent was sitting in the green leather arm chair off in the corner near the stereo, with an Asian looking woman on his lap and a dark-skinned woman with shoulder-length braids trying to balance herself on the arm of the chair. Sharif was in front of the stereo, shuffling through CDs, while behind him a woman with a butt-length blond hair weave and dark brown roots danced in one spot, holding a drink in one hand and a cigarette in the other. Two women, one dressed like a man, were standing in another corner of the room next to a brass floor lamp, whispering to each other, while another woman, Tisha, sat perched in the middle of the glass coffee table, an overflowing ashtray next to her, and an array of half-empty plastic cups scattered around her.

"Mommy, can me and Yusef spend the night at Lucia's house?" Shaniqua ran up behind Brenda and started tugging on the sleeve of her blouse. Brenda swung around to face her daughter, but before she could answer, someone was tapping her on the shoulder.

"Sweetie, Jumah needs changing. He did a number two," her mother said as she tried to push the yawning baby in her hands.

"Hey, Bren." She turned toward the living room, at the sound of Sharif's voice, "Where's your Musiq CD? Let's get something on here besides all this hip-hop crap."

"To hell with you, Sharif," Vincent yelled. "You take that 50 Cent CD off and I'm going to kick your ass."

"Stop cursing in front of all these kids, Vince," the woman sitting on his lap gave him a soft tap on the shoulder.

"How you going to be telling him what to do?" Tisha snapped from her seat on the coffee table. "Vincent's a grown man. Leave him alone."

"Yeah, well, then I'll kick his butt." Vincent ignored the woman and addressed the girl on his lap. "Either way, if he changes that CD I'm going to put a hurting on the boy."

"Miss Brenda, your toilet's got water coming out the bowl," a small light-skinned boy with freckles the size of dimes splattered over his face was saying, "but it's not because I put too much toilet paper in it. But I'm sorry anyway."

"Brenda, I thought you were going to get some ice? Girl, what's the holdup?" Tisha snapped.

"Damn, Tisha, get off your fat ass and get it yourself."

"Was I talking to you, Vincent? I woulda got it, but Brenda said she was. And I'm a guest. So watch your damn mouth. I don't know why you always gotta act so mean to me. Brenda, where's the ice!"

Brenda's hand flew up to her forehead, and she dramatically rolled her eyes up toward the ceiling before leaning against the only bare spot on the wall and slowly sinking to a sitting position on the floor, her legs spread out in front of her and the bowl of ice in her lap.

"Okay," she said putting her hands, palms out, in front of her, looking at no one directly. "I'm not trying to be funny, but I can't take all of this. It's been a long day, and I've pulled this off without any real help, and you guys are just going to have to give me a break."

"I know I'm late, but I'm here!" The front door swung open and a short but voluptuously built copper-skinned woman with a short salt-and-pepper Afro puffed into the apartment. "Y'all better not have cut the cake. Where's my nephews. Bootsy! Shaniqua! Yusef! Jumah! Where's my kiss? Y'all come give your Aunt Pat a kiss."

"Aunt Pat!" Shaniqua ran toward the middle-aged woman and tried to jump into her arms. "Ooh, Aunt Pat, we was waiting for you!"

"Were waiting on you," Brenda corrected her from her seat on the floor. "Hey, Aunt Pat."

"Child, what the hell are you doing on the damn floor?" Pat reached out her hand to help Brenda up. "Where's my kiss?"

"They're trying to wear me out, Aunt Pat." Brenda gave the woman a quick peck on the cheek.

"My sister ain't helping out in here?"

"No, Mommy said since she did the cooking she's sitting the rest of the party out."

"What? Where's she at? Let me set her straight." Pat put her hands and glanced over the crowded living room. "Janet!"

"I'm right here behind you. Just calm down," Mrs. Carver was still jiggling Jumah in her arms. "And Brenda's exaggerating as usual."

"Exaggerating my ass! Look at the poor baby!" Pat swung around to face her sister. "You got this girl working like a dog, and you're just standing around here doing nothing?"

"Well, Mommy is helping me a little," Brenda protested weakly.

"Obviously not enough," Pat stormed. "You look like you're ready to drop dead. She ain't got no business working you like that."

"Pat, please! You just got here, you don't know what's going on and you're ready to start some stuff." Mrs. Carver shook her head. "And I can smell the liquor on your breath a mile away."

"And?" Pat stepped back, raised herself up to her full five feet, and put her hands on her hips. "What you trying to say? You think I'm drunk because I'm trying to defend my niece? Don't make me whup you up in here like I used to do when we were kids. 'Cause I'll do it, you know."

"Hey, Aunt Pat!" Sharif came up behind the woman and grabbed her in a huge bear hug. "How's my favorite lady!"

"How you doing, baby?" Pat gave a giggle, quickly forgetting her sister as she twisted in Sharif's arms to face him. "Where's my kiss?"

"Right here!" Sharif bent down and gave the woman a full kiss on the mouth.

"Aw, sukie sukie now! You gonna make me think you're starting to like women," Pat started laughing, her full breasts almost jiggling free of her low-cut blouse.

"Not likely," Tisha guffawed as she crossed her legs on the coffee table.

"What?" Pat swung around to glare at the woman. "Who the fuck are you? You trying to bust on my Sharif?" She turned back to Sharif. "You want me to get with this little heifer? 'Cause I will, you know."

"Naw, I was only making a joke," Tisha said quickly. "I'm sorry."

"Well, don't be joking about my Sharif. I don't play that shit." Pat huffed at the girl. "And get your ass off that coffee table before you break the glass."

"Hey, Aunt Pat!" Vincent pushed the Asian looking girl off his lap and stood up. "How you doing, baby girl?"

"Now y'all ain't tell me Mac Daddy was going to be here." Pat batted her eyes at Vincent flirtatiously. "Now here's a man I know loves woman."

Vincent laughed and gave Pat a kiss on the cheek, than pointed to the chair he had vacated. "Why don't you sit down? Or would you prefer me to sit and you can cop a seat on my lap, you fine thing, you?"

"Boy, you couldn't handle all this woman," Pat giggled as she sashayed over to the armchair and sat down.

"I've been waiting all my life to try." Vincent grinned.

"You better stop playing, boy, or I'll give you something that'll make you forget all this young pussy up in here." She quickly covered her mouth. "Oops! I forgot there was kids in here." She looked at her sister who was still holding little Jumah. "Janet, pass that baby over here so he can give his Aunt Pat a kiss."

"He needs changing," Mrs. Carver grumbled as she passed the baby to the woman.

"So why ain't you changed him, then." Pat smothered the sleepy baby to her breast, causing him to laugh wildly. "Where's my kiss? Gimme my kiss, you sweet birthday boy."

"I'll change him, Aunt Pat," Lucia suddenly appeared at her side.

"Hey, Lucia, honey. Thank you, baby." Pat passed her the baby then leaned back in the chair, crossing her feet at the ankles. "What y'all got to drink?"

"You want some Kool-Aid, Aunt Pat?" Shaniqua said excitedly. "I'll get you some Kool-Aid."

"No, honey. Your Aunt Pat needs something a little stronger." Pat laughed.

"We have vodka and gin, and I think we have some wine left," Brenda said. "We ran out of rum about an hour ago."

"And you couldn't send one of these grown-ass men in here to the store to get some more?" Pat sucked her teeth and reached down into her pocketbook and pulled out a fifth of Bacardi Light. "Good thing I carry my own shit with me."

"Here, I'll get you a glass of ice." Tisha stood up.

"I thought I told you to get off that table anyway. Your mother ain't teach you better than to come in people's houses and sit on the tables?" Pat looked the girl up and down. "Who's your mother anyway?"

"You don't know her."

"How you know I don't know her? Shit, I know everybody."

"Her name's Bernice Brown."

"I don't know her." Pat shrugged her shoulders. "Yeah, you can get me a glass of ice. Thanks."

Mrs. Carver sidled up next to Brenda who had been watching the goings-on with amusement. "I hope Patricia doesn't start any shit. You know she's already drunk, right?"

Brenda waved her hand. "Aw, Ma. She's just having a good time."

"Okay." Mrs. Carver threw her hands up in the air. "Don't say I didn't warn you. But I think you'd better tell that girl Tisha to get out of here because she's already pissed Patricia off."

Brenda laughed. "Tisha isn't going anywhere while Vincent still's here. She's been trying to get with him all night. And anyway, she's making her peace with Aunt Pat." She nodded at Tisha as the girl walked past her into the kitchen.

"Hmph! Well, you better tell her to watch out," Mrs. Carver said as she walked off toward the back of the apartment. "You know how your aunt can be."

Brenda shrugged and went into the kitchen, and passed Tisha the bowl with the now partially melted ice. "So you met my aunt."

"Yeah, she's a trip." Tisha grabbed a plastic cup from the counter then dipped her hand into the bowl to get two cubes of ice. "I can tell she's all the way live."

"Yeah, she's something." Brenda nodded.

"She and Vincent are real tight, huh?"

"Oh, they play flirt all the time. It's not anything, though. Aunt Pat wouldn't think about doing anything with him. She likes messing with him and he likes being messed with, is all."

"Yeah, he probably thinks of her kind of like a mother figure, huh?"

Brenda looked at the girl and laughed. "Believe me, Aunt Pat isn't anyone's mother figure."

Tisha joined in the laughter. "Yeah, you probably got that right. But I can tell he really likes her, so she must be all right. I'm going to get in good with her, you watch. Hey, remember to give me those pictures before I leave."

"What pictures?"

"The ones of me at the family reunion in Virginia Beach. I gave them to you the other day because you wanted to look at them."

"Ooh, look what the cat finally dragged in! Hey, Brenda! Rosa's here," Lucia shouted into the kitchen.

"Well, it's about time!" Brenda turned, her hand on her hip, and gave her best friend the once over, then reached over and gave her the customary tap on the shoulder. "I thought you were supposed to be down here two hours ago!"

"I'm sorry, *chica,*" Rosa said as she tapped her back. "Mommy called from Puerto Rico, and she talked so long I actually fell asleep with the telephone to my ear. You mad at me?"

"Oh, so you going to tell me your eyes are red from sleeping, huh? Not from smoking that shit, huh? Yeah, I'm mad as hell!"

"Well, get over it and shit," Rosa laughed, then took Jumah from Lucia. "How's my little birthday boy? How's my baby, huh?" She buried her face in his stomach and made a loud blowing sound. "You like that, huh, Jumah? You like your *madrina* to blow on your little tummy? *Te gusta, papi?*"

"Okay, Brenda, I'm heading out." Lucia gave Brenda a quick hug.

"You're leaving and I just got here? Yeah, okay," Rosa said as she carried Jumah toward the living room. "*Hasta mañana.*"

"Oh, great. More of that yin-yang shit," Tisha mumbled under her breath as she also headed into the living room, carrying a glass of ice.

Lucia turned to look at Tisha, and then gave Brenda a quick

nudge. "You know, I changed my mind. I think I'm going to stick around a little bit."

"You just want to see some drama," Brenda chuckled. "But Rosa isn't going to start anything in my house."

"She won't have to," Lucia said as she walked out the kitchen. "Tisha'll start it. Rosa will just finish it off. And good!"

"Hey, Aunt Pat!" Rosa was saying as Brenda walked in the living room. "Long time no see, *Tia!*"

"Rosa, look at you getting all hippy like your mama," Pat said warmly as she took a swig from her drink. "Where's my kiss? What you been up to, girl?"

"I've been trying to get her up to my place," Vincent broke in. "Hey, Rosa. *Da me beso.*"

Rosa cocked her head up at him. "*Besa mi . . .*"

"Don't you say it, girl!" Vincent warned, the smile suddenly disappearing from his face.

"What? I was just going to tell you to *besa mi mano,*" Rosa grinned and presented her hand to his lips. Brenda shook her head. As tight as Rosa was with Vincent, as tight as anyone was with Vincent, everyone knew better than to cross whatever line he set.

"See that? Another black man going after a Puerto Rican woman," Pat rolled her eyes and sucked her teeth. "What? Black women ain't good enough for you anymore, Vincent?"

"I'm with you, Aunt Pat," Tisha piped in. "I'm sick of these *mira mira* babes trying to push up on our men."

"Excuse me?" Rosa whirled around, her eyes blinking rapidly as she hunched her shoulders back in disbelief. "What did you just say?" She hurriedly handed Jumah to Lucia, who was standing next to her, and strode toward Tisha.

"Hold on one goddamned minute!" Pat jumped up from the chair and stomped over to Tisha before Rosa could reach her. Her one hand was balled into a fist, she began jabbing at the girl's chest with the other. "First of all, I ain't your goddamned aunt, okay? I don't know you, and, as you so grandly pointed out a few minutes ago, I don't know your mother. Second of all, who the fuck are you calling a *mira mira* babe?"

"But I was just agreeing with you!" Tisha said as she backed away.

"What the fuck you mean you were agreeing with me? You ain't hear me call Rosa out her name!"

"Y'all get those babies out of there if Patricia's going to be fighting," Mrs. Carver called from the back bedroom.

"No one's fighting, Mommy!" Brenda yelled back as she hurried toward her aunt.

"Don't worry, Aunt Pat. I got this handled." Rosa tried to push past Pat, but Brenda pulled her back just as Sharif stepped in between Pat and Tisha.

"Come on, Aunt Pat. It's okay," he said soothingly as he tried to gently push her back.

"Come on, Aunt Pat?" the woman hollered. "What? Now you turning on me, boy? You gonna take her side over me?"

"Brenda, I mean it. Get those kids in here if Pat's going to start fighting." Mrs. Carver's voice rang out again. "I don't want any of them getting hurt."

"No one's fighting, Ma!"

Sharif raised his hands, palm up, chest level, in a gesture of surrender. "No, no, no, Aunt Pat. I would never take anyone's side against you, you know that."

"Then you don't be pulling on me, boy!" Pat stormed. "You want to pull on someone, you pull on her! Don't be pulling on me! I'm like your blood! Don't you be pulling on me! You got that?" Pat was poking his chest with every step. "Don't make me haul off and hafta slap the shit out of you! You got that?"

"I got it, Aunt Pat, I got it," Sharif said as he backed up toward the armchair.

"You better got it! I love you like a son, but don't you be pulling on me when I'm getting ready to fight! I don't play that!" Pat huffed before plopping down in the armchair. "Brenda, what did you I always tell you about me fighting?"

"Never try to hold you back when you're fighting," Brenda said as she continued to pull on Rosa, who was cursing and still trying to get at Tisha.

"And you gonna tell me Brenda knows it, and you don't?" Pat gave Sharif's foot a soft kick. "Don't make me hurt you, boy!"

"I'm sorry, Aunt Pat." Sharif gave her a sheepish grin. "I musta forgot."

"And don't be thinking because I'm sitting down I won't just get up and kick your ass if you start calling my niece or my nephew names again!" Pat shot at Tisha, who was gathering up her pocketbook.

"I ain't call none of your nephews anything," Tisha grumbled.

"Yes, you did! You called Sharif a faggot!" Pat braced her arms on the chair as if she was going to get up again.

"No, I didn't!" Tisha looked around the room as if seeking confirmation.

"Yes, you did! I heard her!" Rosa screamed, still trying to get past Brenda. "You called me a *mira mira* babe, and you called Sharif a *maricón*. You little bitch. You little *puta*."

"Vincent, can you give me a ride home?" Tisha said as she stepped clear of Brenda and Rosa.

"No." Vincent's face and voice showed no expression as he lit a cigarette.

"Yeah, well, fine. I'll just grab a cab," Tisha snapped. "Brenda, you got those pictures? Let me get up outta here."

"Yeah. Hold on." Brenda disappeared into the bedroom, and returned in a few minutes with an envelope of photographs. "Here you go," she said as she handed them to Tisha.

"Wait a minute. Let me look at those pictures!" Pat had returned to the armchair, but she was still breathing heavily.

"Why?" Tisha asked, a surprised look on her face.

"Oh, I can't even look at your pictures now?" Pat retorted.

Tisha shrugged and obediently handed over the envelope, which Pat immediately stuck in her pocketbook.

"What are you doing?" Tisha stammered.

"I ain't doing nothing but sitting here drinking my drink," Pat took a swig to prove her point. "I thought you was leaving."

"But you've got my pictures!"

"What? I ain't got your pictures," Pat snapped at her before taking another swig.

"You accusing my aunt of stealing your pictures?" Rosa jumped up from the couch where she had been sitting pouting. "You really trying to start some shit up in here, aren't you?"

"What? You sat there and saw here put my pictures in her pocketbook!"

"I ain't see shit!"

"The envelope is sticking out the pocketbook right there!" Tisha pointed wildly in Pat's direction, while glancing around the living room as if for help.

"These are my pictures!" Pat stuffed the envelope further down into her pocketbook.

"Vincent . . ." Tisha turned to him with pleading eyes.

"Huh. I know you're not trying to get me to turn on Aunt Pat." Vincent chuckled and walked out the room.

"Mommy, get Aunt Pat to give that girl back her pictures," Brenda said as Mrs. Carver walked into the room.

"I'm not in it. I'm just coming in here to get the babies," Mrs. Carver said without bothering to look at Brenda. She took Jumah from Lucia's arms. "Come on, Shaniqua. Come in the back with me. You too, Nancy. Your mother will get you when she's ready to leave." She turned and walked out with the children trailing behind her.

"Aunt Pat, please, please, please give me the pictures." Brenda pleaded.

"You don't even know the people in those pictures," Tisha said, near tears.

"Oh, you trying to throw that shit in my face again, huh?" Pat snorted. "I know everyone in these pictures. These are my family pictures. I ain't giving you shit, and you'd better get the hell out of my face before I stomp your ass."

"But, Miss Pat—" Tisha started.

"One more word out of your mouth, and I swear I'm going to knock the shit out of you!"

"Patricia, you're too old to be fighting that young girl," Mrs. Carver called from the safety of the back bedroom.

Pat paused as if in thought, then nodded her head. "Yeah, you're right. I'm not going to be fighting some girl young enough to be my niece." She paused again, and then looked at Tisha through squinted eyes. "What's your mother's address? I'm going to go kick her ass."

Brenda couldn't help herself, and broke out with laughter, as did everyone else in the room, except the bewildered Tisha. Sharif was laughing so hard he was actually doubled up, and Brenda could hear Vincent pounding on the kitchen counter and stomping on the floor with laughter.

"Hey, Aunt Pat. Look at the envelope! I bet her address is on the envelope with the pictures. They make them fill it out at the store," Rosa said excitedly.

"Y'all stop playing now." Tisha said hurriedly.

"Hey, Aunt Pat," Brenda walked over to where her aunt was sitting and knelt down next to her. "You didn't say even ask about the other party boy. Remember? Jimmy?"

Pat's brow furrowed. "Jimmy?" She suddenly clasped her hand to her mouth. "Oh, that's right! That little kid!"

Brenda signaled behind her back to Sharif to get closer to Pat's pocketbook, which was lying on the floor next to the chair. "Uh huh," she continued talking to Pat, "you should have seen him earlier, all excited about having a party. I don't think he ever had one before."

Pat nodded, and then gave a deep sigh and settled back in the chair, "I bet his mother could barely make ends meet. She had a hard enough time trying to feed all those kids. I know she couldn't have been thinking about giving them parties. God rest her poor soul."

"Yeah, it's such a shame," Brenda said as she used her foot to push Pat's pocketbook even closer to Sharif. "But at least he's in good hands now. You know Mommy's taking care of him, right?"

"Is he doing okay? I know he must miss his mother something terrible," Pat said.

"Well, he seems to be doing okay," Brenda shrugged dramatically to make sure her aunt didn't notice Sharif tugging the envelope free of her pocketbook. Rosa grunted, but Sharif shot her warning glance as Brenda continued talking. "He's not really talking, though," Brenda said. "Mommy said he was always quiet, but now he hardly says a word at all."

"Yeah, I'm sure it's the shock," Sharif added. The envelope was now behind his back, and he was stuffing it in his pants.

"Yeah," Pat agreed. "I mean, you can only imagine what the kid's going through. He knows his mother is dead?"

"Oh, yeah," Brenda nodded. "Mommy took him to the funeral and all. Oh, man, Aunt Pat. It was so sad! Those two little coffins next to the big one. Everyone was crying."

Pat sighed, then covered her mouth with her hand, leaned back and shook her head, tears evident in her eyes. "It's such a damn shame is what it is. Just a damn shame," she said in a muffled voice. She let her hand drop to the side of the chair and grabbed her pocketbook, which she plopped in her lap. Brenda shot Sharif an "uh oh" look, but he gave her a short nod to let her know everything was all right. She looked around, and breathed a mental sigh of relief when she realized that Trish had left.

Pat pulled a white handkerchief from her pocketbook and dabbed at her eyes. "I know that must be really hard on him, huh? Seeing his mother and sister and brother all laid out," she said with a deep sigh.

"Oh, girl, y'all must be talking about that funeral the other day. Wasn't that just a shame? Broke my heart seeing them bury them little kids," Brenda looked up to see Miss Jackie, wearing an oversized yellow tee shirt, gray sweatpants, and a pair of men's slippers, shuffle into the room. "Child, brought tears to my eyes. They say God don't take nobody before it's their time, but it makes you wonder, don't it? How you doing, Pat? I ain't know you was here, girl."

Pat looked at her and grunted, before taking a large swig of rum. She leaned further back in her chair then rolled her eyes. "Heifer," she said to no one in particular.

Sharif got up from the couch. "Miss Jackie, you want to sit down?"

"Thank you, baby," said Miss Jackie, as she sat down. "My knees been acting up lately, you know. I can't be standing on my feet too long these days. I gots arthritis and rheumatism. I can't do too much of walking either. I think I might have water on the knee. I'm thinking about getting me one of those scooters.

"So what time you get here, Pat? I woulda been up here earlier myself but Ronald brought his girlfriend over to meet me. A sweet girl. She says she's twenty-five but I swear the girl don't look like she's a day over twenty. But she got manners and all. And that's important. I can't stand some of these young people who ain't got no manners."

Pat grunted again. "Then I don't know how you can stand being around that son of yours."

"Hey, Jackie, come on back in here with me," Mrs. Carver called out from the back bedroom. "Pat's been drinking."

Pat sucked her teeth and shouted back. "Oh, shut the hell up, Janet."

Jackie shifted uncomfortably in her seat, and it looked for a minute like she was going to get up, but she finally sighed and shouted back, "That's okay, Janet. I ain't but staying but a minute anyway."

Pat looked up at Brenda and laughed. "She ain't going back there 'cause she thinks as soon as she leaves I'm going to talk about her or her fucked-up son."

"Oh, come on, Pat. Don't be talking about Ronald. He ain't all that bad," Miss Jackie said defensively.

"He's a jerk, and everyone knows it, including you. Always propositioning all the young girls in here like someone would want his sappy ass." Pat snapped in response. "Ain't that right, Brenda?"

Brenda started chewing her bottom lip and looking at her aunt with a sheepish look.

"Ain't that right?" Pat demanded.

Brenda shrugged her shoulders.

"Yeah, you ain't saying nothing 'cause you don't want to disrespect Jackie, huh?" Pat nodded and took a sip of her rum. "Now, see that's a young person with manners."

Miss Jackie sighed and slowly got up from the couch. "Well, I just wanted to come up for a minute and say hello. I guess I better go ahead and get outta here."

Brenda walked behind her. "I hope everything's okay, Miss Jackie. Don't let Aunt Pat get to you," she said when they got to the door.

"Oh, chile, please. I known Pat before you was born. I know how she gets," Miss Jackie opened the door to leave. "Oh, look, there's my baby now. Hey, Ronald. I thought you and your little girl left."

"You got your pocketbook with you? I wanna put Ginger in a cab." A tall thin man with ashen skin and bulging eyes walked up on Brenda and Miss Jackie. "How you be, Brenda?" he asked as he sidled up close to her, almost pushing her back into the apartment.

"I'm fine, Ronald. Nice to see you. I'll see you later, Miss Jackie," Brenda tried to close the door on the man.

"Hey, hold up. You ain't even going to invite me in to your party?" Ronald put his foot in the door.

"The party's over, Ronald," Brenda tried to keep her voice low. *The last thing I need right now,* she thought, *is for Aunt Pat to realize Ronald is here*.

"Well, we can have a little party by ourselves, then, can't we?" Ronald said in a husky voice. Brenda caught a whiff of his breath, which stank of beer and cigarettes.

"Ronald, look. Why don't you just—" she started.

"Step off, motherfucker, before I put a cap in your ass," Vincent's voice suddenly growled from behind her.

"Yeah. What he said." Brenda grinned.

"Oh, man, you know I was just, you know . . ." Ronald stammered as he stumbled backward almost into his mother's arms. Before he could finish Vincent slammed the door in his face and went back into the kitchen to freshen his drink. He didn't seem the least bit fazed, Brenda noticed.

She turned as the door flew open.

"Ma, can I get a couple of dollars?" Bootsy rushed in, out of breath, with Jimmy close behind. "The ice cream truck's downstairs and Jimmy wants a popsicle."

"Get my pocketbook outta your grandmother's room." Brenda stepped in front of Jimmy before he could rush off behind Bootsy. "What kind of popsicle do you want, Jimmy? Cherry?" she asked as she knelt in front of him. "Orange?"

Jimmy bowed his head so low that his chin hit his chest as he backed up.

"Oh, Jimmy, you don't have to be afraid," Brenda said as she held her hands out to the boy. "You know I—"

To her amazement, Jimmy gave a whine and dashed into the kitchen, where he latched onto Vincent's leg, almost knocking the man down.

"Hey! Yo! What the fuck?" Vincent shook his leg, but Jimmy wrapped his legs around him, and held on tightly, his eyes squeezed tight.

Brenda stood up and giggled. "Vincent, meet Jimmy."

Vincent pointed down at Jimmy. "Yeah. Uh huh. And you want to get him, or what?"

"Come on, Jimmy. It's all right," Brenda said as she tried to pry him off of Vincent's leg. The boy started softly crying, and clung tighter.

Brenda backed away and shrugged at Vincent, who was glaring down at Jimmy. "Don't be mean, Vincent."

"Look, kid," Vincent shook his leg again, and Jimmy started crying louder. "Look, kid!" Vincent bent down and tried to pry his fingers loose. Jimmy used the opportunity to wrap his arms around Vincent's neck and his legs around the man's waist, and started sobbing into his shoulder. "Oh, damn," Vincent said with a bewildered look on his face as he stood up and started gently jiggling the boy. "What do I do now?" he asked Brenda, but she was too busy laughing to answer.

"Okay, kid. Don't cry." Vincent shot Brenda a dirty look. "I ain't gonna let the big bad Brenda hurt you. You want me to beat her up for you? Huh?" He chucked Jimmy under the chin and smiled as the little boy looked up at him with watery eyes. "Let me beat her up for you, okay, kid?"

Jimmy smiled and shook his head. "No. Don't beat her up. I like Miss Brenda."

"Now see that?" Brenda walked over, her arms stretched out, but Jimmy ducked his head back into Vincent's shoulder.

"Ma. You didn't have any singles so I grabbed a five, okay?" Bootsy said as walked into the kitchen.

"You'd better bring me back my change," Brenda said. "I don't want—"

"Booty!" Jimmy wriggled out of Vincent's arms and ran over to Bootsy. "We going outside again?"

"Stop calling me Booty." Bootsy tapped Jimmy lightly on the head.

"Yo! Don't be hitting the kid on the head," Vincent said in a soft growl.

"They're only playing," Brenda said as Bootsy shot Vincent a quizzical look. "Y'all go 'head downstairs and get Jimmy that popsicle."

"Okay, Ma. Bye, Vincent," Bootsy said as he opened the door. "Come on, Little Man."

"Okay," Jimmy said as he darted out after Bootsy, but before the door could close behind him he ran back in and went to Vincent. "Gimme pound," he said as he put his fist out.

"Okay," Vincent chuckled as he lightly hit Jimmy's fist with his own.

"And don't beat up Miss Brenda," Jimmy said, pointing his finger at Vincent. "Okay?"

"Okay," Vincent said solemnly.

"That's a weird little kid," Vincent said as he and Brenda watched Jimmy run back out the door.

"Yeah, he is," Brenda nodded, "but he sure seemed to like you." She turned to Vincent. "I thought you hated kids."

"I never said I hated them. I just don't like 'em." Vincent shrugged and then pulled out his money clip from his pocket. "Here. Your mother told me this party was for Jimmy, too. And I didn't get him anything. Buy him something nice."

"Two hundred dollars?" Brenda's mouth dropped open.

"Yeah. Buy him . . . I don't know . . . a little television or something."

"A television for a four-year-old?

"Or whatever. You decide what to get him. I don't care," Vincent said as he walked toward the living room. He stopped and turned around, and peeled off another bill. "And get something nice for your son for his birthday, too. I forgot to buy him a present."

Brenda stared after him as he walked away. Just wait until Rosa and

Sharif hear about this, she thought with a shake of her head. Stone-cold thug Vincent doing something nice for a child. The world must be coming to an end.

"So, Aunt Pat, why you gotta be so mean?" Brenda said after she returned to the living room.

"Oh, child, please, I'm just keeping it real. And don't think I don't know that you and Sharif gave that girl back them damn pictures," Pat said with a grin. "Now come give your Aunt Pat a kiss."

7

"You don't have to walk me home. I been living here all my life. Ain't nobody gonna bother me," Rosa told her companion as they climbed the subway steps onto the littered sidewalk of 125th Street and Lexington Avenue. "And it ain't even dark." She glanced, adoringly, at the middle-aged blond white man nonchalantly strolling beside her, one hand holding the lightweight blazer slung over his shoulder, the other deep in the pocket of his Banana Republic chinos.

"It's not a problem. Not even really out of my way. And I have about forty-five minutes to kill before my train is due; the trains are spaced out on the weekends. And no use in spending all that time waiting up there . . . ," the man pointed to the elevated Metro North station one block away on Park Avenue, "when I can spend it talking to the most talented thespian in my cast."

Rosa grinned at the compliment. It wasn't every day that an actress with a minor part in the play was called the most talented thespian by the director. And not just any director, but Mitch Jeffries, one of the most prominent movers and shakers on the Great White Way.

The whole cast had been stunned when the original director, a hyperactive Jewish guy who was getting on everybody's nerves, had quit in a huff after a disagreement with the producers. But they almost passed out in shock when, instead of shutting the production down, the producers announced that Mitch was going to replace him. It was a real coup, because the play was being produced on a shoestring budget, and many of the actors—herself included—weren't even getting paid. But it turned out that the playwright was a former student of Mitch's, and when the famous director heard his plight, he decided to donate his services.

The entire cast loved him, because he treated them like they were all marquee actors although most of them didn't have a credible acting credit to their name. And rumor had it that he was actually trying to get backers for the show, which meant they might actually get paid. But from the very beginning he'd shown particular interest in Rosa, and had even persuaded the playwright to expand her role.

"So this is Spanish Harlem, is it?" Mitch asked, looking around.

"Yeah, I guess," Rosa shrugged. "I don't think anybody really calls it that anymore."

"Why not?"

"Well, when my parents first moved up here in the fifties, all the Latinos lived east of Fifth Avenue, and all of the blacks lived on the west side. But nowadays everyone just lives everywhere. It's all just Harlem."

Mitch nodded. "I actually just bought a brownstone on 118th Street, off Malcolm X Boulevard. They're doing renovations, but I'll probably be moving in by the end of the year. So I'm familiar with Harlem, but I've never been up this far east."

"Oh, okay. So you just bought a brownstone, huh? That's nice. I know your wife must be excited," Rosa said in a cautious tone.

"No, it's just for me. I'm not married," he said, and switched his blazer from one shoulder to another. He took a monogrammed handkerchief from his pocket to wipe his forehead, and his Movado watch glistened in the afternoon sunlight. "So, you've lived in this neighborhood all of your life?"

"Yeah. Not in this same building," she said as she pointed to the Ida B., which was now only a block away, "My family moved here when I was like five."

"Really?" Mitch turned to look at her. "So you live with your family, then?"

"Are you kidding?" Rosa snorted. "Now I got my own apartment on the fifth floor. My mom lives on the twelfth."

"Why'd you get an apartment in the same building as your mother? Was it that you wanted to get away but not too far away?" Mitch smiled, causing his baby blue eyes to sparkle.

"Yeah, I guess," Rosa shrugged. "You know, I was pregnant with Eddie, so I didn't want to move too far, because I knew my mother was going to be doing most of the baby-sitting. And I know everyone in the building, so it just made life easier to just stay where I was instead of moving someplace else and having to readjust, and shit." Her eyes widened, and her hand flew to her mouth. "Oh, man, Mitch. You gotta excuse my mouth. I don't usually be cursing," she said quickly.

Mitch waved his hand dismissively. "So you have a son? How old?"

"Eddie's seven." Rosa looked to see Mitch's expression, but the look on his face didn't change. He hadn't made a pass at her, but he'd certainly been very attentive. Maybe that was his way of letting her know he liked her. She wasn't attracted to him, not in the least. In fact she'd never been attracted to white men. But at the same time, if he was interested in her, it could sure help her career, she thought. "Me and his father ain't together. And Eddie's spending the summer in Puerto Rico with my mom." Damn, she thought. I shouldn'ta told him Eddie was away. Now he might be expecting me to invite him up. "What time do you have to catch your train to Connecticut?"

"Six."

"Oh, okay. I just wanted to make sure you don't miss your train."

"Hey, Rosa, yo. 'Sup?"

Rosa looked up as Ricky approached, his hands stuck low in his jeans pockets and a toothpick dangling from his mouth.

"I'm okay," Rosa said before turning to Mitch. "So, you say live in Danbury?" She started walking faster.

"Yo! Ain't you gonna ask me how you doing? Wassup wid dat? Or you too good to be talking to me, all of sudden?" Ricky asked as he fell in step at Rosa's side. "You think your man here going to be mad if you talk to a brotha?" He gave a chuckle at the pissed-off look Rosa shot at him. "You ain't got no problem wid me talking to Rosa, now do you?" he asked Mitch.

"No, of course not. Please go right—" Mitch started.

"Ricky, I know your young ass ain't trying to front on me, and shit." Rosa stopped in the middle of the sidewalk, waving her finger in front of the teenager's face. "You better get your funky ass out of my space. And stop acting like you don't know how to talk good English all of a sudden. " She turned to Mitch. "Excuse my language, I usually don't curse."

"Now, who's trying to front on who?" Ricky laughed as he backed up a few steps. "All I was trying to do was say hi. It's not like I was busting on you about stepping with a white boy when you be brushing brothas off left and right. I thought you only went out with Puerto Ricans."

Rosa started to say something, but paused and took a deep breath, then put her hand—palm out—in front of Ricky. "You know what? I'm going to ignore you. I'm going to pretend you're not even here." She glanced over at the Ida B., and noticed Sharif and Brenda standing out front. "Mitch, come on. I wanna introduce you to some of my friends."

She put her arm around Mitch's elbow and started walking away from Ricky, then turned her head to mouth, "I'm going to kick your ass."

"Oh, what?" Ricky cupped his hand to his ear. "What's that you say? You're going to kick my ass." He doubled up with laughter when she reached her hand behind her back and gave him the finger as she walked on.

"Hey, *chica*. Hey, Sharif. I want to introduce you to someone." Rosa stepped back and gave a slow and expansive wave in Mitch's direction as if she were presenting a prize on a game show. "This is Mitch Jeffries," she said with a satisfied smile.

"How do you do?" Brenda shifted Jumah to her hip, and extended her hand to Mitch, who gave it a gentle shake.

"And you are?" he said with a smile.

"Oh, I'm sorry," she stammered. "I'm Brenda Carver."

"And this is Sharif Goldsby," Rosa pointed to Sharif who gave a nod, and continued to sip juice from a sports bottle.

"Mitch is the director for the play I'm in," Rosa said looking directly at Sharif. "And he's one of the most famous directors on Broadway. All the producers be trying to get him to direct their plays."

"Wow, that's really nice," Brenda said as she jiggled Jumah who was squirming wildly. She almost jumped when Bootsy, who had come out of the building, Jimmy happily trailing behind him, tapped her on the shoulder.

"Ma, Grandma's sending me to the store to get some bread. You want something while I'm there?"

"Oh, well, yeah, pick me up a bag of flour, and make sure it's Gold Medal. I'm going to fry chicken tonight." She reached into her jeans and pulled out a crumpled five-dollar bill, looked at it, then stuck it back in her pocket. "Take it out of Grandma's money. I'll pay her back."

"Okay." Bootsy started down the street. "Come on, Little Man," he called over his shoulder to his little protégé who obediently trotted to catch up with him.

"Bootsy, make sure you hold Jimmy's hand when you cross the

street," Brenda called after them. "And don't buy any more candy at the store. You're gonna give that boy diabetes."

Rosa acted as if the interruption as hadn't occurred, continuing where she had left off. "And even though Mitch's worked with all the veteran actresses and all he said I'm one of the most talented actresses he's met," she nudged Sharif on the shoulder. "Ain't that something?"

Brenda gasped. "Really? Oh, you go, girl!" she said excitedly. "I always knew you had it in you. I can just see you in the movies."

"Well, I don't think I'm going to be doing movies. I think I'ma stick to the stage. You know, be a serious actress." She flashed a smile at Mitch.

"Well, a lot of great actors switched between the stage and movies," Mitch said. "Jessica Tandy. Richard Burton. Sir Lawrence Olivier. All of them great actors."

"And Paul Robeson," Sharif said with a glare.

"Yes, and of course Paul Robeson," Mitch nodded. "One of the most talented actors of all. He could act, sing. Do it all."

"Yeah, I know, and he was an athlete and a political activist, too. I don't need you to teach me his history," Sharif snapped.

Rosa stared at Sharif in disbelief. Why was he acting so damn hostile, she wondered. She looked at Brenda, but the question in her eyes went unanswered as her friend gave an almost imperceptible shrug, and started jiggling Jumah even faster.

"Mitch," Rosa said turning to the man who seemed unperturbed by Sharif's behavior. "You know, Brenda's a writer. Maybe one day you'll be directing a play she wrote. Wouldn't that be nice?"

"Well, I don't write plays," Brenda said slowly.

Mitch gave Brenda an appraising look. "Oh, you write books, then? Have you been published?"

"No not yet. I'm not finished with anything," Brenda said shyly.

"Oh, well, that's understandable," Mitch nodded. "In what genre do you write?"

"Well, I haven't actually started writing anything yet. I mean, I guess I will be writing a novel," Brenda said sheepishly. "The thing is, I don't know what to write about."

Mitch looked at her a few seconds before finally saying, "Well, take your time because I'm sure it'll come to you. But most young writers start out by writing about what they know."

Sharif grunted. "That's what I told her."

"Oh." Mitch turned to Sharif. "Are you a writer?"

"No. Do you live around here?"

"What?" The question seemed to catch Mitch by surprise. He glanced at Rosa before answering. "No. I live in Connecticut. Danbury."

"Really? I would have guessed you to be one of those liberal artistic types moving into Harlem," Sharif stared straight into Mitch's eyes as he spoke. "You know the people I mean, right? The ones proud to say they live uptown with the blacks, to show how progressive they are. Oh, I'm sure you're familiar with the type. The hypocrites who then encourage all their friends to move to their block so they're not actually surrounded by the darkies whose culture they're so eager to soak up."

"Damn it, Sharif," Rosa stamped her shoe on the ground. "Why you gotta be so hostile all the time? *Mierda*. The man's nice enough to walk me home and you gotta go all angry black man on him?"

"How's he walking you home and he lives in Connecticut?" Sharif demanded.

"I use Metro North," Mitch said calmly. "The 125th and Lexington subway stop puts me only a block away. And I had some time to kill so I walked Rosa to her building. All quite innocent, you see."

"I thought you guys were rehearsing in the Village. You could have caught the train from Grand Central." Sharif snorted, and then took a long swig from the sports bottle. "I'm heading upstairs. I'll catch y'all later." He turned around and walked into the building without looking back to see Rosa and Brenda staring at him in disbelief.

"Ahem," Mitch cleared his throat and took a quick look at his watch. "Well, it's about time for me to head to the train. It was nice meeting you, Brenda." He turned to Rosa. "Thank you for allowing me to escort you, Rosa. I'll see you Tuesday. Okay?"

Rosa mentally rolled her eyes, but tried to keep a straight face as she nodded at Mitch. Damn Sharif for acting so fucked up, she thought. Now she'd never know if Mitch was going to try and invite himself up, or if he was only interested in her acting ability. "You know what?" she said suddenly. "I'm going to walk you to the train."

"No, doesn't make sense. You're home," Mitch protested, though he was smiling expansively.

"I insist." Rosa linked her arm around his elbow. "Brenda, I'll see you later. Come on."

"Look, I gotta apologize for Sharif," Rosa said after they walked a few feet. "He's funny like that sometimes. But he's a real sweetheart when you get to know him."

Mitch nodded. "I'm sure he is. He seems like a very interesting character. What does he do for a living?"

"Sharif? He sells incense, oils, and shea butter . . . stuff like that," Rosa said with a wave of her hand.

"And he makes enough to live?" Mitch asked in a surprised tone.

"Oh, yeah. He used to work at a stand on 125th Street until a couple of months ago, and when he closed it down he kept all his customers, except now they come to him or he goes to them," Rosa explained. "But he spends most of his time doing volunteer stuff, and helping people out in the building."

"Is that right?" Mitch slowly rubbed his chin as he walked. "What do you mean by helping people out in the building? Handiwork?"

"Yeah, well, some of that, but Sharif ain't good with his hands," Rosa said. "But he's a good brain, and a real good heart. If someone has a problem he tries to help them out. Like go to court with them, or write letters for them, or help them with resumes. He checks on the old folks in the summer to make sure they at least got fans. He does a lot of stuff."

"He sounds like a really nice guy. Helping out the other residents like that."

"Well, we're all pretty close in the building. I mean we argue and fight with each other sometimes. But we're all kinda tight, too, because we're all in this together. You know what I mean? There ain't no doctors or lawyers living at the Ida B., just people trying to make it. I mean, shoot, it's subsidized housing, ain't nobody there got no real money. So most of the time everyone's scrambling to take care of themselves, but when someone's in trouble, we all try to help out. Like a couple of weeks ago, a woman killed herself and two of her children."

"My God!"

"Yeah, it was a shame," Rosa said nonchalantly. "But anyway, she didn't have any relatives or anything, so Sharif took a collection to help pay for her funeral, and Brenda's mother took her youngest son in. Jimmy. The little boy that was with Brenda's son. And everyone in the building is chipping in buying him clothes and stuff. We're a pretty tight group."

"It must be quite nice living in a building like that. Where everyone looks out for each other. I suppose it's like having a huge extended family."

"Yeah. Kinda like that. There's rumors that they're going to tear the building down, though. But I'm hoping it's just a rumor."

Mitch nodded. "I hope so also. So was that Brenda's only child?"

"No, she has four kids."

Mitch whistled. "That's quite a handful. Is she married?"

"No, but she's okay. Her mom lives in the Ida B., too, and she helps her out. But anyway, enough of that. I wanted to ask you about my acting career. I mean, what do you think I should be doing next after the play closes?"

They had reached the foot of the stairs leading to the elevated train. Mitch leaned against the railing, crossed his arms, and stared at Rosa a few seconds before answering.

"Yes, yes, I wanted to talk to you about that," he said slowly. "Have you taken any acting lessons, Rosa?"

"Well, yeah. Don't it show?" Rosa looked at the man in disbelief. "I used to take an acting workshop at the Martin Luther King Recreation Center over on Seventh Avenue."

"Well, I'm sure that was helpful, but I was thinking of a more structured program, like—"

"Wait a minute, just a little while ago you were telling me I was one of the most talented actresses you know," Rosa said in a hurt voice. "Now you telling me I gotta take lessons? What, you was like lying to me before?"

"Rosa, calm down. I haven't been lying to you." Mitch put his hand on her shoulder. "You are a great talent. You're wonderfully talented, and you have great depth which you can draw on. If I didn't know that before, I certainly know it after walking you home today. But what you have is raw talent. I'd like to see you really develop that."

"Well, damn, that's what I thought I was doing. I mean, I'm doing this play for no money, just to get the experience," Rosa said sullenly. She started twirling a tendril of her hair, her eyes downcast.

"Yes, I understand," Mitch said gently. "All I'm saying is that right now you can really impress an audience, but with some training you can totally own an audience. You can command them to laugh or to cry, to be angry or happy." He moved his hand from her shoulder and moved a few steps away from her. "With a toss of your head," he tossed his head for effect, "you can make them forget about their housing project or their penthouse, and pull them into the world you create for them. With a gesture of your hand," he gestured appropriately, "you can make every man love you like they've never loved another woman, and make every woman want to be you. And with a tear in your eye," he paused before saying slowly, "you can make every man, woman, or child willing to die in order to make sure you never shed another tear."

"Yeah, yeah, that's just what I wanna do," Rosa said in a husky voice.

"And *that*," Mitch pointed his finger at her, "is exactly what you will do, Rosa."

"But I gotta take acting lessons, huh?" Rosa chewed her lip for a second. "I don't have a lot of money to be paying for a lot of fancy acting classes, though."

"I know the perfect one. It'll be starting in September, and I can guarantee you'll be accepted. And it won't cost a dime," Mitch grinned.

"Really? Where?" Rosa asked cautiously.

"At the Mitch Jeffries Acting Workshop."

"Get out!" Rosa stepped back in surprise. "You got a workshop?"

"I will in September, and I would love to have you as a student," Mitch placed his hand on her shoulder again. "I'm taking a special interest in your career, Rosa."

"Wow," Rosa shook her head in disbelief. "Kinda like that guy, what's his name, that became Marilyn Monroe's acting coach."

"Lee Strasberg. Yes, kinda like him," Mitch smiled. "So what do you think?"

Rosa jerked back from him. "What do you mean, what do I think? I'm there, baby. 'Cause I'm going to be owning the audience and shit, and letting them know when to laugh and cry, just like you said." She snapped her finger in the air, a haughty look on her face. "I'm going to be the next Jennifer Lopez."

Mitch laughed. "Forget Jennifer Lopez, you're going to be the next Nicole Kidman."

"You know, you're exactly right." Rosa snapped her finger. " 'Cause Nicole gotta lotta depth, just like me."

"That's exactly right." Mitch looked at his watch. "But now I have to catch my train. I'll see you at rehearsal Tuesday, okay?"

Rosa watched him trot up the stairs, before turning to walk back to the Ida B. "Yeah," she said out loud. "Me and Nicole Kidman."

8

The Black United Front. Yeah, that's a good one,* Sharif decided as he took another long toke off the reefer joint. *Yeah, I'll give them that last five grand. Split it up fifty-fifty between the New York chapter and the one in Philadelphia that's just forming.* Although maybe he should break off a little for that library they were trying to form in Cleveland in memory of Queen Mother Moore and Robert F. Williams. That would be nice, he thought. If any two contemporary icons needed an institution in their honor, it would be these two activists who devoted their life to the movement. Yes, he decided, picking up the yellow pad next to him on the couch to jot down his latest changes, it would be good use of the insurance money Gran left. He couldn't believe she had really taken out a policy for $50,000. She should have known he wouldn't want the money. He wouldn't want to profit from the death of the person who had meant the most to him in life.

The old Spinners' song "Sadie" played softly on the stereo as he let his gaze fall on the five-by-seven photograph of his grandmother that he had placed on the living room table in front of him. It was one of those black-and-whites which had been colorized, but the many creases on the picture revealed its true age. She was in her long flowing white wedding gown, surrounded by the bridal party, holding a corsage and smiling lovingly at the handsome soldier at her side. Sharif never knew his grandfather. He died just a year after the wedding, in 1953, while serving in Korea. His son was born two months later, and Gran had to find work as a live-in maid, scrubbing other people's floors and raising their children while leaving her own son with relatives. It broke her heart to see her son only on weekends, but it was hard for a black woman—with only a third-grade education—to get a good job in the 1950s, so she suffered through. When her son started shooting heroin as a teenager she quit her job, and held his shaking body as he tried to kick cold turkey. There were no drug programs back then for poor black heroin addicts, and she had to go through the cold-turkey process three times before he finally was able to stay off the drug. She then went through it twice more for the woman her son had married. The proudest day in her life, she often told Sharif, was the day his father became a deacon in the church. The saddest day was when he and his wife were killed by police in a drug raid on the wrong apartment.

If there's a heaven up above
I know she's teaching angels how to love.

Tears welled up in Sharif's eyes as he heard the lyrics, and the lump that had been in his throat since Gran died once again began to swell. He grabbed the worn picture from the table and pressed it against his face, kissing it and wetting it with his tears. "Oh, man, Gran," he said through his tears. "Why'd you have to leave me?"

It was a few minutes after the song ended before he was able to compose himself. He wiped the tears from his face, then put the photograph in the pewter frame he'd just bought. He sniffed as he put the picture on an end table next to a vase of fresh flowers, and then lit the white candle centered on the table.

"Light, peace, and progress to your spirit, Gran," he said solemnly.

"You loved me, no matter what. You supported me, no matter what. You gave and gave, and never expected anything in return. You were the most wonderful person who ever lived, and I know God is proud to have you as his personal angel." He tapped the table three times and then kissed his hands.

The phone rang, interrupting his thoughts. He sighed, gave one more look at the newly made altar, then walked over and picked up the receiver.

"Peace."

"Sharif. The police done picked up my Ricky and they won't tell me what's happening! Sharif, they probably beating up my baby! You gotta help me!"

"What? Miss Rose? Slow down, tell me what happened." Sharif quickly grabbed the notepad he'd been writing on earlier, pulled a pen from his back pocket, and sat down on the couch. "When did they pick up Ricky?"

"I don't know exactly. I came home from work and Miss Jackie told me they picked him and a couple of boys on the corner," the voice on the other phone said hysterically. "Sharif you know that boy ain't selling no drugs. He just hanging out with the wrong crowd. Oh, Sharif, they done locked up my son."

"Okay. Just take it easy, Miss Rose," Sharif said in a soothing voice. "We're going to get this straightened out. It was probably just one of their regular sweeps, and he's probably right down at the thirty-fifth precinct."

"But he didn't do anything. Miss Jackie said one of the boys told her when the police pulled up he just started running because everybody else did. He even said that Ricky ain't had nothing on him."

"I believe you. I know how Ricky is, and I know he wasn't carrying anything or even holding anything for someone else. He wants to be down, but he isn't stupid. I'll call down to the thirty-fifth and see what's going on."

"I called down there, Sharif. They won't tell me anything!" Miss Rose said, tears in her voice.

"Well, I'm going to call down there now. I'll call you right back. Just stay there and try to calm down."

Sharif hung up, and sighed, then picked up the phone and dialed.

"Yes, this is Sharif Goldsby. I'd like to speak to the desk sergeant. Hello, Sergeant Murphy? This is Sharif Goldsby, and I'm trying to get some information on a fifteen-year-old that I understand was picked up by some of your officers this afternoon. His name is Ricky White . . . On the corner of 126th and Lexington . . . So you're saying that officers in your precinct are conducting sweeps and you don't know about them? . . . All right, let me speak to someone who does know . . . I'm not trying to tie up your lines with bullshit, I'm trying to find out what's going on with one of the young people in my community . . . Okay, let me speak to your community affairs officer. Better yet, take a message, let him know that Sharif Goldsby called—he'll know who I am—and that I'll be down there in about fifteen minutes with a hundred people in the community to hold a rally in front of the precinct to protest the disregard the police have for the people they're hired to serve. . . . Watch your mouth, Sergeant Murphy . . . Yes, I'll be glad to hold on. . . . Oh, Ricky is there? Good. His mother and I'll be there to pick him up in ten minutes. . . . A bench warrant, huh? Well, we'll see. That kid's an honor roll student at the Bronx High School of Science and has never been in trouble before, and I know for a fact that he didn't have any drugs on him. We'll straighten it out when I get there, but I really believe you should just let him go with his mother and we'll all just forget about it. . . . Okay, like I said, we'll talk about it when we get there. Bye."

Sharif cradled on the receiver, and sighed before he slowly stood up. He looked at the ingredients for the shea butter lotion and musk oils he was supposed to be mixing for some of his regular customers, and suddenly remembered the grant proposal he was supposed to be writing for the rites of passage program that was supposed to be starting at the neighborhood recreation center. He had also promised to take Bootsy to the new Ice T flick that was opening at the Magic Johnson Theater on 125th Street. And most importantly, he needed to go over, once again, all the information he'd gathered about Chest Park Inc., the development company that was pressuring the city to sell the land on which Ida B. stood.

He picked up his backpack and slung it over his shoulder, his body sagging though the backpack was almost empty. I'm really feeling overwhelmed, Sharif thought. I've got to sit down and meditate to clear my head. *As soon as I find some time.*

"So let me get this straight," Sharif tapped his ballpoint pen on the yellow legal pad as he spoke. "You were standing on the corner with some of your friends, a police car pulls up and two cops jump out and you start running?"

"I'm telling you, G! One of the po-pos had his baton out, and the other had his hand on his holster like he was reaching for his gun, Dawg!" Ricky stood in the middle of the floor waving his hands wildly. "Ouch!" he grabbed his head and looked accusingly at his mother who had just delivered a sound blow with her pocketbook.

"His name ain't G, and his name ain't dawg. You call him Mister Sharif like you've got some kind of manners up in here," Miss Rose said. "And what the hell is a po-po?"

"That's what we call police, Ma. And why I gotta be calling Sharif 'mister'?" Ricky danced out of the range of the pocketbook just in time. "Come on now, Ma!"

"Come on now, Ma, nothing. I raised you to call adults 'mister' or 'miss' to show some kind of respect." Miss Rose put her hands on her hips and advanced toward the retreating Ricky as she spoke. "And I raised you to go to school, get good grades so you can get a scholarship and go to college and get a good job. I ain't raised you to be hanging out on no corner with no bunch of drug dealers and running from the police and getting locked up."

She turned to Sharif, who still sat on the couch, doodling on the legal pad. "Do you know this boy brought home a report card with all A's last month?" she asked, pointing at Ricky. "Do you know he won the National Merit Award for Science two years in a row? Do you know he got the brains enough to be president one day?" She stopped and took a long look at her son, and took a deep breath. "But instead," she started swatting him on the shoulder with her pocketbook as if to emphasize each word, "he wants to hang out with these no-good-for-nothings so he can wind up in prison with them."

"Come on, Ma!"

Sharif chuckled before getting up from the couch and putting his arm around the woman.

"Miss Rose, I totally agree with you. But I don't think beating him with your pocketbook is going to make any difference," he said as he gave the woman a kiss on the cheek. "Come on, sit down by me so I can show you some ideas I've come up with." He led the distraught woman to the couch. "And you," he said pointing to Ricky. "Cop a squat on the chair."

"Okay," he said when they were both settled in. "Why don't we write up a contract between you and Ricky?"

"A what?" Rose asked.

"Get outta here, Sharif. You tripping," Ricky waved him off.

"A contract," Sharif continued. "The two of you would discuss what it is you expect each from each other, and what kind of support would be needed to make it happen. It's a sign of mutual respect for each other."

"I don't know, Sharif. This all sounds crazy," Miss Rose shifted uncomfortably in her seat. "That's my son, and he better do what I say. And that's all there is to it. I don't need no damn contract."

"Yeah. That's what I'm—" Ricky started.

"Shut your mouth, boy!" Miss Rose glared at him before turning back to Sharif. "So like what kinda stuff would be in this contract, anyway?"

"Well, for instance," Sharif leaned back in his seat. "You don't like Ricky hanging out on the corners. For obvious reasons, of course. But, Ricky grew up with most of the guys that are out there. So we'd have to try and see if we can reach a compromise that both of you can live with."

"Yeah. Like I can hang out with whoever I wanna, and she can't say anything since I'm not selling drugs," Ricky piped in.

"Like hell you say," Miss Rose started to rise up off the sofa but Sharif put his arm out to block her.

"What if we tried a compromise like this," he said calmly. "Miss Rose, Ricky is fifteen, right?"

"Sixteen, Dawg."

"He's fifteen, and stop referring to peoples as animals," Miss Rose snapped. "I don't know why these young kids wanna rush to get old. Then when they old they wanna try and act like they're young."

"Ma, I'm going to be sixteen in two months." Ricky threw his hands up in the air.

"And in two months you can say you're sixteen. Until then you're fifteen. Now, shut up before I rap you in the mouth for talking back to me." Miss Rose narrowed her eyes at Ricky as she spoke, and the boy obediently leaned back in this chair.

"Yes, ma'am," he said out loud, then mumbled something inaudible.

"What did you say?" Miss Rose demanded.

"Nothing." Ricky's expression remained sullen.

"Okay, so Ricky's fifteen. Do you have a curfew for him?"

"He's supposed to be home by nine o'clock. And I think that's a fair time." Miss Rose crossed her arms in front of her. "Ain't nothing to be doing out after that but trying to get in some kind of trouble, and I ain't having it."

"But Ma, none of my other friends have to be home until eleven."

"And I ain't raising none of your other friends, now am I?" Miss Rose snapped.

"But see, Ma, that ain't right!" Ricky slapped his hand against his thigh. "I can see it during school, but it's summer now. And I never get to see my friends during school because I have to go to school way up in the Bronx with all them white folks, and they're all down here in Harlem. Summertime is the time I can catch up with them, Ma. I gotta stay down with my peeps. I don't wanna turn out like no white boy."

"You know, you talk the stupidest shit some time," Miss Rose huffed up.

"How am I talking stupid when all I'm saying is I wanna be around the people I feel comfortable with, Ma? I mean . . ." Ricky threw his hands up in the air. "I mean, dag, come on. I'm not trying to get in any trouble. I hear you when you say you wanna make sure I get in college. I wanna go to college, too. I ain't gonna mess that up."

"Well, what time do you think would be a fair time for your mother to expect you in?" Sharif broke in.

"I mean, like, you know, two AM sounds fair," Ricky looked straight at Sharif as he spoke.

"Boy, have you lost your mind? Ain't no son of mine going be hanging out in the street after midnight." Miss Rose chuckled.

"Okay, so the issue seems to be that you don't want him hanging out, and not knowing what he's doing, because he could be getting in trouble, right?"

Miss Rose nodded.

"And your issue is that you don't intend to get into any trouble, you just want a curfew that allows you to spend time with friends who don't have to get in as early as you do, right?"

Ricky nodded.

"Okay, you think he should be home at nine, and he thinks he should be able to stay out until two," Sharif tapped his pen against the notepad. "How about a midnight curfew during the summer?"

"That boy ain't got no business being in the street at no midnight!" Miss Rose sat up and put her hands on her hips as she turned to Sharif.

"I ain't got no problem with that." Ricky rubbed his chin and grinned at Sharif.

"Well, I gotta problem with it," Miss Rose reiterated.

"It's just a suggestion. But hear me out," Sharif said soothingly. "What if the deal was he could have a midnight curfew, and he couldn't be home even one minute past midnight, and he would check in by telephone at, let's say nine, and let you know where he was and what he was doing?"

"Aw, man, that's like having a parole officer!" Ricky said with disgust.

Miss Rose took a deep breath and shook her head. "I don't know. Maybe. Yeah, I guess I could live with that."

"Okay, Ricky," Sharif turned to the teenager. "Can you live with it?"

"I don't like that checking in part," Ricky grumbled. "But yeah, I can deal with it."

"So, if we were to make up a contract, we could put that down as one of the first items, right? Miss Rose, you agree to let Ricky stay out until midnight, and in return, Ricky, you agree to check in and let your mother know where you are and know what you're doing."

Both Miss Rose and Ricky nodded.

"Now, see, that's how a contract would work. We'd write it up, and both of you would sign it. And everyone is clear about what is expected of them."

"But I don't want him hanging out on that corner," Miss Rose glared from Sharif to Ricky. "I want that in the contract, too."

"Aw, come on, Ma. Now you not being fair," Ricky stomped both his feet on the floor and flopped back in the chair. "You know I ain't selling no drugs, Dawg. Can't you tell her?"

"He ain't gotta tell me shit." Miss Rose scrambled off the couch and Sharif quickly got up to step in front of her before she could get to Ricky. "Ain't you learn nothing from what happened today? You ain't gotta be selling drugs for them to haul your ass off to jail."

"It's okay, Miss Rose. Just sit down and we'll talk this out." Sharif managed to get the woman back on the couch, where she sat breathing heavily and glaring at Ricky, who sat in the armchair, tapping his feet and biting his lip.

"All right, Ricky," Sharif said after he was also seated. "What about the corner? Your mother has a point. You don't have to be dirty to get busted. And you were lucky today. There's a lot of brothers doing big time because of drugs that cops planted on them because they needed a bust to get promoted."

"Aw, Sharif man, yo," Ricky protested weakly, never looking at Sharif or his mother.

"Naw, it's not about Sharif man, yo. You're talking about wanting to go to a good college. You think Columbia or NYU is going to accept you if you have a rap sheet for drugs?"

"Columbia, nothing," Ricky chuckled. "I'm heading to Harvard or Yale."

"Well, if you're trying to make it to the Ivy League, you got some decisions to make, little brother. And I'ma tell you, the corner just isn't the way to go," Sharif said gently. "And you already know that, don't you?"

Ricky nodded, then sunk his chin in his hands.

"Okay, so both of you agree that Ricky needs to stay off the corner, right?" Sharif picked up the notepad again. "So how about—"

"Hey, Sharif!" There was a pounding on the door.

"Excuse me just a minute." Sharif got up and opened the door to find Bootsy and Jimmy leaning against the doorsill.

"Hey, Sharif, how you doing, man?" Bootsy extended his hand for a pound.

"Hey, Reef. How you do, man." Jimmy echoed pounding his fist against Sharif's elbow.

"Everything's everything, dudes," Sharif tousled Jimmy's hair, causing the little boy to duck behind Bootsy. "Listen, I'm in the middle of something right now. Y'all want to come back a little later?"

"We just came up because Grandma wants you to move her refrigerator for her," Bootsy bounced the basketball a few times. "I could've moved it, but you know how she is."

"I coulda moved it, too," Jimmy piped up from behind Bootsy.

"Yeah, I know you could, Little Man," Sharif smiled. "Tell your grandma I'll be down in a little bit. I've just got to finish some business."

"Hey, Ricky! Waddup, dawg." Bootsy yelled into the apartment.

" 'Sup, dawg," Ricky waved at him.

" 'Sup, doggy!" Jimmy called.

"These young boys calling each other animals. Don't make no sense," Miss Rose sucked her teeth.

"Hey, Miss Rose. I ain't see you there. How you doing, Ma'am?" Bootsy said in a lower voice.

"I'm doing fine, child. Tell your mama I said hello."

"Okay, I will. A'ight, catch you later, Ricky. Catch you later, Sharif," Bootsy turned and started bouncing the basketball down the hall.

"Catch you later," Jimmy yelled as he ran behind Bootsy.

Sharif chuckled as he watched them disappear around the corner. Then he closed the door and turned to face Miss Rose and Ricky.

"Okay," he said wearily. "Back to business."

It was a little past midnight when Sharif, stretched out on the couch fully clothed, woke up to a ringing telephone.

"Peace," he said as he picked up the receiver.

"Sharif. Is Jimmy up there?" The urgency in Brenda's voice was unmistakable.

"Jimmy? What? No." Sharif sat up, rubbing his eyes and trying to clear his head. "What's going on?"

"We can't find him. He's been missing since like nine o'clock. I've been calling you for hours."

"I was asleep," Sharif apologized. "Last time I saw him he was with Bootsy. That was earlier this evening. About six, I guess."

"Well, Bootsy went out to play ball with some friends, and he didn't want to take Jimmy. Me and Mom thought he was in the bedroom sleeping, but when she went to check on him he was gone. He must have slipped out looking for Bootsy. We've been looking for him ever since. Bootsy got home about an hour ago and he's just hysterical. He searched all over the building and went to the stores he's ever taken him to, all the playgrounds and everything, but no one's seen him." Brenda started crying. "Oh, God. Please don't let anything have happened to that boy. I would just die."

"Have you called the police yet?"

"Yeah, Mom called them. They were here and took a report, but you know they're not going to do anything to try and find him."

"Okay. I'm going to hang up. I'm on my way down."

9

Brenda ran her hand over her hair as she walked back and forth in the living room talking on the telephone. Her eyes were red and swollen, and she kept rubbing her hands over her face. "Yeah, Daddy. I'm glad you called. And I'm gonna try and calm down, but I gotta get off the phone so I can keep the line open. I really appreciate you talking to me, it's really helped, but let me go. Call me tomorrow, okay? I love you, Daddy."

Brenda hung up, and walked to the window. She could see packs of women and men hunting through alleys with flashlights, and she heard them calling out Jimmy's name. Even the corner where the young dope dealers plied their trade was deserted, save for one lone young man "holding it down" while the others joined the search for the little boy who had captured so many hearts. She wiped her eyes and picked up the telephone, but before she could dial, Rosa burst into the apartment.

"Ay, *Dios*, this is too fucking crazy. Me and Bootsy knocked on every door in Ida B. We woke everybody up but no one's seen that boy. Where the hell can he be?" Rosa flung her pocketbook on the couch, and grabbed her hair with both hands. "How the fuck can a little boy just disappear like this?"

"Oh, God, I don't know, Rosa," Brenda stared at the telephone, trying to remember who it was she was going to call, then finally put the receiver down.

"But I mean it's not like he knows a lot of places around here, except the playgrounds and stuff, and we searched all of those. And Sharif even got the candy store owner's home phone number and made him come back and open up, just in case Jimmy went there and got locked in 'cause no one noticed him, and shit. *Ay, chica,* you should see Bootsy. He's all broken up and crying, thinking it's his fault because he didn't take Jimmy with him."

"Yeah, I keep telling him it's not his fault, but he won't listen," Brenda wiped her eyes. "Where's he now?"

"He and Ricky went over to the schoolyard. And then they said they was going to look in the subway stations and then head back here and search the building again. Sharif's getting security to let him into all the vacant apartments, although I don't how the hell Jimmy could have gotten into a locked vacant apartment."

"He's just trying to cover all the bases," Brenda said sadly as she sat on the couch. "I feel so useless being here while everybody else is out looking, but someone's gotta stay here in case Jimmy comes home. Mommy is downstairs in her apartment, but Sharif and them said I should stay here since Jimmy's been spending the night with Bootsy lately."

"Oh, man, how is your mother?"

"Oh, Rosa, she's just so upset! She's been calling here every ten minutes to see if I've heard anything. And you know she's called all the newspapers and television stations already. She must have left a hundred messages for that woman on Channel Seven she's always watching. That action lady, or whatever. Shaniqua, Yusef, and Jumah are down there with her, and I'm sure she's driving them crazy. They're kids, though, so they can handle it." Brenda got up and walked back over to the window. "Rosa, can you stay here for just a couple of minutes? It's almost two a.m. I gotta get out there and do some looking or I'm going to go crazy."

There was a cool breeze blowing as Brenda walked out of the building, and she actually shivered for a moment before she wiped the perspiration from her forehead that she hadn't realized was there. The lobby had been teeming with people, some in their robes, who had been searching the building looking for Jimmy and were badgering the security guard for updates. The security guard, a minimum-wage worker who was used to reading comic books on duty, was doing his best to be helpful. Even he had taken a liking to Jimmy, who would yell " 'Sup" to him whenever he went by with Bootsy. The lobby door was unlocked, and held open by a wedged newspaper as people flowed in and out.

Bootsy. She sighed and crossed her arms to hold herself as she thought about her oldest son. Big bad Bootsy hadn't shed a tear in public since he was five, but he was bawling his eyes out when he set out on his search. Shaniqua, Yusef, and Jumah may have been his siblings, but Jimmy—in the few short weeks he had been staying with them—had become his special little buddy. Poor Bootsy.

"Brenda. Why aren't you upstairs?"

She swung around to see Sharif approaching her.

"Rosa's up there. I just needed to feel useful." Brenda wiped her eyes again. "Anything new?"

"No. I've even—"

They both jumped as a loud howl came from the building, a painful howl that made the hair on Brenda's neck stand on end. The first howl lasted about ten seconds, and Sharif and Brenda were already running back into the Ida B. when the second howl started. "Oh, God, Sharif, that's Bootsy!"

They ran to the laundry room, where the howling had started, and pushed through the crowd that had gathered there. Brenda's heart almost stopped as she saw her son on his knees in front of one of the dryers, tears streaming down his anguished face. He was cradling Jimmy's lifeless battered nude body in his arms.

"He's dead!" Bootsy wailed over and over. "He's dead!"

"It's okay, Bootsy. Put him down," Sharif reached over to touch Bootsy's shoulder but the boy violently jerked away.

"Get off me. Get off me," he yelled at the top of his lungs as he struggled to his feet. "Just stay off me. I'll kill if you touch me."

"Oh, my God. Bootsy, baby!" Brenda ran over and pulled her son into her arms. Instead of fighting, he buried his face in her bosom. "Someone killed him, Ma. Someone killed him and put him in a dryer like he was just laundry."

"I know, baby. I know," Brenda cried along with her son as she rocked him back and forth.

10

Coño! I'm coming. Don't knock down my damn door!" Rosa wrapped a robe around her nude body, her skin still wet from the shower someone was interrupting.

Rosa peeked out the peephole and saw two middle-aged men—one white and one African-American—standing in front of her door. Both wore slacks and shirts and ties, and both looked bored as all hell. So why were they banging on her door at ten o'clock in the morning, she wondered. "All right already! Who is it and what do you want?"

"I'm Detective Michael Ralston, and this is my partner, Detective Al Lopez," the white detective said, holding his badge up to the peephole for inspection. "We'd like to ask you some questions about the body that was found in the building earlier this morning."

Al Lopez, huh? Rosa thought as she looked Wright's partner up and down through the peephole. He coulda fooled me. She could usually spot a fellow *boriquo*, no matter the skin color, but this guy's Latino heritage had eluded her. Maybe he was Dominican or something, she decided. She opened the door to find out.

"Come on in." She waved them toward the living room. "Let me just put on some clothes and I'll be right out. *Está bien?*" she asked, addressing the detective who had been identified as Lopez.

"I don't speak Spanish," he said curtly.

Shit. He sure set me straight. But he didn't have to do with such a fucking attitude. She curled her lip as she watched him walk over to the sofa and sit down. "Yeah, well, why don't you, you know, just take a seat, and shit."

"Uh, thanks," Detective Ralston said uncomfortably. He took a seat on the sofa, a cushion away from his partner. Lopez said nothing.

Rosa sucked her teeth and walked into the bedroom.

"So you say you've known Mrs. Carver how long?" Detective Ralston asked as he scribbled on his notepad.

"About fifteen or sixteen years. Twenty years. Something like that. Like I already said, ever since I moved here," Rosa said impatiently.

"And you say she's really good with kids, right? What do you mean by that? I mean," Ralston gave a chuckle, "I'm a father myself, and I know sometimes the little tykes can really work your nerves. Have you ever seen Mrs. Carver, well, lose her temper with the children she takes care of?"

"No, never," Rosa shook her head emphatically. "And I'm telling you, she loves kids. I even let her baby-sit my Eddie. He's not here now," she added. "My mother took him with her to Puerto Rico for a couple of months."

"Yes, of course. I understand," Ralston said with a nod. "So you say Mrs. Carver called you shortly after nine to ask if you'd seen Jimmy?" Ralston asked as he continued his scribbling.

"Yeah. I think it was about that time. I'd just gotten back from rehearsal. I'm an actress in a play."

"Really? Imagine that." Detective Ralston smiled. "When you opened the door I thought I was looking at Rosie Perez."

"A lot of people tell me I look like her," Rosa ran her fingers through her damp hair, then brushed of an imaginary piece of lint from her yellow tee shirt. "I'll probably get more parts than her though, because I don't have that Brooklyn accent. I mean, she could never get a part playing someone from, like you know, someone from Boston and shit. For instance, I'm playing an Italian woman in the play I'm in now. She could never get away with something like that." She looked over at Lopez to see his reaction now that he found out that he was in the presence of a somebody, or someone on the verge of being a somebody, but he just sat there stone-faced.

"Makes perfect sense to me." Detective Ralston nodded. "But back to Mrs. Carver and Jimmy. So she called you around nine, and . . . tell me again exactly what she said."

"Well, you know," Rosa leaned forward in her chair. "She sounded really concerned. I wouldn't say she was hysterical, but then she just thought he was wandering the building, maybe, or had went to someone's house. You know, someone he knew, and shit. So she said, 'Rosa, have you seen Jimmy?' And I told her no, that I had just gotten in. And she said that he had been in the bedroom sleeping, but that when she looked in on him to make sure he was okay, he was gone. So like I went downstairs and me and Brenda started looking around the building, and then when Bootsy came home he started looking, too. And pretty soon the whole building was searching. Oh, and you know what I didn't already tell you? What's really fucked up?"

"What's that," Detective Ralston asked.

"I looked in the laundry room myself. Twice. And I looked in the washing machines and shit, but I didn't check that dryer because it was stopped and had white sheets and I think a bedspread on top of it. But I guess by the time Bootsy went in there again the blood had started seeping through. Oh, my God! Can you imagine!" Rosa leaned over and slapped Ralston on the knee. "I mighta been the one who found Jimmy's body. I woulda died!"

"Oh, yeah. That would have just been terrible for you," Lopez said with a snort.

Rosa glared at him. "Oh, yeah, well look. I'm an actress, not a police officer or a detective, okay? I'm not used to finding dead people, all right?"

"Ma'am, I think what my partner meant—"

"What I mean," Lopez cut him off. "Is that you're sitting here cooing and preening when we're trying to investigate a serious crime."

Rosa stood up and stamped her foot. "I'm not cooing! I haven't cooed not once." She turned to Ralston. "Have I cooed at you?"

"No, not at all," he said hurriedly.

"You're just mad 'cause I thought you was Spanish. And I don't know why, 'cause it's an honest mistake since you're named Lopez. And like someone mistaking you for Spanish is some kind of insult. What are you?" Rosa crossed her arms and started tapping her foot, "Latino-phobic or some shit?"

"Miss, the only thing I am, *and shit*," Lopez said, not bothering to look at Rosa, "is sick and tired of you trying to make this interview about *you* rather than a four-year-old dead boy."

"Oh, now, you hold up a minute," Rosa put a hand on her hip and started waving her finger in Lopez's face, "Don't you try to make like I don't care about Jimmy. I do care! And what *I'm* sick and tired of is you motherfuckers interviewing me to try and dig up on Miss Janet when you should be out there looking for the *hijo de puta* who killed him!"

She turned to Ralston, her hand still on her hip and cocked her head to the side. "You're not a motherfucker, but he is, with his fucked up attitude," she said pointing to Lopez.

"Mrs. Rivera . . ." Ralston started.

"You know what?" Rosa walked over to the front door and swung it it open. "You know what? Now that I think about it, you're a motherfucker, too. Trying to pin this on Miss Janet, and shit. So both of y'all can get out my house.

* * *

Rosa sat her crock pot of *arroz con pollo* down on the aluminum card table already almost overflowing with casserole dishes and soup tureens. She glanced over at the table next to it, filled with cakes and pies, and made a note to fix some flan since there were no puddings evident. She hadn't gotten any sleep, and judging by all the freshly cooked food in the apartment, no else had either. It looked like everyone had been up all night cooking in order to bring down food to the apartment as a gesture of sympathy and support.

She sighed as she looked across at the room where Mrs. Carver sat in an armchair wiping her eyes, with six or seven women hovering over her, rubbing her shoulders and clucking sympathetically.

"How you doing, Miss Janet?" Rosa walked over and knelt down to give the woman a hug.

"Oh, well. I'm not doing so well right now. They had me over at the police station all night asking me questions," Mrs. Carver said weakly. "But, I'll be okay."

"Of course you'll be okay," Miss Jackie said as she passed Mrs. Carver a tissue. "It's just such a shock, isn't it, honey? Such a tragedy, isn't it. But God has his way. We just gotta learn how to deal with it. And the city's probably ain't gonna give you no more foster kids either, huh? Such a shame."

Rosa stood up and looked Miss Jackie up and down, then snapped, "I don't think Miss Janet is thinking about foster kids right now, Miss Jackie."

"Oh, no, of course not," Miss Jackie said hurriedly. "I'm just making conversation. I didn't mean no harm." She turned to Mrs. Carver. "You know that don't you, honey?"

Mrs. Carver simply nodded and wiped her nose and eyes.

Rosa shifted from one foot to the other, wondering what she would say. She'd never been good at situations like this, watching someone in pain and not being able to do anything about it. "You want me to do anything, Miss Janet? I took off from work to help out."

"Oh, Rosa, you're such a sweetie." Mrs. Carver put her hand on Rosa's arm. "You didn't have to do that. I think we got everything covered."

"Well, I wanna do something. I tell you what, I'll straighten up the kitchen for you, okay?"

Miss Gracie, who was standing next to Mrs. Carver spoke up. "I got that kitchen set up just the way I want it. Don't you set your foot in there."

"Oh, okay." Rosa shifted uncomfortably. "Well, you want me to run some errands or anything for you?"

"Honey, just fix yourself a plate and sit down," Mrs. Carver said. "There's plenty of food here." She turned to the woman who had spoken earlier. "Gracie, can she fix her own plate, or do you want to make it for her?"

"Come on now, Miss Janet," Rosa pleaded. "I gotta do something. Let me clean up, run errands," she looked around the apartment desperately. "Let me clean the bathroom . . . something."

"Now you know Janet keeps this house clean as a hospital, ain't no need for you be trying to be doing no cleaning," Miss Marcie said as she put her hands on her hips.

"Okay, Miss Marcie, but I . . ." Rosa said dismally.

Mrs. Carver smiled. "Why don't you go in the bedroom and talk to Brenda. Maybe she needs some help with the phone calls, and all."

"No, I don't need any help. Everything's taken care of."

Rosa turned around at the sound of her friend's voice. "Hey, *chica.* You okay?" She walked over and tapped her on the shoulder before giving her a quick hug.

"Yeah, I'm as fine as can be expected under the circumstance," Brenda said with a grimace that Rosa knew was supposed to pass as a smile.

"And how's Bootsy?" Rosa asked gently.

"Oh, Rosa," Brenda's shoulders sagged. "He's so messed up. He keeps blaming himself. And nothing I say, is changing is his mind."

"Yeah, I know. And then for him to be the one to find Jimmy." Rosa shivered. "Brenda, I swear I checked that laundry room at least twice, but I never thought to check in a dryer that had clothes in it."

"Yeah, whoever did it arranged a bunch of sheets on top," Miss Grace said. "You know that was Mrs. Harris's wash what was in the dryer, right?"

"No! Get out!" Rosa stepped back in surprise.

"Oh, child, yeah," Miss Jackie broke in. "I went and told her myself because I didn't want the police coming to her door and telling her. The poor woman woulda had a stroke. Plus, God knows what they would have done if they heard them dogs in there barking and all, 'cause you know we ain't supposed to be having no dogs in here. And can you imagine what woulda happened if she let them in and they saw all that stuff she had in there. They probably woulda locked her up on the spot,"

"Ooh, chile, ain't that the truth," one of the women answered.

"And that crazy grandson of hers, Vincent, woulda probably went down to the police station and try to shoot the place up for them locking up his grandma," Miss Jackie continued. "Child, yeah, that's why I went and told her before the police came, so she could get herself together and lock everything up. You know I don't want to see no trouble."

"Ooh. I know she must have been really upset, huh?" Rosa said, looking at Brenda for a response.

"Well, you know how she is, especially when someone had to wake her up like I did." Miss Jackie answered before Brenda could say anything. "She wouldn't open the door, not even a crack. So I had to shout it through the door. I thought she was going to have a heart attack right there on the spot. I could her gasping and coughing through the door."

"Oh, girl no," the woman in the flowered dress said.

"Child, yeah. I had to go get Sharif. You know he's the only one besides Vincent she'll let in late at night and what them dogs won't attack. He got her to let him in and made sure she had her nitroglycerin pills, and all. Then he called Vincent so he could come and stay with his grandma. Child, it's been one hell of a night. I ain't had but two hours sleep."

"It's two more than I got," Mrs. Carver sighed. "Brenda, did you fix the kids a plate?"

"Yeah, Shaniqua and Yusef are eating in the spare bedroom and I'm getting ready to feed Jumah now," Brenda said wearily. "Bootsy's upstairs with Sharif, but I'll fix him a plate when he comes back down."

"Mmmm."

Rosa turned to look at Miss Jackie, who stood with arms crossed and shaking her head.

"What now?" she demanded not too nicely.

"Well, I don't mean to get in anyone's business, but you saying Bootsy's up there alone with Sharif?" Miss Jackie said through pursed lips.

"I don't know if they're alone, but he's up there," Brenda said.

"Well, I don't know. Do you really think that's a good idea?" Miss Jackie asked.

"What are you saying, Jackie?" Mrs. Carver pulled herself up in the chair, a worried look suddenly appearing on her face.

"Look, I ain't trying to start no mess, but you know they saying that Jimmy was molested, 'cause he was naked, and he had all that blood on his little butt. And I'm just saying," Miss Jackie looked around the room as if to make sure her words were going to have the impact she felt they deserved, "I'm just saying, Sharif is the only one in the Ida B., that I know of, that likes little boys."

"Ooh, well, now you know . . ." Miss Marcie started.

"Oh, shut up!" Rosa spat. "Just because he's homosexual doesn't mean he like little boys."

"It's the same difference," Miss Jackie said emphatically. "If he likes doing it with men then he likes doing it with little boys. And I'm not saying he did it, but it woulda had to been someone who lives in the building, and I'm thinking he's the most likely cause he's a pervert."

"Brenda. Call Sharif and tell him to send Bootsy down here," Mrs. Carver said urgently.

"What? I'm not going to do that," Brenda's mouth dropped open.

"Miss Janet, don't be listening to her," Rosa said, pointing to Miss Jackie. "She's crazy. You know Sharif ain't do nothing."

"Mmm, I don't know, though," Miss Grace said. "She might have a point. It had to be someone who's a homo to do that to a little boy. And it's better to be safe than sorry, I always say."

"Miss Grace!" Rosa stamped her foot.

"I know Sharif didn't have anything to do with it," Mrs. Carver said lamely. "But Bootsy needs to be with his family at a time like this, anyway."

"Janet, I gotta go 'cause I promised I'd take my sister to the clinic," the woman in the flowered dress said. "Marcie, you coming with me?"

"Mama! I can't believe you're buying into this!" Brenda shouted at her mother, not paying attention to the departing women.

"You know what? You always starting some shit." Rosa walked up close to Miss Jackie and started pointing her finger in the woman's face. "Just wait until I tell Aunt Pat. She's gonna kick your ass."

"Stop cursing, Rosa," Mrs. Carver said weakly.

"Miss Janet," Rosa swung around to face Mrs. Carver. "I'm sorry, 'cause you know I don't usually curse in front of my elders, but I can't just stand here and let her accuse Sharif like this. It ain't right, and shit." Rosa caught herself, and crossed her arms as she looked down at the ground. "Sorry for cursing again."

"Mama, Sharif is like your son, and now you gonna let her poison your mind against him like this?" Brenda demanded. "What's the matter with you?"

"I'm not being poisoned, and Brenda, lower your voice when you talk to me." Mrs. Carver braced herself on the arms of the chair as she slowly pulled herself up. "And go call Bootsy to come down and get something to eat. Or are you going to make me call?"

"You're gonna have to call because I'm not," Brenda crossed her arms and looked at her mother. "And you know what? That's my son, and I don't have a problem with him being up there so he can stay right where he is."

Miss Jackie looked nervously between Brenda and her mother. "Brenda," she said hesitantly, "why don't you just call Bootsy so your mother doesn't get any more upset than she is? You don't have to tell him. Just tell him to come on down and we'll just leave it at that."

"I'm not doing it!" Brenda shouted at her. "And you should just mind your damn business! You're the reason she's upset!"

"And that's what I'm talking about." Rosa snapped her fingers just inches from Miss Jackie's face. "Go home, Miss Jackie. Your presence is no longer required."

"Brenda, if you're going to talk to me like that get the hell out of my house," Mrs. Carver shouted, her face reddening. She suddenly sagged back down in the chair. "This is all just too much for me."

"Now look, y'all gonna stress this poor woman to death." Miss Grace walked behind the chair and started massaging Mrs. Carver's shoulders. "All y'all stop all this shouting. Don't make no sense."

"Mama," Brenda knelt down in front of her mother. "I'm not trying to stress you. And you know I love and respect you more than anyone on this earth, but I'm not going to treat Sharif like he's some kind of molesting murderer because of Miss Jackie. Let's just leave Bootsy up there, and drop this, okay?"

Rosa walked over to the window. "Ooh, look. Aunt Pat just got outta a cab."

"Well, girl, I need to get outta here," Miss Jackie started shuffling toward the front door. "They got that police tape over the laundry room door, and I gotta get my wash down. I'ma have to go all the way down to 123rd Street, so I gotta go get Ronald up so he can help me haul it. I'll see y'all later."

"Knock, knock," Sharif said as he opened the unlocked front door. "Peace, y'all."

"How you doing, baby?" Miss Jackie said sweetly.

"Well, you know, I guess I'm doing okay," Sharif responded.

Rosa sucked her teeth. "Oh, please. Don't be talking to that old hag."

"Rosa, please," Mrs. Carver sighed.

"I'm sorry, Mrs. Carver," Rosa said politely.

"Janet, as God as my witness, I don't know what's wrong with some of these young folk, talking all outta turn and being disrespectful," Miss Jackie said as she pushed past Sharif and headed out the door.

"I gotta go, too," Miss Grace said as walked past Sharif, carefully avoiding his eyes.

Sharif looked at Brenda, Rosa, and Mrs. Carver. "Someone want to tell me what's going on?"

"Oh, nothing really," Rosa walked to the middle of the room, facing Sharif. "I wouldn't say it was nothing at all. Just that she, you know, just accused you of killing Jimmy."

"Rosa!" Mrs. Carver said.

Sharif's head jerked back. "What?"

"Yeah," Rosa said with a twirl of her hand. "She said you're the only one in the building who likes little boys, so you had sex with him and then killed him. 'Cause, you know, you're a homo. And that's what homos do. At least, according to Miss Jackie."

Sharif slapped his hand across his forehead, then raised his hands toward the ceiling. "Why, dear Lord. Just tell me why?" he said mockingly.

"Well, hmmph! I'm glad you think it's funny because me and Brenda were down here defending you, you know," Rosa huffed.

"How you doing, Sharif?" Mrs. Carver said with a slight wave of her hand.

"I'm doing fine, Miss Janet. And how are you?" Sharif bent down and kissed Mrs. Carver on the cheek. "You holding up okay?"

"I'll be fine. You heard anything else from the police?"

"They're working on it. Two detectives came up to my apartment a little bit ago to see if I had any more information."

"Don't tell me. Lopez and Ralston, right?" Rosa started. "I threw them out my place 'cause they started accusing Miss Janet of killing Jimmy."

"What!" Mrs. Carver jumped out of her chair.

"Uh-huh." Rosa nodded her head. "Well, they ain't accuse you right out, but they was dropping hints like nothing. And you know I wasn't having it. I would have said something to you sooner, but I wasn't gonna give Miss Jackie nothing else to gossip about. It's bad enough that she's going around saying it's probably Sharif."

"They think I did it," Mrs. Carver looked around the room as if in a daze. "They think I would hurt that little boy?"

Sharif put his arm around her and led her back to the chair, then knelt down in front of her and rubbed her arms soothingly. "It's just normal procedure. They always look at the caretaker first. They know it's not really you."

"Is it true he was molested?" Brenda asked.

"Yeah," Sharif sighed. "I managed to get that out of the detectives."

"Well, then they have to know it's not me!" Mrs. Carver said excitedly. "It has to be a man."

"Sharif! Where's Bootsy?" Brenda asked suddenly.

"I don't know. He came upstairs but the detectives were there so I told him I'd come down and talk to him later. He's not here?" Sharif stood up suddenly.

"No!" Brenda ran to the front door. "I'll check to see if he's in my apartment."

She swung open the door to find a sullen-faced Bootsy. "Oh, baby. I was so worried." She tried to hug him, but the boy pushed her away and stormed past her into the middle bedroom, barely looking at the people congregated in the living room.

"What the hell?" Brenda started after him, but he reappeared from the bedroom, holding something behind his back.

"I'm okay, Ma," he said with a strained smile. "Go ahead back in the living room. I wanna show everybody something," he said waving her back.

"What is it, baby?" Brenda asked as she walked over to couch where Sharif was sitting.

"Sharif," Bootsy said with a teary smile. "This is for you!" With that he lunged at Sharif with the hammer he'd been hiding. Sharif managed to dodge partially out of the way, and the blow that was meant for his head grazed his shoulder instead.

"Ay, *Dios!* What the fuck!" Rosa ran toward the boy, but Brenda had already grabbed him in a bear hug from behind.

"Bootsy!" Brenda struggled with the boy, trying to swing him away from the couch. "Drop the hammer."

"No. I'ma kill him. I'ma kill that faggot."

"Drop the hammer!" Brenda yelled again.

Rosa bent down and bit down hard on Bootsy's hand.

"Ouch!" Bootsy bent down so low that Brenda who was still holding him from behind almost slipped over his head to the floor. They both tumbled to the floor.

"Well, I made you drop the hammer," Rosa cried as she fell on the floor beside him and Brenda. "Sharif. You okay?"

Sharif was kneeling on the floor, rubbing his shoulder and grimacing. "Damn, damn," he whispered over and over again.

"Oh, good Lord! Sharif are you all right?" Mrs. Carver rushed over to him and started rocking him in her arms.

"I'm okay," Sharif said through clenched teeth. "I don't think he hit the bone."

"Let go of me! I'ma kill him!" Bootsy was still struggling, though Rosa had him in a headlock and Brenda had his hands pinned behind his back.

"No one's letting go of you until you tell me what the hell is wrong with you," Brenda said between clenched teeth.

"He killed Jimmy! He raped him and then he killed him so he wouldn't tell anyone!"

"What? Bootsy, stop talking nonsense," Mrs. Carver said. "Who told you that nonsense?"

"It's not nonsense. Let me go!" Bootsy managed to squeeze out of Rosa's headlock and was trying to struggle to his feet. "He's the only one in the building who does men."

"Oh, God, he's been talking to Jackie." Mrs. Carver shook her head as she stroked Sharif's hair. "That woman ain't nothing but trouble."

"Bootsy, you know better than to listen to that woman," Brenda allowed Bootsy to scramble to a sitting position. "You know she doesn't know what she's talking about."

"She didn't tell me nothing," Bootsy said, pulling his arms out of her hands.

"Then who did?"

"Ronald," Bootsy said sullenly.

"Oh, well, yeah. Then that's the gospel," Rosa threw her hands in the air.

"Bootsy." Sharif slowly stood up, though still gingerly rubbing his shoulder. He shook his head as if to shake off the pain, and then sat down on the edge of a chair. "Look, Bootsy. I didn't hurt Jimmy. You know I wouldn't hurt him. My God! You've known me all your life and you really think I'm capable of doing something like this?"

"Fuck! I don't know! Someone killed him." Bootsy cradled his chin in his hands and stared off into space.

"Bootsy, watch your mouth," Mrs. Carver said sternly.

"It's okay, Ma," Brenda started rubbing her son's back. "Bootsy. You know Sharif didn't kill Jimmy, right?"

Bootsy stared straight ahead, his lips quivering.

"Bootsy," Brenda continued massaging her son's back.

"Aw, Ma. I don't know," Bootsy sighed. "Someone did."

"But you know it wasn't Sharif, right?"

"Well, who was it, then?" Bootsy wiped at the tear that was forming in the corner of his eye, and turned to bury his face in his mother's arms. "Then who was it?"

"Baby, I don't know. But we're going to find out. And then he's going to be locked up so he won't hurt anyone else."

Rosa stood up and looked at Bootsy, her eyes welling up with tears as she did so. Too see her best friend in such pain, and to see her best friend's son in even more pain was almost too much to bear. Before she could decide what to do next, Mrs. Carver gently pushed her aside and bent down to help her daughter and grandson to their feet, and then the three grouped into a teary swaying hug.

"Come on," Rosa motioned weakly to Sharif. "Let's go up to your place.

"Fine." Sharif slowly stood up and followed Rosa to the door, pausing just before leaving the apartment. "Bootsy, man. We're still okay. All right, man?"

Bootsy lifted his head toward Sharif and gave a slight nod before lowering his eyes.

11

"I can't believe Bootsy attacked you like that, Sharif," Rosa said as she placed a towel wrapped around ice cubes on Sharif's shoulder. "He musta lost his mind, and shit."

"Can you blame him?" Sharif raised his arm a little to test his shoulder, and then grimaced in pain. "I can't even imagine how I would feel in his place. He feels responsible for Jimmy's death."

"*Pobrecito,*" Rosa sighed.

"What?"

"*Pobrecito*. Poor little one. Poor foolish little one." Rosa explained. "Blaming himself like that."

"He's a kid," Sharif said as he readjusted the makeshift icepack. "Are you sure I'm supposed to have ice on this, and not heat?"

"You gotta put ice on it so that it doesn't swell." Rosa sat down on the chair. "And I know he's just a kid, and he feels guilty, but I'm still not understanding how he could be so quick to think you did it, and shit. I mean, just because Ronald told him some shit? He don't even like Ronald. And everyone knows you've been almost like a father to him. And he hits you with a hammer? That's fucked up."

"Yeah, I know," Sharif exhaled slowly. "But at the same time I understand why he did it."

"Oh, you do," Rosa said with a smirk.

"Yeah. It's important to him to find someone else to blame beside himself. He's gotta beat someone else up so he can stop beating himself up, poor kid. I'm sure he wouldn't have paid Ronald any mind if he was thinking straight, but right now he's messed up emotionally." Sharif's voice trailed off and he suddenly seemed lost in thought.

"So?" Rosa said after a few moments.

"So, what?" Sharif directed his attention back to her.

"So, who do you think did it?" Rosa asked as she rolled a joint.

"Damn if I know," Sharif shook his head. "It had to be someone who lives here, though.

"No way," Rosa said with a wave of her hand. "I'm not believing that someone at Ida B. would hurt Jimmy. Everyone in the building loved that kid."

"Yeah, that's true. But I don't think someone from the outside would come in and rape and kill him, and then stick him in a dryer. They would have just left him wherever it was they assaulted him. It had to be somebody who was worried about being found with his body."

"*Coño.*" Rosa jerked her head back. "That makes sense, though. I hadn't even thought about it like that."

Sharif snorted. "Stop smoking all my reefer and maybe you'd think a little clearer."

"Someone here at Ida B.," Rosa said slowly. "But why put the body in the laundry room? Why not take it out the building?"

"Maybe he was afraid of someone seeing him. Maybe he started to, but got cold feet about walking past the security guard. I mean, the laundry room is right on the first floor, so maybe he was trying to get the body out of the building but had to settle for the laundry room instead." Sharif leaned forward in his seat, forgetting the pain in his shoulder. "What if he wrapped Jimmy's body in something and put it in a box or something to take it out the building, but then got cold feet before he passed the security desk? So he ducks into the laundry room to get his nerve back, and then got the bright idea to leave Jimmy there."

"But Jimmy's body wasn't wrapped up in anything."

"Right. He unwrapped him before he put him in the dryer. Because he realized whatever he wrapped Jimmy in would lead the police right back to him," Sharif said eagerly. "So it might be that he still has incriminating evidence in his apartment." He paused. "Actually, he could have gotten it out this morning. If it was a sheet or blanket he could have sneaked it out in a shopping bag without suspicion."

"Damn. You got this all thought out and shit, huh, Sharif?" Rosa flicked the last ash of her reefer and stubbed it out in the ashtray. "But I got a question. How could he get the body in the laundry room without anyone noticing him? I mean, there were a bunch of people running all around the building looking for Jimmy."

"But what if he did all this before anyone even realized Jimmy was missing? Remember, Miss Janet said she didn't know when Jimmy slipped out, just that he wasn't there when she went to check on him at nine. Bootsy left the apartment at six, right? So whoever this guy is, he had plenty of time. And you know like I know, most people don't do their laundry on Sunday nights. Or not usually, anyway. So whoever it was took a chance, and it paid off."

"Hmph. Well, you got this all figured out, huh? I guess all those detective comic books you used to read paid off, and shit." Rosa stood up and walked toward the window, and peeked through the curtains. "You know what? I ain't even high. All this shit going on is stopping me from getting my head bad. What a waste of good marijuana." She turned back around to look at Sharif. "So, Sherlock. Absolutely no idea who it could be, huh?"

Sharif sighed and shook his head. He leaned back on the sofa. The towel that had held the ice for his shoulder was on the cushion next to him, soaking the material through, but he didn't even notice as he chewed the inside of his lips and strummed his fingers on his knee. His thoughts were interrupted by the ringing of the telephone. He reached for it, and winced as pain shot through his shoulder.

"Peace . . . Yeah, I'm up here. What's going on? . . . Where are you? . . . Yeah, come on up." He put the phone back on the cradle. "Vincent is on his way up."

"I gotta call Mitch and tell him I'm going to miss rehearsal today." Rosa reached for the telephone and stopped. "Wait a minute. Tell me what was up with you the other day? Why'd you break on Mitch, and shit?"

"Yeah, I knew you were going to bring that up," Sharif said almost dismissively.

"Oh, hell, yeah, I was going to bring that up." Rosa stamped her foot.

"Why do you always stamp your feet whenever you want to make a point?" Sharif chuckled.

"Because that's what I do," Rosa said. "Now don't change the subject. Why were you tripping the other day?"

"I don't know. There was something about him," Sharif said grudgingly.

"Oh, so you just insult people 'cause you don't like the way they look, and shit." Rosa glared at him.

Sharif started rubbing his shoulder again. "Rosa, could you get me some aspirin? They're in the medicine cabinet. And I didn't say I didn't like the way he looked. I just said there was something about him. Don't put words in my mouth."

"Same thing," Rosa snapped.

"Girl, will you just go get me the damn aspirin." Sharif picked up a magazine from the coffee table with his good arm and threw it at Rosa.

"So if it wasn't the way he looked, what do you mean there was something about him?" Rosa crossed her arms and tapped her foot she glared at Sharif defiantly.

"Hmph. There goes that foot action, again."

"Sharif, if you don't quit playing with me, and shit, I'm going to—"

"Man, Rosa. I don't know. But when you told us his name, it just sounded real familiar," Sharif put his feet on the coffee table, and crossed and then uncrossed them. "And wherever I'd heard it before, I knew it wasn't good."

"Of course you heard his name before." Rosa stamped her foot. "He's a famous theater director. The most famous theater director alive."

"It wasn't in that context, Rosa," Sharif grumbled. "Like I said, wherever I'd heard the name before it was connected to something negative. Now will you please get me the aspirin?"

"Why don't you get it yourself? Ain't nothing wrong with your feet." Rosa shot back over her shoulder as she headed toward the bathroom.

"Because I'm trying to change the subject," Sharif said in a low voice he knew Rosa couldn't hear.

He looked up as he heard someone banging on the door.

"Yo. Come on in. It's not locked," he yelled.

Vincent quickly walked into the apartment, letting the door slam after him as he strode into the living room. "Get your shit, bro. We got some business to take care of."

"What? What's up?" Sharif jumped up from the couch. He knew the look on his old friend's face, and he knew that when Vincent wore it something really serious was about to go down.

"It was Ronald, man," Vincent said through clenched teeth. "Ronald killed that kid."

"What? Ronald?" The uncapped bottle of aspirin Rosa was holding fell to the floor. "How do you know?"

Vincent swung around to look at her standing in the hallway between the bathroom and the living room. "I didn't know you were here. You'd better split."

"How did you know it was Ronald?" Rosa demanded again.

"Rosa, get the fuck out before you get hurt," Vincent said in almost a whisper. "And don't say shit about what you just heard. You and I go way back, but if I hear this again, I'll slit your throat. Got that?"

Rosa strode past him and picked up her pocketbook and swung it over her shoulder, then turned toward the front door. "Yeah, we do go way back. And you ain't had to threaten me, and shit. Fuck you," she said as she walked out.

Vincent watched as the door slammed, then turned back to face Sharif. "I'll apologize later. You cool?"

"Yeah, bro," Sharif nodded. "But how'd you find out it was Ronald?"

The cold glint returned to Vincent's eye. "One of the girls I used to use in one of my cons, Sookie, turned crack ho awhile back. Last night she fucked a janitor in the utility closet in the laundry room for ten bucks. He left, and then she was supposed to walk out five minutes later, but she decided to stick around and smoke her shit. Sookie said she was about to split when she heard someone come in. She ducked back into the closet, but she kept the door open a crack. She figured if it was a man she could offer up a blow job and make a few bucks. She saw Ronald come in."

"Damn! And she was sure it was Ronald?"

"Yeah. Sookie said he's a regular trick. He pays her extra to take it up the ass. She said she was going to say something to him when she first recognized him, but the way he was breathing and looking all nervous she knew something was up. So she just kept peeking through the crack in the door. That's when she saw him put the body in the dryer."

"Oh, shit! Shit." Sharif could feel a dark cloud enveloping him, the cloud that preceded rage, and his fists clenched and unclenched as he struggled to fight back the urge to run downstairs and drag Ronald out of his apartment. He slowly sat back down and started drawing deep breaths, trying to make the cloud disappear so he could think rationally. "How come she didn't say anything?" he asked finally.

"Didn't you hear me say she was a crack ho? What the fuck's wrong with you?" Vincent said. "She caught me up on 145th Street and was hitting me up for money is the only way I found out."

"Right. Right," Sharif nodded numbly although his mind was racing.

"Now, we gotta take care of this shit," Vincent continued. "All I need you to do is go down there and tell Ronald some shit to get him to meet you somewhere. Then whatever time you tell him, make sure you're somewhere else. Somewhere where people can see you so you can have an alibi. I'll be meeting him instead and I'll take care of him in my own special way. "

Sharif looked at Vincent through narrowed eyes. "You'll take care of him?"

Vincent looked at him and said nothing.

"You know we could just go to the police," Sharif said slowly.

"Man, Sharif, what the fuck is wrong with you?" Vincent demanded. "This motherfucker raped a little boy and killed him, and then put him in my grandmother's laundry."

"Yeah, but . . ."

"Yeah, but shit. Sharif, you know this little pervert gotta get what's coming to him. If I go around asking for him I'm gonna be fingered when he winds up dead. And I can't trust anyone else on this shit but you. So you tell me now, you got my back or what? Either way, I'm gonna handle my business. That was a sweet little kid he fucked up," Vincent paused and took a deep breath. "A sweet little kid. And that heart everyone says I ain't got? It hurt like shit when I heard what happened. And I'm gonna make that motherfucker pay."

Sharif looked up at Vincent, and chewed his lip.

"Sharif, I know you're down with all consciousness shit, and trying to be law abiding, and as much as I tease you about it, I admire that shit. But you gotta step outta that consciousness mode for a fucking minute, and then step back in it when this shit is done. I ain't asking you to do nothing but get that motherfucker somewhere I can get to him. There's some motherfuckers who just deserve to die, and you can't tell me you don't think Ronald is one of them after he did that shit to an innocent kid."

Sharif was barely listening to Vincent as his mind continued to race, and the cloud began to again form. Justice, every nerve in his body was screaming at him, there's got to be justice. A picture of Jimmy's watery smile flashed in front of his eyes, and the picture seemed so real he wanted to reach out and grab him into a bear hug. All of his life he'd tried to look out for the innocent, and if there ever an innocent, it was that sweet kid who had just begun to open up and trust the people around him. And that trust had been betrayed in the most vicious manner. There had to be justice for Jimmy. But even if they turned Ronald turned over to the police and he got the death penalty it wouldn't be good enough. A nice little injection, where Ronald could drift off into a peaceful death? No, that fucking pervert had to suffer. Vincent was right, street justice was what Ronald deserved.

"Yeah, that motherfucker gotta pay," he said finally as he stood up.

"Solid," Vincent said as the two men gave each other a pound. "You always been my nig—"

"Don't say that word in my house." Sharif cut him off. "Ronald's been bugging me to put him down with my shea butter business. I'll tell him to meet me so we can discuss it in private. Where do you want me to tell him to meet?" Sharif asked as he stood up.

Before Vincent could answer they heard someone banging furiously on the door.

"Y'all better come quick," Rosa yelled out breathlessly. "Someone shot Ronald in the fifth-floor hallway."

12

"Bootsy saw it," Brenda said in a whisper after she was huddled in the foyer of her apartment with Rosa, Sharif, and Vincent. She'd pulled them from the grisly hallway where Ronald's body lay sprawled, the top of his head almost blown off, and insisted they come with her.

"He saw what?" Rosa asked excitedly. "What did he see?"

"He saw Ronald get shot."

"What?" Sharif almost shouted.

"He was on the sixth floor hallway tagging again, when he heard some voices on the fifth floor. He said he was getting ready to run up the stairs, but then he recognized one of the voices, so he looked down the stairway. He saw Ronald get shot!" Brenda said all in a rush.

"Get out of here. Oh, shit. Who did it?" Rosa asked.

"You're not going to believe it," Brenda said in an even more hushed tone. "It was Ricky."

"What?" Rosa's hand flew to her forehead, and she leaned against the wall. "*Madre de Dios*. Ricky? He's just a kid."

"Damn," was all Sharif could say.

Vincent chuckled. "Go ahead, youngblood."

"How can you think it's funny, Vincent?" Brenda hit him on the arm. "Bootsy said he hauled ass out of there, and he didn't think Ricky saw him, but what if he did? You think he might come after Bootsy?"

"Where's Bootsy now?" Sharif said urgently.

"He's in his room lying down. I think everything that's been happening just taken everything out of him," Brenda answered. "And I think he's just plain scared."

"Don't worry," Vincent said soothingly. "Ricky's not going to bother Bootsy."

"Oh?" Brenda put her hands on her hips. "And just how do you know that? I mean, why did he shoot Ronald?"

Vincent looked at Sharif. "You're thinking what I'm thinking, right?"

"Yeah," Sharif nodded. "But how did he find out?"

"How did he find out what?" Brenda asked.

"Ooh!" Rosa put her hand over her mouth and looked at Sharif and Vincent.

"Ooh, what?" Brenda demanded. "What's going on? What is it, Vincent?"

"Ricky musta found out that Ronald killed Jimmy," Vincent said with a shrug of his shoulders.

"What? Ronald killed Jimmy?" Brenda looked at Sharif for confirmation. When he nodded his head she whirled back to Vincent. "Do the police know?"

Vincent shrugged again. "Hell if I know. I'm wondering how Ricky found out."

"Well. I mean, well . . ." Brenda struggled to find words but her head was spinning. All of her blood seemed to speed to the top of her head, then plummet down to her feet, only to charge upward again, as the events of the past few days sped through her mind. Ronald killed Jimmy. And Ricky killed Ronald. She leaned against the door, staring wildly at her friends. "I mean, these are all facts, right? It's a fact that Ronald killed Jimmy. And it's a fact that Ricky killed Ronald because of it?"

"The first is a fact. We don't know about the second for sure," Sharif put his good arm around Brenda and pulled her into the living room, with Rosa and Vincent following.

"Well, it looks like my business is handled even if I ain't handle it myself. Huh, Sharif?" He winked at Sharif and looked at his watch. "I'ma get up on outta here."

Brenda turned her head when she thought she heard the sound of a light tapping on the door. "Is that someone knocking?" she asked no one in particular. She got up and walked toward the door and looked through the peephole. "Oh, shit!" She ran back to the living room. "It's Ricky. He's at the door."

Vincent grabbed Brenda by the arm and propelled her back to the door where the tapping had hardened to a soft knock. "Open it and let him in," he said in a whisper.

"I'm not letting that boy in my house!" Brenda whispered back. "We still don't really know for sure why he killed Ronald."

"Don't worry. I got it covered," he said as he positioned himself behind the door. "I promise he won't hurt anyone. Just let him in."

"Yo, Vince," Sharif started, but Vincent motioned him to be quiet as Brenda took a deep breath and opened the door.

"Ricky, come on in," Brenda tried to force a smile as she waved the boy in. He gave a furtive look up and down the building hallway before quickly stepping into the apartment.

"Brenda. I got to talk to you—"

Before Ricky could finish, Vincent caught him in the back of his head with the palm of his hand, and forcefully pushed him—face first—against the wall. The boy didn't even have time to yell before Vincent was up against his back, quickly patting him down.

"Oh, my God, Vincent!" Brenda covered her mouth with her hands, but didn't otherwise move.

"He's clean," Vincent finally said as he took a big step back from Ricky.

"Damn it, Vince," Sharif strode over and pulled the still silent boy from the wall. "Ricky? You okay, man?"

Ricky stood before him, blood gushing from his now broken nose, his mouth gaping open, his arms limp by his side, as he stared—wide-eyed—at the people in the room.

"Oh, shit, he's in shock." Sharif quickly led him to a chair. "Somebody get me a glass of water."

Rosa darted to the kitchen, and Brenda could hear the faucet running. She bent down next to Ricky. "Are you all right, Ricky?"

He nodded slowly, and took the glass that Rosa handed him and slowly brought it to his lips. It wasn't until he tried to drink the water, and saw that blood from his face had dripped into it, that he seemed to realize his lip and nose were busted.

"Aargh!" He dropped the glass and grabbed his face.

"Stop acting like a baby. Your nose isn't broken," Vincent said with a scowl.

"Actually, I think it is," Sharif said as he gently pulled Vincent's hand down so he could examine him closely.

"Oh, well," Vincent said with a half-smile. "He'll live."

Sharif looked up at Vincent and shook his head. "So much for that heart everyone says you don't have."

"Whatever." Vincent shrugged.

"That's all you can do is shrug?" Brenda stood up and glared at him.

"Shit. You're the one who said you were afraid." Vincent leaned against the wall and pulled a cigarette from a gold case. "Now, let's hurry up and get this over with. I got business to take care of."

"Let me go check on Bootsy. I can't believe he didn't wake up with all this ruckus." Brenda walked down the hall and eased opened Bootsy's bedroom door and peeked in. Her son lay curled up in a semi-fetal position on his bed, his bony chest slowly rising and falling with his deep breaths. Her mother was right, she thought. That boy can sleep through an earthquake. *Actually, this is the first time he's slept since*

Jimmy . . . Brenda shuddered as she watched him. She tiptoed in and sat on the side of Bootsy's bed. He was sleeping so soundly he didn't even budge when she ran her hand over his face. God, what would have happened if it were Bootsy that found out what Ronald did? Would her son now be shaking like a leaf in someone's living room after killing another human being? The words in her father's last letter seeped back into her mind. *Only twelve years old and he thinks he's a man. Harlem will do that to a boy, and don't I know it.*

She wasn't going to let her children wind up so like many kids did. Selling drugs, sticking up people, or . . . she shook her head. Or worse.

She shuddered. Poor Ricky, she thought as she got up and closed the door behind her.

"We got to get him to the hospital," Rosa was saying as Brenda walked back into the living room.

Ricky sat slumped in the chair, a bloody dish towel pressed against his nose. "Naw, naw, I don't need to go to the hospital. I'm okay," he said in a muffled voice.

Brenda sidled up close to Sharif. "Is he going to be okay?" she asked quietly.

Sharif nodded. "He just got the street scars he's been wanting all his life."

"Well, if you guys are through babying him, maybe we can find out what the hell is going on." Vincent walked over and lifted up Ricky's chin.

"Does it hurt when you talk?" he asked.

Ricky nodded.

"Okay, then talk fast." Vincent took a few steps back. "You killed Ronald, huh?"

Ricky nodded.

"Good job. Saved me the trouble," Vincent chuckled.

Ricky looked around at everyone as if to gauge their reaction. "I didn't mean to kill him. I mean, I went up there to kill him, and I wanted him dead, and when I shot him I wanted him dead," he looked around again and then dropped his head to his knees. "But then when he was dead, I don't know. It's like I didn't really realize he would die. I never really wanted to kill anybody." He sat back up. "I mean, you know, that's not me. It isn't." He turned to Sharif. "You know that, right? I mean, I know I did it, and . . ." Ricky leaned back in the chair and crossed his arms over his face but the tears that streamed down his swollen cheeks were still visible.

Instead of comforting him, Sharif walked over and sat down on a chair across from Ricky. "Why'd you do it?"

"Because he killed Jimmy," Ricky said with some difficulty.

"How do you know?" Sharif demanded.

"Sookie was begging for some product on the corner and no one would give her any play, until she said she had the four-one-one on Jimmy's murder. Taz gave her a ten-dollar rock and she spilled the beans. She told all of us she'd seen Ronald dumping the body in the dryer," Ricky turned his head, wincing as he did so, to look at Brenda. "I wanted to pay him back."

"Why'd you do it, though?" Sharif shook his head. "Why didn't you just go to the police?"

"I don't know. I just thought it had to be handled in the streets . . ."

"Oh, right. And all of a sudden you're Mr. John Q. Street?" Brenda stood in front of Ricky, her arms crossed. "What the hell were you thinking about?"

"Leave him alone," Vincent exhaled a puff of smoke. "He did a good thing."

Brenda looked at Sharif and Rosa. "Ricky," She said slowly. "Did anyone see you? I mean, when you . . . uh . . . killed Ronald."

"Yeah, like, I think Bootsy was in the hall when I smoked him," Ricky answered, finally removing his arms from his face. "I didn't see him, but after I shot Ronald I heard someone running, and when I ran up the stairs there wasn't anyone there, but I saw someone had been spray painting on the wall. It said 'RIP Little Man,' so I figured it was Bootsy."

Brenda closed her eyes and lifted her chin toward the ceiling. "Oh, God," she muttered.

"So you was coming over here after Bootsy, and shit," Rosa stormed over and hit Ricky on the back of the head.

"Ouch! I was not!" he cried out as he bent over in pain. "Brenda," he said turning back to her. "You know I wouldn't hurt you or yours. I was just coming over because I wanted you to know what happened. I know Bootsy would never dime me out, but I knew he was going to tell you, and I just wanted to make sure you understood why I did it."

"Okay, now we understand why you did it," Vincent said as he stubbed his cigarette out in an ashtray, "so now what are your plans?"

"What do you mean?"

Sharif edged forward in his seat. "Rick, you just took somebody's life, man. What are you going to do now? You can't just make like it never happened. What? You were just going to go home and have dinner with your mother like it's just another ordinary day?"

Ricky groaned. "If Ma finds out she's going to beat the living crap out of me."

Vince laughed. "Look at that. He just killed a man and now he's worried his mommy going to give him a beating."

"That was just a metaphor," Ricky looked around quickly as if to see if Brenda had been paying attention. "She doesn't beat me. I'm too old to get beatings."

"Hey, Sharif. Ain't that some shit," Vincent said with another laugh. "All this trouble he's in and he's still trying to impress some pussy."

"Vincent!" Brenda said turning to him with a glare. "Why do you always have to be so damn crude?"

"So where you'd get the gun?" Vincent asked, ignoring her.

"I asked Taz to lend me his piece."

"Are you crazy?" Sharif jumped up. "You told Taz you were going to kill Ronald?"

"No," Ricky said quickly. "I just told him I needed to take care of some business downtown. And even if he figures it out he ain't gonna say anything. You know Taz. He's down. And no one saw him give it to me."

"Yeah, right. Down until the police pick him up for drugs again, then watch him give you up so he can get his own ass off," Sharif strode over to the window, then back to the chair where he sat down and bent his head down to his knees. "Damn!"

"That piece that Taz gave you . . . was it a thirty-eight?" Vincent asked urgently.

"Yeah," Ricky answered in a scared voice.

"Well, your boy just fucked you up. That gun belonged to that cop that got shot in the Bronx a couple of weeks ago. And it's got another body on it since then."

Sharif raised his head. "Tell me you're kidding."

"Wish I could." Vincent shook his head. "Taz got it off a crackhead last week who ripped off the guy who shot the cop. He told me he was keeping it as a souvenir." He turned to Ricky. "Where's the gun now?"

"I . . . I . . . I threw it in the garbage chute." Ricky was trembling as he spoke. "I wiped off all the . . . all the . . .the prints. I wiped it clean."

"In the garbage chute in the building?" Brenda asked. When Ricky nodded she turned to Sharif. "Maybe we can get it back?"

"Naw, naw, that would be the wrong move. Just leave it where it is." Vincent slowly rubbed his chin as he spoke. "Might be that no one will find it when they haul off the trash."

"All right. What do we do now?" Sharif said, gazing from face to face.

"Well, obviously we're not going to give him up to the police," Rosa said with a shrug.

"Obviously," Vincent said dryly. "I say he goes home and makes like nothing happened. I'll talk to Taz and make sure he doesn't say shit to anyone no matter what. Ricky's right. Taz is cool, and he ain't gonna run off at the mouth, even when he's heard Ronald got shot. And he ain't gonna use him as a Get Out of Jail Free card if he knows he's gonna have to deal with me if he does."

"I appreciate that, man." Ricky held out his fist and he and Vincent exchanged pounds.

"So how does it feel to have popped your guy?" Vincent smiled as the boy's eyes widened and then his head dropped down to his knees. "Not so good, huh? Don't worry. It gets easier each time."

"Vincent, stop it!" Brenda said as the boy raised his head, and looked as if he were to cry.

"I'm just fucking with him," Vincent said with a laugh.

"Well, how is Ricky going to explain his face?" Brenda dabbed at Ricky's nose again with the towel.

"I can probably get Taz to alibi him. Say that they got into it and he busted up his face," Vincent offered.

"Aw, naw." Ricky shook his head. "I don't want my boys to think I got punked like that.

"Well, what do you suggest?" Vincent asked.

"I could, uh, say I walked into a door. Or that I fell down the stairs," Ricky said hopefully. "I could say that when I heard Ronald got shot I ran down the stairs to see for myself, and fell down."

"That might work," Sharif nodded. "Especially if someone saw you fell."

"Someone like who?" Brenda asked.

"Someone like me." Sharif got up and started slowly pacing the floor while rubbing his chin. "I could say that he was up in my apartment when someone knocked on the door to tell me what happened, and we didn't want to wait for the elevator because it takes so long, so we ran down the stairwell, and Ricky fell."

"Yeah, okay." Rosa stepped up to Sharif. "I can say like, you know, when I ran to tell you about Ronald that Ricky was with you in your apartment, and shit. That way he got two people alibiing him."

Sharif shook his head. "No, you just tell the truth. You banged on my door and said Ronald was shot and then ran off. We don't need you get caught up in this."

"My man's right," Vincent nodded. "The less people involved in this the better. Besides," he walked over and slapped Sharif on the back, "if Sharif says Ricky was with him, ain't nobody gonna doubt it. You know everyone thinks he's a saint."

"He is a saint," Brenda said under her breath. It was hard to believe that Sharif was actually putting the credibility he worked so hard to earn on the line. And it was wrong what he was doing. It was wrong what they were all doing—protecting Ricky after what he'd done. But at the same time it was the right thing to do. Ricky was one of them, and they protected their own. *And besides, who in this apartment wouldn't have done the exact same thing if they'd had the opportunity.*

Sharif sighed and started rubbing his shoulder, as if finally remembering his physical pain. "Ricky, you really got us all into a lot of shit, you know that?"

Ricky nodded. "Man, I'm sorry, you know," he said, trying to fight back a sob. "And I appreciate y'all having my back like this."

"Okay. I'll call your mother at work and tell her you got hurt, but that you're okay. And you and Brenda should walk downstairs, so everybody can see you and make sure you tell them about you falling down the stairs."

"Why do you want me to go downstairs with him?" Brenda asked.

"To make sure he doesn't do or say anything stupid. Put him in a cab and get him the hell away from the Ida B." Sharif answered curtly as he picked up the telephone."

"Hurry up with the phone," Rosa said as she started tapping her foot. "I still gotta call Mitch."

13

I'm not trying to insult you. I'm just saying that you are, well, the epitome of the Puerto Rican stereotype."

Rosa eyed the cashmere-sweatered redhead who was leaning over the rust-stained sink, applying eyeliner in the dimly lit bathroom which served as the dressing room for the actors. She'd taken a dislike to Cissy Arlington from the first day of rehearsal. The woman always went out of her way to be extra nice to Rosa, patronizing even, especially when people were around. But it was an act, Rosa knew, and Cissy wasn't a good enough actress to pull it off.

"I'm not saying I'm insulted. I'm just saying I'd like you to explain what you mean." Rosa tried to keep her voice light as she sat on the closed lid of the toilet. She crossed her legs "You know . . . I'd like you to, how do you say it, *expound* on your statement."

"Well, let's see," Cissy balanced the eyeliner wand on the edge of the sink, and peered more closely into the mirror. "Stereotypically, Puerto Rican women are, well, very colorful, if you know what I mean. They wear rather tight clothes, very bright, lots of reds. They're emotional and verbal. A fiery temperament. All of which, you have to admit, describes you to a tee." Cissy picked up her tube of lipstick and started painting her lips a pale peach as she talked,

"What do they call it? Latin spitfires? Yes, that's it. " She pouted into the mirror.

"A Latin spitfire, huh?" Rosa stood up and raked her fingers through her hair. "But I'm not supposed to be insulted?"

"Oh, no! Of course not." Cissy's eyes met Rosa's in the mirror. "Chita Rivera won an Oscar playing a Latin spitfire in *West Side Story*, remember?"

"Rita Moreno." Rosa crossed her arms.

"I'm sorry?" Cissy said as she puckered her lips in the mirror.

"Rita Moreno won an Oscar for *West Side Story*, not Chita Rivera," Rosa snapped. "Not that I'd expect you to know the difference. I'm sure we all look alike to you." She walked over to the sink and stood in front of the mirror, pushing Cissy aside with her hip. "And as far as me being a stereotype, you can kiss my ass." Rosa raked her fingers through her long hair. "I wear bright colors because I like bright colors, and shit. And I wear *tight* clothes because I got a figure worth showing off." She turned and looked Cissy up and down. "But I don't expect you'd understand that, huh?"

"Oh, now see, you're taking what I said the wrong way, Rosa." Cissy flashed a smile as she lightly placed a hand on Rosa's shoulder. "I'm just saying—"

"Oh, I know exactly what you're saying, and shit. And did I give you permission to touch me?" Rosa made a face in the mirror, and Cissy hurriedly removed her hand.

"I'm just saying that I think it's nice that you don't try to act like someone you're not." Cissy's smile seemed a bit more nervous, though she held her ground.

Rosa examined her makeup in the mirror, and then opened her mouth to inspect her teeth and make sure there was no lipstick on them, ignoring the woman who had one hand on the door as if she wanted to leave. *Now see, if I wasn't so much of a lady I woulda kicked her phony ass. I should kick it anyway.* She flashed an icy look at Cissy in the mirror. *But she'd probably like that so she can run and yell about the "crazy Puerto Rican chick" and try and get me kicked out of the show. She's just jealous as shit because I got a major role in the show, and she's just an extra and a prop girl.*

"Well, I guess I'm finished. I'm going to go ahead and make sure everything's together on the stage," Cissy said as she picked her tube of lipstick off the sink. "And I might run out and get some coffee. Can I bring you back something?"

Rosa turned and looked at her. "Well, sure. How about you get me a, let's see, what is it we Latin spitfires drink? Oh, yes, a shot of tequila. Yeah, bring me back a shot of tequila."

"Rosa, come on . . ." Cissy started, then sighed. "Look. I'm sorry you took my words as an insult, because believe me, that wasn't my intention."

"Whatever. I'd love to hear what you'd have to say if an African-American ate a piece of watermelon in front of you, though." Rosa started applying her eye shadow. "Now if you'll excuse me, you're in my light."

"Hey, Sharif. I see you're still looking miserable," Rosa said as she sidled up to Sharif, who was leaning on the unmanned security desk in the lobby of Ida B. reading a newspaper. "You heard anything new?"

Sharif looked up and shook his head. "The police are still asking questions, but I get the impression they really don't give a damn about Ronald being killed. They're just going through the motions."

Rosa nodded, knowing that the police had heard the same thing that everybody in the building had heard as word spread on the street, that it was Ronald who had killed Jimmy.

"But that's a good thing, that the police don't really care, right?" Rosa said in a low voice.

Sharif gave a slight shrug, and started leafing through the newspaper again.

Rosa felt a twinge as she looked at her friend. All of them had been going through hell since that afternoon in Brenda's apartment when they found out what Ricky had done, but no one more than Sharif—probably because Sharif, who had always been known for his honesty and forthrightness, was actually involved in the cover up.

"Ay, *mijo,*" Rosa put her arm around Sharif's waist. "Everything's going to be okay. *Sabe?* Just hang in there, okay?"

Sharif nodded, but said nothing.

"Well, look you'd better get in a better mood," Rosa said in a lighter voice. "Mitch is stopping by later and if you happen to see him you'd better not start some shit!"

Sharif grinned. "Mitch and Rosa up in a tree . . ."

"Shut up," Rosa said as she punched him in the arm. "It's professional. He's stopping by to give me some direction for the play."

Sharif rubbed his chin and looked at Rosa. "What's Mitch's full name?" he said slowly.

"Mitch Jeffries. You know that."

"Yeah, but what is Mitch short for?"

"Mitchell, I guess." Rosa shrugged her shoulders. "Why?"

"Remember when I told you that his name sounded familiar?" Sharif waited until Rosa nodded. "Well, now I know why."

"Okay," Rosa said expectantly. "Why?"

"Because," Sharif said as he turned around and leaned his back on the desk, "There's a Mitchum Jeffries listed on the board of directors of Chest Park Incorporated, the company that's pressuring the city to tear down the Ida B."

Rosa's head jerked back. "What? I don't believe it. I mean, how do you know it's my Mitch?"

"I'm not sure it's *your* Mitch." Sharif nudged Rosa's leg with his foot. "So, why don't you ask him when he comes over tonight?"

"All right, you two. Where's my kiss?"

Rosa's face broke into a grin before she even turned around. "Hey, Aunt Pat. How you doing?"

"I'm doing okay. Even with all this craziness going on." Pat shook her head. "You know, Janet told me that damn Jackie stopped her in front of the building today, talking about her son ain't kill that little boy. Saying you can't believe that girl 'cause she uses crack." Pat took a tissue from her pocketbook and wiped drops of perspiration from her forehead. "Just 'cause the girl uses don't mean she's lying. I wish Jackie would come up to me with that shit."

"Well, when the police come back with the DNA evidence, Miss Jackie will just have to face the facts," Sharif said.

"Shit. Sometimes I think about kicking her ass just 'cause she brought that damn pervert in this world." Pat's heavy bosom started heaving. "That was a sweet little boy, that Jimmy. Ain't nobody should have to die like that, and him just a little kid." Pat turned her head and quickly dabbed at her eyes. "I'm glad someone killed that fucking Ronald. I only wish I coulda killed him my damn self. And it wouldn't be as quick as a shot to the head. I woulda made that motherfucker suffer." Pat's eyes narrowed almost to a slit and her face flushed to a bright red as she spoke. "I woulda taken that gun and shoved it up his—"

"Aunt Pat, Aunt Pat, calm down." Rosa put her arm around Pat's shoulders. "You're getting your blood pressure worked up. Come on, there's the elevator. Let's go on upstairs." She started leading the woman toward the elevators. "I'll talk to you later, Sharif."

"Okay, Rosa." Sharif waved. "And don't forget to ask . . ."

"Yeah. I will. But you're wrong. Watch." She said over her shoulder. She turned back around. "*Coño*, we missed the elevator."

"He's wrong about what?" Pat asked as Rosa repeatedly pushed the elevator button.

"Aw, he's got this crazy idea that—"

"Aw, don't tell me I just missed the elevator."

Rosa turned to see Miss Marcie puffing up next to them.

"You know there's only one elevator working, right? And you see there ain't no guard at the desk. I tell you this building is going to pot." Miss Marcie shook herself slightly if trying to collect herself. "Pat. How you doing, girl?" She said after a few moments.

Pat gave a little nod.

"What's wrong with you?" Miss Marcie put her hands on her hips. "All I get is a nod? As many times as I had to carry your drunk ass outta bars?"

Pat paused a moment, then started giggling. "You ain't shit, Marcie. I had to carry your ass a few times, too."

"Uh huh." Miss Marcie turned to Rosa. "I ever told you about the time when we living on 145th Street and Pat got thrown outta the Lickety Split because she hauled off and slapped the bartender when he told her she couldn't put her own bottle on the bar." Marcie started chuckling as she spoke. "I wasn't there, but they told me it took five grown-ass men to pick her up and throw her out. I mean literally! I was coming up Seventh Avenue, and I can still remember, it was in the middle of winter. I see someone sprawled out, spread eagle, on a mound of snow. I walked on up, and sure nuff it was Pat, passed out, and on the verge of frostbite. Good thing I'm built like a horse," she straightened up to her full five feet eleven inches and wiggled her massive shoulders. "I had to haul the heifer on my back."

"Oh, no, you lying, Miss Marcie!" Rosa burst out laughing.

"Oh, yeah, you wanna tell tales, huh?" Pat put her hands on her hips. "What about the time they had to call the police on you over at the Lido? Girlfriend here thought some chick was making eyes at the guy she was with, and she waited until the girl went in the bathroom, barged in behind her, locked the door and commenced to kicking the girl's ass. The police had to finally kick the door down. And then it turned out that girl was Marcie's guy's sister."

"Oh, my God," Rosa covered her mouth with her hand. "So what happened?"

"He got over it." Miss Marcie shrugged. "He married me, didn't he?"

"That was Mr. Roy? You beat up his sister?" Rosa shook her head. "Hmph. I'm afraid'a both of y'all."

"Rosa, girl, we was in our twenties, then. Those days are long behind us." Miss Marcie chuckled and looked at Pat. "Well, at least long behind me. I can't talk for this crazy woman here."

"I calmed down, too. I just ain't get all sanctified and stop drinking like you." Pat smiled. "Going to church and volunteering at the hospital."

Rosa smiled and shook her head as she looked at the two women, still clucking and slapping each other on the shoulder. Miss Marcie was probably the only one who could get with Pat like that, but it was good to have a friend who could.

"So, Marcie," Pat said as they stepped into the elevator. "I heard you didn't go to Ronald's funeral."

Miss Marcie's head jerked back. "Aw, hell, no. Hardly anybody in the Ida B. did. I hope that motherfucker rots in hell for what he did."

Rosa raised her eyebrow but said nothing. She'd never heard Miss Marcie curse before.

"And someone needs to slap the shit out of Jackie," Miss Marcie continued. "Going around swearing her son ain't do it. And she was the first one to try and say it was Sharif." She looked at Rosa. "You were right there, that morning at Janet's house. Am I lying?"

"No, she said it," Rosa agreed.

"Now, see, I ain't know that shit." Pat took a deep breath and exhaled slowly. "Now I want to kick her ass even more than I did before."

"But I'm going to tell you," Miss Marcie started waving her finger in the air. "I still hope they found out whoever killed him, cause I don't feel safe knowing there's a murderer still hanging around here."

"Well, I'm not worried, 'cause whoever shot him did the world a favor, and shit," Rosa cut in. "He should get a medal or something. In my opinion, anyway."

"It ain't nobody's place to be taking nobody's life," Miss Marcie said as she put one hand on her hip. "He should've just waited for the police to take care of him."

"Oh, you trust that the police and courts would take care of it?" Rosa rolled her eyes. "I don't. And why should he be allowed to live and spend the rest of his life in jail when he took Jimmy's life?"

"In case you forgot, New York State has the death penalty," Miss Marcie said.

"In case you forgot, Ronald already got it," Rosa shot back.

"You better watch your tone," Miss Marcie's eyes narrowed. "I'm still old enough to be your mother."

"All right, all right, you two," Pat said soothingly as she held a hand out in front of the two of them. "Just calm down."

Rosa retreated into a corner of the elevator. "I'm sorry, Miss Marcie," she said sullenly. "I didn't mean to raise my voice."

"Yeah, I know. Everybody in the Ida B.'s worked up right now," Miss Marcie said in a reluctant tone. "But don't you raise your voice to me again."

She turned as the elevator bell rang to announce they were at the sixth floor. "Pat, stop by my apartment on the way out," she said as she got off.

Pat swung around to Rosa as soon as the elevator doors were closed. "You know who did it, don't you?" she said in almost a whisper.

Rosa thrust her chin upward and avoided looking at Pat. "No. I don't know who did it, Aunt Pat. I was just saying we shouldn't be trying to judge the person before we even know who it is," she said in a defiant tone.

"Look at me," Pat demanded. She stepped closer to Rosa and put her hand on the woman's face. "Look at me, and tell me that it wasn't none of my family involved."

"But," Rosa said weakly. "I really don't know—"

"Don't you lie to your Aunt Pat," Pat's hand moved from Rosa's cheek to her chin, and tightened. "Now you tell me if my family had anything to do with this."

"I don't know who did it, but I . . . I'm pretty sure no nobody in your family did," Rosa said slowly.

Pat released her hold on Rosa's chin and stepped back. "And of course you know that I consider you and Sharif my family, right?" She stared straight into Rosa's eyes as she spoke.

"I know, Aunt Pat." Rosa breathed a sigh of relief as the elevator's door opened at the tenth floor. To her dismay, Pat jammed her finger into the OPEN DOOR button. Seconds passed with neither woman saying anything.

"Look," Pat said as the elevator gave an annoying buzz notifying the entire floor that its doors were being held open too long. "If you need me, or someone else I know needs me, I'm here. And I'll go to the wire with them."

Rosa nodded, still avoiding Pat's eyes. "I know."

Pat serious expression turned into a weak smile. "Well, as long as you know, and you better act like you know, then okay. Now give your Aunt Pat a kiss."

14

The thing is, Gran, I feel as guilty as if I'd pulled the trigger myself. Because I would have." Sharif wiped his eyes as he sat in front of the makeshift altar he'd set up in memory of his grandmother. "And I know you raised me better than that." He looked at the flickering white candle and sighed. "And I know I'm wrong to lie to help Ricky, but I don't have a choice." His shoulders sagged as he spoke. "He was wrong, but he only did what I wanted to do, and what Vincent was going to do with my blessing. Ricky's murdered Ronald, but he's not really a murderer. He's just a kid who got caught up and now is scared out of his mind. He messed up, but he's a good kid with a good future, and I can't see that future being thrown away because of someone like Ronald."

He wiped his eyes again, then tapped his hands three times on the end table and stood up. "Light, peace, and progress, Gran. Please look out for me, and keep me strong. Keep me true."

Sharif walked into the kitchen and poured himself a glass of iced tea. What a mess, he thought, as he leaned on the refrigerator and took a short sip. Vincent was right, no one questioned it when he alibied Ricky, because everyone knew he strove to live in an upright way, and that didn't include lying to protect someone who murdered a man. Or shouldn't include it, anyway. But there were some things worth compromising his integrity over, and saving Ricky's ass was one. And he wasn't really compromising his integrity, he mused as he jiggled the ice in his drink. He was being true to his own roots.

He downed the rest of the iced tea and picked up his satchel, making sure he had all of the shea butter and musk oil orders his customers were expecting, and headed out the door.

He grimaced when the elevator doors opened in the lobby, and he saw Miss Jackie standing in front of the security desk talking to the guard on duty. He walked straight ahead, hoping the woman hadn't seen him.

"Sharif? Hold on a minute, honey. I need to talk to you."

Sharif obediently turned around and walked over to the woman. "How you doing, Miss Jackie?" he said politely.

"You know how I'm doing. Everyone in this building knows how I'm doing," Miss Jackie looked him up and down. "Don't tell me you don't know what they're saying about my boy."

Sharif bit his lip, but said nothing.

"I want you help me tell these people that Ronald didn't do this," Miss Jackie said putting her arm through Sharif's. "Everybody knows you and they know you ain't gonna lie."

"Miss Jackie, no offense. But I can't tell anybody anything," Sharif said slowly. "How am I supposed to know if Ronald did it or not?" Damn, he thought as soon as the words were out of his mouth. I could have been a little more diplomatic than that.

"Because you know my Ronald wouldn't have killed that little boy," Miss Jackie said insistently. "And I don't want people dirtying his name like that. It ain't right."

"Well . . ." Sharif started.

"I just want you to know that people was going around saying it might be you what did it," Miss Jackie stepped back from Sharif. "And I defended your name, least you could do is defend my son's."

Miss Jackie turned when the security guard chuckled loudly. "What are you laughing at?"

"Nothing," the man said with a grin. "Except it was you who told me you thought Sharif did it."

"No, I didn't. And I ain't gonna let you sit up there and lie on me like that. If you security people woulda been doing your job wouldn't nobody got killed up in here," Miss Jackie thundered. "So don't be talking that mess to me. As much as I always tried to help everybody in this building they all done turned against me." She turned around and gave Sharif a scathing look before storming off.

"Hmph. That old busybody's been talking about everybody in this building for years, and now she can't take it when everybody's talking about her," the security guard said after she'd left.

"Yeah, well, you didn't have to bust on her like that," Sharif said as he shook his head.

The security guard shrugged as he picked up a book and started reading.

"Vincent, man. You ever thought maybe that chick lied?" Sharif exhaled a long puff of smoke from the large blunt he'd just rolled. "Maybe she was just trying to frame Ronald."

He handed the blunt to Vincent and waited while he took a quick drag.

"Naw, man," Vincent said after he exhaled and passed it back to Sharif. He leaned back in the chair and closed his eyes.

"What? You hooked her up to a lie detector or something?" Sharif flicked the ashes from the blunt into an ashtray.

"Nope. I ain't gotta do that." Vincent started slowly moving his head to the music pouring out of Sharif's stereo. "I told you she and I go a little way back. She'd know better than to lie to me. And if she wanted to lie, she wouldn'ta picked Ronald. She didn't even know I knew him." Vincent opened his eyes and put his hand out toward Sharif who obligingly handed him back the blunt. "Who's that you playing, man? She's sweet as shit."

"Randy Crawford's 'Rio de Janeiro Blues.'"

"Randy Crawford, huh? Never heard of her." Vincent said while exhaling. "Oh, yeah. She did the song "Street Life," right? My mom used to play that all the time before she died. That was her song, man. Is that cut on this CD?"

"Yeah, man."

"Yeah, I ain't heard that in a minute. Play that one next."

Sharif picked up the remote and pointed it at the stereo.

I play the street life
Because there's no place I can go

"Man, I still miss my mom sometimes. She was fine as all hell, wasn't she? And had a smile . . . hmph . . . used to just make me feel good whenever she smiled," Vincent spoke as if he were in a daze. "Made me feel like the most important thing in the world was to keep her smiling. Ain't that some shit?" Vincent stopped and looked at Sharif. "Aw, man I'm sorry to be talking about this when your grandmother just died."

Sharif waved his hand. "It's okay, man. I'm okay."

Vincent nodded his head, then leaned back in the chair again. "I'm glad your gran died peacefully. That's the way to go. Not like my mom. Throat slit open by her fucking pimp. All that blood, man." Vincent shook his head. "Remember all that blood?"

"Yeah, I remember." Sharif nodded his head. "You okay, man?"

"Helluva thing for a ten-year-old to be coming home from school for lunch and finding his own mother's body on the living room floor," Vincent continued his reverie. "At least you was with me, man. At least you was with me."

Sharif nodded but said nothing.

"It took me two years to run into that motherfucker again. But when I did, I handled my business, didn't I?" A satisfied smile crept to Vincent's face. "First man I ever killed, and it felt good."

"First man I've ever seen killed, and it felt like shit." Sharif's mind drifted back to the memory. He and Vincent were only twelve when they saw a tall light-skinned man coming out of Porters, a clothing store on 125th Street right next to the Apollo Theater. Vincent stared for a moment, then bent down and cracked the bottle of soda he'd been carrying on the sidewalk. Holding the bottle behind his back, and without saying a word to Sharif, he walked over to the man and punched him square in the crotch. The man yelled and doubled over, and Vincent took the opportunity to swing the jagged edge of the bottle into his throat.

Sharif stood horrified as people around them screamed, and the man sank to the ground, clutching his throat as if to hold back the spurting blood. Instead of running, Vincent stood over the man saying nothing, just smiling.

It wasn't until another man tried to grab Vincent from behind that Sharif's limbs were once again able to move. He ran over and punched the man in the kidneys. Then he grabbed Vincent by the arm and the two sped around the corner to 126th Street. They ran into a building and hopped roofs until they were safely away. The two of them had been friends before, but after that incident they were officially tight. When Sharif came out of the closet ten years later, Vincent's friendship never wavered. Although Vincent teased him about his homosexuality from time to time, everybody knew better than to tease him when Vincent was around.

Vincent was almost a living legend in Ida B., and indeed around Harlem. The legend began when he was nineteen. He had accompanied his grandmother to the post office, so she could make her monthly purchase of money orders. When a clerk berated Mrs. Harris for wanting to fill out the money orders right there and then in front of him, Vincent stepped up and confronted the man. The clerk had taken one look into Vincent's eyes and started apologizing profusely, but a cocky young police officer, who happened to be in the post office to do a change of address, stepped up to tell Vincent to mind his business. The mistake he made, though, was pushing Mrs. Harris aside to get to Vincent. Mrs. Harris almost fell, and before anyone knew what was happening, Vincent swung around and decked the officer, who fell against a wall and pulled out a gun. But before he could clear it from his holster, Vincent was on him. A quick punch to the jaw, and another to the left ear, and the officer was sliding to the floor, but that wasn't enough for the enraged Vincent. He grabbed the gun and actually started pistol whipping the dazed cop into unconsciousness, to cheers from a crowd who had too long felt victimized by police, and by this officer in particular. And no one was cheering Vincent on louder than Mrs. Harris.

It was also Mrs. Harris who threw aside her cane and flung herself over her grandson when other police officers, notified by the post office management, burst into the post office, guns drawn. Vincent tried to struggle free of her, but she hung onto his neck as if for dear life, screaming. "Oh, Lord. They gonna shoot me and my baby. They gonna kill an old woman and her only grandson. Oh, God, yes they is."

At the station house Vincent was beaten unmercifully. But broken ribs and a dislocated shoulder were nothing compared to what usually happened to anyone who had viciously assaulted an officer. Sharif was a student at City College and president of the African-American Student Union at the time, and when he heard what happened he convinced the group to congregate outside the precinct to make sure Vincent wasn't badly hurt. Sharif even arranged to have one of the law professors at City College defend his friend. Vincent didn't need him, though. To everyone's surprise he plunked down a $25,000 retainer for one of the best criminal defense lawyers in the city. What everybody found even more surprising was that Vincent's high-powered attorney managed to beat the assault charge by claiming self-defense. The only charge that stuck was a federal one, for having an illegal gun on federal premises. Only Sharif, and maybe Mrs. Harris, realized it was the same gun Vincent used just two months before in his first two bank robberies. He'd only gotten away with $7,500 in the first one, but netted a whopping $158,000 in the second. More than enough to pay the attorney's fees. Vincent got off with a year's probation.

The second federal charge was a bum rap. Vincent, who'd never bothered to get a driver's license, bought a brand new Ford Expedition from a drug dealer who was trying to raise money for bail. He thought it was a deal, only $17,000 for a $30,000 vehicle, until he was stopped for speeding on the New Jersey Turnpike. He was charged not only for driving without a license but also for money laundering. The cops' reasoning was that the original owner had bought the car with drug money, then sold it to Vincent to get clean cash. It was a bum rap, and wouldn't have stuck if the police hadn't wanted to get Vincent on something for beating up an officer two years before, but it stuck. The lawyer he had used before had gone on to become a city councilman, but Vincent was able to obtain another top-notch attorney, who managed to get him another year's probation.

"Play that again, man," Vincent said when the song went off. "Better yet, don't. That reefer must be fucking with me. Making me take a trip to the past. Ya know?"

"Yeah, but I don't mind, man." Sharif wiped his face with his hand and then stretched. It was the first time he'd gotten high since Jimmy's death, and his rumbling stomach told him that that munchies had set in. "I'ma order some Chinese, you want something?"

"Yeah, I'm hungry as shit. Get me some chicken chow mein, some ribs, some fried dumplings and some beef fried—"

Both he and Sharif stopped as they heard a knocking on the door.

"Who is it?" Sharif shouted out, though he made no move to get up.

"It's your aunt Pat! Open up."

Sharif grabbed the ashtray and quickly dumped it into a wastebasket. "Hold on, I'm coming." He lit an incense stick and waved it around in the air before planting it in the incense holder and then walked over and opened the door.

"How you doing, Aunt Pat," he said as the woman breezed past him and into the living room.

"Y'all been smoking that shit up in here, huh?" She waved her hand in front of her nose.

"Hey, Beautiful," Vincent started to get up, but Aunt Pat stopped him.

"Don't bother getting up," she said, and then turned and looked at Sharif.

"Sit," she demanded.

"What's wrong?" Sharif asked as he moved back toward his chair.

"No. You sit there," she pointed at the sofa. "I'm taking the chair."

She waited until Sharif sat down, then threw her pocketbook on the chair and walked to the center of the room. Swinging around to face them, she opened her mouth as if to say something, then paused and took a deep breath before speaking.

"Look," she said in a rush. "I just spoke to Rosa, and so I already know."

"Already know what?" Sharif said slowly.

"I know that you know who killed Ronald," she said as she walked over to him. "And," she peered into his eyes. "And you're involved, aren't you?"

Sharif struggled to keep his face expressionless, but Vincent chuckled.

"Aunt Pat," he said as he took out a cigarette. "You been drinking, again?"

She glared at him. "Not enough to stop from knocking the shit out you, if you try disrespecting me again, Vincent Harris."

Vincent put the cigarette back in the case and mumbled, "Sorry, Aunt Pat."

She turned and faced Sharif again. "I wanna know what the hell is going on, and the first person that lies is gonna get my foot stuck straight up his ass."

"Aunt Pat, I don't know what you're talking about . . ." Sharif started.

"Don't you lie to your aunt Pat," she said, her eyes narrowing. "I know you're involved in it, and I also know you ain't the one that shot that boy."

She looked at Vincent. "And I know it weren't you that done it, 'cause Rosa wouldn't been so worried, 'cause she knows you can take care of yourself."

She turned back to Sharif. "And I know it ain't Brenda, 'cause she ain't had the guts to do it, and Janet ain't had the sense." She sat up and straightened her shoulders, pushing her bosom out as she did so. "And so that narrows it down quite a bit, doesn't it. So I want you to tell me straight," she paused as she looked Sharif in the eye. "Did Bootsy shoot Ronald?"

"No, Aunt Pat," Sharif shook his head. "He didn't. I swear."

Pat looked at him intently. "And you're not lying?"

Sharif shook his head again.

She looked at Vincent. "Is he lying?"

"Why you asking me?" he answered nonchalantly.

"Because I'm asking, is why."

Vincent sighed, making Sharif smile. There weren't many people who could get to Vincent, but Aunt Pat was one. Had always been. Everyone else, young or old, might have been afraid of Vincent, but not Pat. She could get away with saying things to him even Sharif would hesitate to say.

"I asked you a question, Vincent," Pat reminded him.

"No, Aunt Pat," Vincent sighed again. "Bootsy didn't do it."

"Uh huh," Pat said looking at him sternly. "And you know this because you know who did it, right? And don't you put on them damn shades," she added when Vincent reached over to the table for his sunglasses.

"Aunt Pat. Yes, okay?" Vincent threw up his hands. "Bootsy didn't do it. I know who did it. But I can't tell you who. All right?"

Pat looked at Vincent and then at Sharif. "So then it was Ricky, huh?"

Sharif's mouth opened, and Vincent just rolled his eyes.

"What—what makes you say that?" Sharif sputtered.

"Because, you wouldn't go out on a limb like this for just anybody, and so I figured it was in the family, or a kid. And I know how close you are to Ricky, Sharif," Pat said as she picked up her pocketbook. "And I saw his face. Fell down the stairs my ass. I ain't never seen no one fall down the stairs and bust his nose, but ain't bust his chin open."

Vincent covered his eyes and started laughing.

"Ronald tuned him up before Ricky got a shot off, huh?" Pat asked, as she looked at Vincent.

Vincent shook his head, still laughing.

Pat looked at him for a minute, and then giggled. "I swear, there's some people who just can't handle their smoke."

She walked to the door. "Look, Ricky ain't no family of mine, but if he killed that fucking pervert 'cause of what he did to Jimmy then I'm down with protecting him." She chewed her lip for a minute. "And I mean that. I'm down. Let me know what I can do." She flashed a smile at them before walking out the door. "Y'all thought y'all was going to get something on your old Aunt Pat, huh? Just cause I'm over thirty don't mean I'm stupid. Now y'all come over and give your Aunt Pat a kiss."

"Vincent, man," Sharif said after she left. "You gotta tell me, you just gotta tell me. You're scared'a Aunt Pat, right? I ain't never seen you let no one talk to you like that."

"Sharif," Vincent said with a smile. "I ain't saying I'm scared of no mutherfuckas, but there are three women I've always had to give their props, because I know they'd cut you as soon as say hello. My grandmother's one. My mother was another. And so is Aunt Pat. And she's got the razor in her pocketbook to prove it."

Sharif smiled. "Yeah, I know. I've seen it."

"What about that Chinese food? I'm hungry as shit."

Sharif picked up the telephone and dialed, then put the receiver to his ear. "Oh. I'm sorry. I didn't hear the phone ring . . . What?" Sharif jumped up from the chair. "When . . . where is he now? . . . okay, I'm on my way." He slammed down the phone.

"Vince, get your shit," he said as he headed for the door. "The police just picked up Ricky."

"Damn. That's fucked up," Vincent said as he got up and picked up his sunglasses from the coffee table. "Look, police stations ain't my thing. But I'll drop you off on my way to the Chinese."

15

"Sharif says he wants some of us to go around the back, just in case they try to sneak him out that way," Brenda said as she shooed a group of women towards the back of the police precinct. "Y'all go, and Miss Marcie," she turned to the woman who was breathing as hard as if she'd just run a marathon. "Make sure you yell loud enough for us to hear you if they do come out."

"Oh, you don't have to worry," Miss Marcie nodded furiously as she tried to catch her breath. "If they try to haul my nephew out in a paddy wagon I'm going to yell loud enough for all of Harlem to hear."

Brenda looked around as Miss Marcie hurriedly strode off. It looked like all of Harlem was already out here. At least everybody who lived in the Ida B. There had to be at least five hundred people yelling and throwing things at the police station. Sharif had done a good job of rallying the troops. He'd been thrown out of the precinct twice for yelling at the desk sergeant and insisting that he be told where they were keeping Ricky. They told him if he tried to enter again, they would arrest him. No doubt they would have already if they hadn't thought it might start a riot.

Brenda looked up when she heard a loud whirring sound above her. "Oh, my God, that's a police helicopter," she said to no one in particular as she pointed upward where a helicopter hovered only a couple of hundred feet above.

She looked around for Sharif, and saw him in the front of the crowd, one arm around Miss Rose in a comforting manner. He was yelling into a large white megaphone.

"Mr. Pig! Patriot Act be damned, it is still unconstitutional to interrogate a minor without his guardian or lawyer present," he enunciated each word clearly. "We may live in Harlem, but we are still citizens of the United States of America, and we know our rights. We will not let you railroad one of our youth."

He looked around the crowd and held his fist in the air. "No justice! No peace!"

Chants of "No justice! No peace!" filled the air.

Brenda waited until Sharif lowered the megaphone from his lips before tapping him on the shoulder. "How long before that lawyer friend of yours gets here?"

"He should have been here thirty minutes ago," Sharif growled. "I just made a call to try and get another guy here."

"And we're sure he's in there? We're sure they didn't take him somewhere else before we got here?"

Sharif nodded. "One of the black officers, when he was escorting me out, hipped me. Said the detectives had him up on the second floor, grilling him. They're trying to get him to confess."

Brenda shuddered. "We've got to get him out of there."

"Er. Excuse me. Sharif?"

Brenda turned around to see Mitch Jeffries, looking cool and unruffled. She was shocked he was still around. When she had called Rosa to tell her what was going on, the woman was knocking on the door almost before she hung up. Surprisingly, Mitch was with her, and Rosa had explained they were running some lines when she called. She thought he would go home once they all got downstairs, but instead he had walked over to the police station with them.

"Sharif, I just wanted you to know that I called my lawyer, and he's on the phone now with the police commissioner. I'm on hold," Mitch held up his cell phone. "Why don't you talk to him when he gets back on the line?"

"Oh, shit, yeah!" Sharif said, grabbing the telephone.

But before he could bring it to his ear, there was a shout among the crowd as the uniformed community affairs officer appeared on the steps of the precinct.

"I only want to speak to Mrs. White. Please stand back," he said as a horde of people swarmed around him. "Just Mrs. White."

"I'm here! I'm here!" Miss Rose cried as she elbowed her way through the crowd. "I'm right here."

"Please come with me," the man put his arm around her and started to draw her into the station house.

"Hold on a minute, Jerry!" Sharif ran up the steps after her, still holding the cell phone and megaphone. "I'd like to come with her."

"Sorry, Sharif. I'm only allowed to bring in Mrs. White," the man said apologetically. "Come on," he said as he once again proceeded to lead Miss Rose inside.

"No." Miss Rose pulled away from the man. "I want Sharif to come with me."

"Mrs. White, I'm going to be straight with you," the man said sternly. "I can bring in you, and only you. Now it's up to you. If you don't want to come in because Sharif's not allowed, then I'm not going to be able to let you see your son." He looked at Sharif and then again at Miss Rose. "I've known Sharif for quite awhile now, and I'm sure he would advise you that you should take this opportunity to see your son."

"So then you admit you've been holding him there all this time!" Sharif shouted. "You admit that you've been lying to us!" he waved his hand at the crowd and a roar went up from them.

"They've been lying! They have Ricky!" someone yelled.

"They're probably in there beating him!" someone else screamed. "They been in there beating that boy!"

"Calm them down," Jerry pointed his finger at Sharif. "Calm them down right now, or I swear I'll have you arrested for disorderly conduct."

"Oh, no, you're not arresting Sharif!" Aunt Pat's voice screamed out. She ran in front of him. "You gonna have to arrest me before you take him."

"And they gonna hafta arrest me too!" Rosa scrambled beside her.

Mitch walked up to the officer. "Just for the sake of peace, can't you talk to your superiors, and see if he'll let at least one person go in with Mrs. White?" he said in a soothing voice. "I'm sure he'll understand that we don't want any trouble. We just want to make sure the boy is okay."

The officer glared at him, and then at Sharif who was trying to push Aunt Pat and Rosa aside. "All right," he said turning to Mitch. "For the sake of peace, you can come in with Mrs. White." He opened the door and Mrs. White and Mitch started to follow behind him.

"What!" Sharif exploded. "You're gonna let a white boy who doesn't even know Ricky in there but not me?"

Rosa nudged Mitch on the shoulder. "He didn't mean that in a bad way, you know."

"Oh, no, I understand." Mitch hurriedly nodded. "And he's perfectly right. I probably shouldn't be the one going in."

"Well, then pick someone else," the officer said with a sigh. "Sharif, it wouldn't be a good idea for you to come inside. You need to stay out here to keep everyone calm." He looked at Brenda. "What about her?" he said pointing in her direction.

"Me?" Brenda looked around at Sharif, and when he nodded, she stepped forward and grabbed Miss Rose by the arm. "Okay. I'll just let you know everything when I get back."

They moved past dozens of police officers, some in riot gear, who were lined up in the station house, and walked up the stairs to a beat-up office door marked "Detectives." Miss Rose was shaking so bad, Brenda thought she was going to topple over. But the woman took a deep breath, as if trying to calm herself before the officer opened the door. When she saw her son she let out a piercing scream.

"Oh, God, Ricky!" she ran over to the boy who was sitting in front of a desk, his cuffed hands in his lap. "What did you do to him?"

Brenda's mouth dropped open as she walked over. Ricky's face was puffy, and his eyes were almost swollen shut. He was slumped so far forward in the chair it looked like he was about to slide to the floor. He looked up at the sound of his mother's voice, and made a weak noise as he tried to get up, but lost his balance and fell to the floor.

"They beat him. They beat my baby." Miss Rose cried as she threw her body over her son. "I want a lawyer. I'm going to sue."

"Mrs. White," a detective pulled her off the floor. "He's fine. No one beat him. Just ask him."

Another detective grabbed Ricky by the elbow and snatched him to his feet.

"Don't handle him like that! Can't you see he's hurt?" Brenda ran over and tried to hug Ricky, but Miss Rose had already grabbed him in her arms.

"Oh, my baby. My poor baby," she said over and over again as Ricky sobbed into her bosom.

"Mrs. White, if you let go of him you'll see he's fine." The officer who had escorted them upstairs tried to pry the woman away from her son.

"What do you mean? Just look at his face," Brenda said.

"That's just from crying." A detective pulled Ricky back into the chair.

"Are you hurt, baby?" Miss Rose knelt down next to the chair and started wiping at Ricky's face. "Did they hurt you?" She tried to pull his head to her chest again, but the boy pulled away.

"I'm sorry, mom," he said in a hoarse whisper.

"Sorry? Oh, baby, you don't have anything to be sorry for." Miss Rose hugged him around the shoulders and started rocking him. "Everything's going to be okay."

"Can we take him home now?" Brenda said as she stepped in front of one of the detectives who seemed to be in charge.

"Sorry. No can do." The detective slapped a yellow legal pad on the desk. "He just confessed to killing Ronald Johnson."

"What?" Miss Rose jumped up. "No he didn't. You're lying." She swung around to Brenda. "They're lying. Ricky ain't kill that man."

"I know he didn't!" Brenda almost shouted. "You had to have . . . had to have . . . you had to have beat him to make him confess to something he didn't do."

"Ricky," the detective said almost nonchalantly, "did anyone beat you?"

The boy shook his head dismally.

Oh, God, he actually confessed. Oh shit, oh shit. What do I do now? What would Sharif do if he were here? Brenda looked around, trying to think of something to say. "You had no business interrogating him without his lawyer. Or even his mother," she said finally. "You violated his rights. We're going to call our . . . our . . . our city councilman. Our congressman."

"You can call whoever you want." The detective shrugged. "Mike, take him down and book him."

"I want you to know that's it never, ever, ever, okay to kill someone." Brenda sat on the side of the bed, patting the sleeping Jumah on the back, speaking to Bootsy, Shaniqua, and Yusef who sat on the floor looking at her. "What Ronald did to Jimmy was very wrong, but, well, it's never right to try and take justice in our own hands. It's up to the courts to decide what should have been done to him. Do you understand?"

Shaniqua and Yusef nodded solemnly, but Bootsy shifted nervously.

"I want you all to get ready for bed and—"

"Mommy, is Ricky going to get the death penalty," Shaniqua interrupted.

"What? No, of course not."

"What's that?" Yusef asked.

"You're only four so you can't know," Shaniqua snapped.

"Yes, I can!" He jumped up and started tapping Brenda on the knee. "Mommy, what's that?"

"It's when the court says that Ricky should die because he killed Ronald," Bootsy said sullenly.

"*Allegedly* killed Ronald," Brenda shot Bootsy a warning look.

Bootsy shrugged and said nothing.

"Mommy? The courts are going to kill Ricky?" Yusef's eyes welled up with tears.

"No, baby, no one's going to kill Ricky," Brenda shifted Jumah to one shoulder and reached out and pulled Yusef close to her. "Everything's going to be fine, okay? And you know what I want you to do?" She looked at Shaniqua and Bootsy. "You know what I want all of you to do? When you pray to God tonight, say a little extra prayer for Ricky, okay?"

"So that when they kill Ricky he'll go to heaven?" Yusef asked.

"No. So that police will hurry up and let him go so he can be home with his own mommy, okay?" She gave Yusef a kiss on the cheek. "Now hurry up and put on your pajamas. All of you."

Bootsy lingered after Shaniqua and Yusef left.

"Ma," he said after a few moments. "What do I do if they want me to testify against Ricky? To tell them what I saw?"

"Hopefully it won't get to that." Brenda put Jumah on the bed and took off his pants. "Hand me a Pamper, Boot."

"Why won't it get to that?" he handed her the Pamper and sat down on the bed.

"Well, how would they even know you saw him?"

Bootsy shrugged and started playing with Jumah. "I don't know. But what if they do?"

Brenda stopped diapering Jumah and looked at her son. "Bootsy," she said, pausing to peer into her son's eyes. "You didn't tell anyone besides me, did you?"

Bootsy's head snapped up. "No, Ma. I swear I didn't. You know I don't have a big mouth like that."

Brenda released the breath she hadn't realized she was holding. "Okay, then, we'll just cross our fingers they don't find out." She picked up Jumah and walked over and put him in the crib, then turned to Bootsy and smiled. "It's been a really long night, hasn't it? Want to stay up awhile and talk?"

"Naw, I'ma go ahead and get to bed." Bootsy walked over and gave her a kiss on the cheek. "Night, Ma."

"Night, baby." Brenda watched him as he walked out the room, his head bowed and shoulders sagging. "Bootsy, come here a minute," she called out after him.

"Yeah, Ma?" Bootsy stuck his head in the door.

"Baby, you want to sleep with me tonight? So we can talk?"

"Oh, come on, Ma!" Bootsy waved his hand at her. "Stop trying to treat me like a baby."

"Okay. But just knock on the door if you change your mind." Brenda smiled and kissed him on the forehead. "You know, if you want to, you can bring a blanket and pillow and camp out on my floor."

Brenda sighed as her son closed the door behind him. It was getting harder and harder to connect to Bootsy. She knew he was going through a lot, first with Jimmy being murdered, then actually witnessing Ronald being murdered, and now Ricky getting locked up. But it was hard as all hell trying to get him to open up and let anyone in. *Bootsy's almost thirteen, a teenager. I guess it should be expected that he would start withdrawing from his mother, rebelling even. And hell, I should know about rebelling teenagers. I was pregnant with him when I was about his age. With him.* Brenda rubbed her temples as she slipped out of her bedroom slippers. She sighed and looked at the notepad on her nightstand. She hadn't written anything in it since Jimmy's death. She picked it up, and grabbed a pen, but then put them both down. She just didn't feel like writing. Being a mother wasn't easy, and the older the kids got, the more difficult it became. She didn't regret having Bootsy, or any of her children—she loved them all dearly. And that's why it was so hard now that Bootsy just couldn't seem to relate to her anymore. Maybe when her father came home in two weeks he'd be able to break through to Bootsy. Maybe he'd be able to relate to a man.

"Ma? Can I come in?"

"Sure, Bootsy. Come on."

"Um, Ma." Bootsy held a pillow and blanket in his hands. "That Spike Lee movie you like, *Crooklyn,* is on TV. You wanna watch it in the living room, 'cause it's bigger than yours. You can lay on the couch and I can be on the floor keeping you company."

Brenda smiled as she slipped her slippers back on. "Sure, baby. I'll microwave some popcorn."

16

Rosa sat cross-legged on the floor, looking around her. Sharif's apartment was packed. People who weren't able to sit on the couch or chairs were sitting on the floor, or window sills, or leaning against walls. Tired faces all, most of whom had gone with Miss Rose to One Police Plaza and waited while Ricky was booked and then carted off to a holding cell. All of whom were waiting on Sharif to figure out what to do next.

Rosa glanced at the clock. Four AM. Dawn would be breaking soon. She nudged Mitch, who was sitting on the floor next to her. "You doing okay?" He nodded, and started to say something, but just then Sharif picked up his yellow legal pad and stood up.

"People, the most important thing we have to do now is to keep pressure on the police and the courts," he said passionately. "Let them know that we're following their every move. We need as many people as possible to be there tomorrow morning—well, later this morning—at Ricky's arraignment, so they know this is not just some kid they can railroad. This is a young man who has community support. You'd be surprised at how much that can help."

"But what if he's guilty?" a man standing in the kitchen doorway shouted. "We're supposed to support him if he killed Ronald?"

"You shut your damn mouth right now!" Miss Marcie jumped up. "James Murphy, you know damn well my nephew ain't killed nobody."

"He's only asking a question, Marcie," a woman sitting on the couch said wearily.

"Well, he shouldn't be asking that question, Miss Helen!" a young woman sitting on the windowsill snapped.

"Why don't you just keep quiet, Chante? Ain't nobody ask you nothing."

The woman whirled around and snapped at the overweight man leaning over the couch. "You shut up, Buddha. I gots my opinion and I'm going to give it."

"Folks," Sharif held his hand up, "I don't think we even need to have this conversation right now . . ." He looked down when he felt someone pulling on the leg of his pants.

"Better to let them go at it for at least a little while," Mitch said quietly. "Let them get it out of their system."

Sharif glared down at the man, then sighed and nodded.

It's a good thing Sharif persuaded Aunt Pat to take Miss Rose home, Rosa thought. She certainly didn't need to hear this.

Sharif stood there patting the legal pad against his knee, listening to what everyone was saying. Rosa knew he was ready to jump in if it got too heated.

"Well, I'm with James. I think we really oughtta sit down and consider if that boy killed Ronald before we talking about picketing and carrying signs and acting all crazy and then find out he done it," Miss Gracie piped up from the couch. "We'd be looking like fools."

"You're an old fool anyway, Gracie. And everyone here knows Ricky couldn't have done it. He's an honor roll student! He's going to college. You think he's going to throw that all away, throw his future away like that?"

"Just 'cause he gets good grades don't mean he ain't a killer."

"And besides, he confessed."

"That don't mean nothing. The police gots ways of making people confess, even if they don't beat them. They tricks them."

"That's right! Like them boys that got locked up after they confessed to killing that Central Park jogger chick. All them years and then come to find out they didn't do it."

"Well, I'ma tell you the truth. I don't care if he did kill Ronald. Someone needed to kill that bitch."

"Watch your mouth, Michael. We got parents and grandparents in here."

"Well, I'm a damn grandparent myself, and I say she's right. I don't condone no murdering as a rule, but I say if he killed that asshole then good for him. And he shouldn't fry for it."

"New York ain't got the electric chair anymore. They use the needle."

"Same difference, and you know what I'm talking about, so don't be funny."

"We don't even know for sure Ronald killed that boy."

"Well, actually, we do." Sharif held the legal pad in the air. "I got a call from a friend in the police lab this afternoon. The DNA came back with a one hundred percent match."

A hush fell over the room. Rosa looked up at Sharif, and he answered the question in her eyes with a nod. He was telling the truth.

"I knew he did it. He always was a pervert. And remember how he used to stick firecrackers up cats' asses? That was a sick little motherfucker," someone said finally.

"The boy was always strange," a woman said with a little nod. "But I sure ain't figure him to do something like that."

"May he burn in hell," another woman muttered.

"And Ricky right along with him if he killed him," James said.

Rosa jumped up. "I ain't been saying nothing, cause I been listening to what everybody said really intensely, and shit." She walked to the center of the room. "But I got something to say now."

She pointed at James. "Mister James. Let me ask you something. What if it was your little girl, Ness, who was raped and killed by Ronald? You telling me you wouldn'ta wanted to track him down and shoot him?"

"My daughter wouldn't have been roaming the building at night by herself."

"Oh, oh," Rosa started walking around, waving her hand in the air. "So you telling me that you think it was Miss Janet's fault, huh? Is that it? The same woman who's done baby-sat for almost every child in Ida B., a lot of times for free, and shit, and cared for each and everyone of them like they was her own. You telling me it was her fault? That woman who's been upstairs crying her eyes out since this happened. It's her we should be blaming, you trying to tell me?"

"Oh, hell no, it ain't Janet's fault that boy wandered off like that. She ain't got eyes in the back of her head," Miss Marcie said as she crossed her arms and looked around, shaking her head.

"And any decent person seeing him wandering around woulda just took him home," a woman piped up.

"Exactly!" Rosa pointed at the woman. "Any decent person." She turned around and pointedly looked at all the people in the room. "But Ronald wasn't a decent person, was he? Instead, he found that poor little boy, who had just lost his mother and brother and sister, and he took that little boy by the hand," Rosa held her hand out and walked around the room as if holding an imaginary hand, "and instead of bringing little Jimmy back to Miss Janet's house, he brings him to his apartment or someplace, and he molests him." Rosa looked around wildly. "He pulled down that poor baby's pants, held him down, and he raped him. Tore him apart. He didn't care about him crying and screaming. He got off on it. The more poor little Jimmy screamed, the more he enjoyed it."

"Sweet Jesus," a woman moaned.

"Rosa, don't . . ." Sharif started, but Rosa ignored him.

"And then, then when he was finished, when that little boy lay in front of him crying his poor heart out, he killed him! He probably picked him up by the legs," Rosa bent down and picked up an imaginary body from the floor, "he probably picked him by the legs, threw him up in the air, and then smashed his head on the concrete floor."

"Oh, God, Rosa, please!" Miss Gracie shouted.

"And you're going to tell me," Rosa walked quickly over to James and pointed her finger in his face. "You're going to tell me that if he had did your daughter like that, you're going to tell me you wouldn't track him down and shoot him? That if it was Ness's body that was found in a laundry room that you wouldn't kill him?" She stopped and took a deep breath and took a step back from the man. "You're going to tell me you would let your Nessa's death be unavenged? You would let the man who savagely raped and kill your child live?"

The man looked down but said nothing.

"That's what I thought," Rosa nodded at him, then looked around the room again. "But poor Jimmy didn't have a mother or father who would want to avenge him. But can we really curse someone who shot Ronald for raping and killing Jimmy, when each and every one of us would have done the same thing if Ronald raped and killed our child? I know I can't." Rosa sighed and wiped at the corner of her eye, then walked back to the center of the room.

"I'm sorry about getting all emotional, and shit. But I had to get that off my chest." Her hand flew to her bosom. "But what I also wanted to say is that I know for a fact, *a fact*, that Ricky didn't kill Ronald. And how do I know that?" She swung around to Sharif. "Tell him."

"Because he was with me in my apartment all afternoon going over college applications," Sharif said as he stood up.

"And when I ran to get Sharif, just minutes after Ronald was killed, I saw Ricky there," Rosa said with finality. She avoided looking at Sharif's eyes, knowing he'd be angry that she had made herself part of the alibi. "So I say, let's get back to what we should be doing. And that's finding out what we can do to help Ricky. Who should be out here thinking about college instead of locked up in some cold hard jail cell, framed for killing someone who should never have walked the face of this earth in the first place."

"That's right. That's right." Miss Marcie stood up. "We gotta get that boy outta jail."

"He's a good kid. Shouldn't be locked up like that," James said slowly.

Rosa nudged Mitch to make sure he heard, then flashed him a satisfied smile. *How's that for owning an audience, and shit*, she thought. *I bet I impressed the shit outta him*.

"Does he have a lawyer? I can call my nephew. He just handled a murder case."

"Yeah, Arthur, but he lost."

"Well, yeah, but that dude was guilty. Ricky's not."

Sharif stood up. "The good news is we have a lawyer." He looked down at Mitch. "Thanks to this man."

"Who the hell is he?" Chante demanded.

Rosa shot Chante a dirty look and stood up. "His name is Mitch Jeffries, and he's a theater director." She started to announce that he was directing her play, but stopped herself. She didn't want anyone to realize that she had just put on a performance for them.

Mitch stood up. "Yes, hello everybody." He gave a short wave. "I asked a friend of mine, Jonas Goldman, to take the case pro bono, that means free, and he's agreed to do so."

"We know what pro bono means," someone said with a snort.

"Yes, of course," Mitch said unabashedly. "Jonas will be meeting with Ricky later this morning, and I can assure you all he's a top-notch attorney."

Rosa gave his hand a quick squeeze when he sat back down on the floor. She still couldn't figure out if Mitch was interested in her as a woman or just an actress, but he sure as hell was impressing the shit out of her.

"Jonas Goldman is very, very good," Sharif nodded, "and well connected. We're lucky to have him. But now what I want you all to do is go on back to your apartments, don't go to sleep if you don't think you can get back up in a couple of hours, and be prepared to all meet downstairs at eight so we can go to the arraignment together."

"Sharif," Rosa whispered as people began to trail out of the apartment. "How did the police know about Ricky?"

"I don't know. Vincent's working on finding out now." He gave her a kiss on the cheek. "You were wonderful, Rosa."

"Oh, yeah, I know," Rosa grinned as she walked out the door. "I'm good."

17

What did you find out?" Sharif asked before Vincent even took a seat in the booth at the Lenox Lounge. "Who gave him up?"

Vincent signaled the drink waitress over. "Scotch on the rocks." He looked over at Sharif. "You good?"

Sharif held up his orange juice and nodded.

"Then, fuck it, make mine a double." Vincent threw a hundred-dollar bill on the table.

The waitress, a twenty-something woman who could have passed for Vanessa Williams in her prime, was dressed in a low-cut black one-piece leotard and a skimpy white apron. She bent over and picked up the money, sexily shaking her shoulders as she did so. "Any particular brand? Or do you want shelf?" she asked, smiling at Vincent.

"You figure out what I want, and bring it," Vincent said as he licked his lips and gave her a slow once-over.

"I'd say"—the waitress let her hand slowly slide down from her chest to her waist—"that you look like a man who'd want only the best."

"Then, baby, bring me the best." Vincent watched her as she sashayed off. "Nice fat booty."

"Was it Taz?" Sharif tapped his knuckles on the table to get his friend's attention.

"Naw. I spoke to him. He fucked it up, but he ain't rat Ricky out." Vincent shook his head. "It was some punk named Bo-Bo. He was there when that stupid-ass Ricky asked Taz for the gun, but he wasn't there when Taz passed it." Vincent shook his head and snorted. "Thank God Taz got some smarts even if Ricky ain't."

"So what do you mean when you say Taz fucked up?"

Vincent lit a cigarette. "Turns out that punk, Bo-Bo, ratted out some brothers from Detroit a couple of years ago. Taz runs that corner. He shoulda checked out Bo-Bo's resume before he put him down." He inhaled, then let the smoke slowly seep through his lips before speaking again. "So Ricky caught a break. Bo-Bo is out on the street, so Taz is going to handle his business, so he ain't gonna have to worry about him showing up trying to testify." Vincent put up his hands. "And before you say anything, I ain't got a nickel in that dime. Taz had made up his mind to take care of Bo-Bo before I even talked to him. So just say 'oh, well,' and move on." He nodded dismissively as the waitress placed his drink in front of him and redirected his attention to Sharif, ignoring the indignant look she shot him before walking off. "What I wanna know is why Ricky confessed? Got a case of the guilties or some shit?"

Sharif slumped in his seat. "Naw, man. I got a chance to talk to him at the arraignment. The police told him they had the gun and it had his fingerprints all over it."

Vincent raised his eyebrows. "Get the fuck out. How'd they come up with the gun?"

"Man, that's the thing. They don't have it. They bluffed him out." Sharif banged his fist on the table.

"Yeah, okay, and you know they ain't got it, how?" Vincent asked. He waited, but Sharif said nothing. "You went and got the piece from the trash chute, didn't you?"

"Yeah. I just wanted to make sure no one else found it," Sharif shrugged. "Good thing I did, too. Otherwise the lawyer would have to wait until discovery before they found out the police lied."

"Not the way I woulda handled it, but, yeah, whatever." Vincent took another sip of his drink. "So he's lawyered up?"

"Yeah. Jonas Goldman. He's doing it pro bono cause he's a friend of a friend of Rosa."

"Yeah, I heard of him. He's supposed to be good," Vincent nodded. "Always good to get a Jewish lawyer. They got the hook-up. They be playing golf with the judges, and shit."

"That's so much bullshit. A black lawyer is as good as a Jewish lawyer any day."

"So you say, but I always get the Jew boys to handle my shit. 'Cept that time I got in some trouble in Philly a couple years back. I used an Italian lawyer then. Peruto, or some shit. Got them to drop the charges like that." Vincent snapped his fingers. "Set me back eight thousand, but I ain't give a shit." He leaned back in the booth, a faraway look on his face.

"You okay, man?" Sharif asked after a few moments.

"Yeah, man. I just got some shit on my mind. Nothing I can't handle. But I'ma go ahead and split." Vincent took another sip, then put the glass down and stood up. "You know that bitch ain't bring me back my change? And I gave her a benny."

Sharif grinned. "Maybe she thought it was a tip."

"She's fine, but she ain't that fucking fine." Vincent waved at the waitress who was serving drinks to another table. She smiled and held out her finger to signal she'd be right over. "Man, collect my dough for me, and don't give the bitch a tip. Trying to play me like I'm a fucking trick." He reached down and picked up the glass again and gulped down the contents. "I'm out."

Sharif sipped his orange juice while he waited for the waitress to come over, and thought back to the arraignment earlier that morning. Jonas Goldman was indeed good. He'd called Miss Rose right before she was getting ready to walk out the door and told her to bring Ricky a change of clothes. Not a suit, he said, because he didn't want it to be too obvious, but a good pair of slacks and a light button-down shirt and matching belt and shoes.

Ricky still looked pitiful when he entered his not guilty plea to the judge, but at least he didn't look like a thug, with his droopy jeans and oversized tee shirt. And better for him to be looking pitiful than trying the wannabe gangsta act—acting like he didn't give a damn.

Goldman was ecstatic when he saw how many Ida B. tenants had turned out for the arraignment, and after warning them all not to make any kind of scene, he strategically placed all of the older ones in the front of the court room. He was rewarded for his efforts when they all clucked sympathetically when a teary-eyed Ricky was led—handcuffed—into the chambers.

The judge—an older Latino woman—had even shown compassion, asking if Ricky had been treated all right at the detention center, and Jonas immediately jumped on it, asking the judge to let Ricky out in the custody of his mother. The prosecutor had objected of course, saying this was a homicide case, but Jonas drove home the fact that Ricky was only fifteen, had no priors, and was an honor student at one of the most prestigious public high schools in the city. The judge looked at the smug white, yuppie-looking prosecutor, and then at the pathetic-looking African-American teenager, and scheduled a bail hearing for Friday, before banging down her gavel. Sharif had two days to get as many character reference letters as possible, but he knew it wouldn't be a problem since Ricky was such a well-liked kid. With any luck, Ricky would be going home with his mother Friday afternoon.

Sharif shook his head and wondered if he'd done the right thing by telling Ricky not to reveal the truth to his mother. With any luck, Ricky would be able to beat the rap, and there was no use in his mother knowing the truth about what her son had done. It was bad enough it was going to haunt Ricky for the rest of his life. Let the poor woman have some peace of mind.

"Where's your friend?"

Sharif looked up at the smiling waitress leaning on the edge of the table with one hand, the other sexily placed on her hip.

"He was running late for an appointment, so he had to leave. He asked me to collect his change for him."

"Shoot!" The woman rolled her eyes. She paused for a moment, and then grabbed a napkin from the table and hurriedly wrote down a telephone number. "Give him this for me," she handed the napkin to Sharif and started to walk off.

"Excuse me, Miss!" Sharif gestured her back. "You forgot to give me the change?"

"Well"—the waitress flashed a toothy smile—"tell him he can pick it up after he calls me and we get together."

Sharif looked at her and shook his head. Vincent was right. The idiot really did have an overblown image of herself. "You don't want me to tell him that." He held out his hand.

She sucked her teeth and reached into her apron and pulled out a wad of bills and started counting it out into his hand. "How much should I take for my tip?" she asked before placing the last ten dollar bill in his hand.

"Zero," Sharif said with a smile. "He'll give you the tip himself *if* he ever calls you and the two of you hook up." He usually tried to be nice, but this woman really grated his nerves, and needed to be taken down a notch.

The waitress sucked her teeth, threw the ten on the table, and stomped off.

"I notice ain't nobody knock on my damn door to go to that meeting at your apartment last night," Miss Jackie snapped as Sharif walked into the lobby of Ida B. "What you ain't think I was gonna find out? I still got some friends in this damn building."

She looked bad, Sharif noted. She hadn't bothered putting on her wig, and graying pigtails peeked underneath the dirty red scarf haphazardly tied on her head. The bags that had begun to appear under her eyes after Ronald's death now almost reached her the top of her cheekbones, and a bit of spittle was nestled in the corners of her snarling lips.

"How you doing, Miss Jackie?" He put his hand out to touch her on the shoulder, but she jerked away.

"And I notice ain't nobody knock on my door this morning so I could come to court today, huh?" Miss Jackie's eyes narrowed into a slit. "I woulda told that judge woman a little something for sure. I woulda told her to lock his ass up and throw away the key. I woulda told her to—"

"Miss Jackie, it wasn't Ricky who killed your son," Sharif said in a calming voice. "And the longer the police hold him, the more time the real killer will have to get away."

"Stop your lying!" Miss Jackie shouted. The few people in the lobby looked over in their direction, and the usually absent security guard looked up from his book. He slowly stood up as if he was going to take some action. Sharif waved for him to sit down, and continued talking calmly to the woman.

"Miss Jackie, I'm telling you that Ricky couldn't have done it. He was with me in my apartment when your son was shot."

"And I said stop lying," Miss Jackie spat. "You never did like my Ronald. You and your damn grandmother. Always lying on him and trying to get him locked up for something he ain't do. She was jealous cause he was a fine upright young man and youse a goddamned faggot."

"Now look, Miss Jackie—" Sharif tried to grab the woman by the hand, but she backed away.

"Don't you touch me! You probably was in on it. You probably put Ricky up to it, didn't you? You and that goddamned Vincent. Both of you probably—"

Before she could say another word, a large heavy cane seemed to come out of nowhere and thumped her soundly on the side of her head, knocking her backwards onto the floor.

"I would advise you to keep my grandson's name out of your filthy mouth," Mrs. Harris said, looking down at the dazed woman. "And you should be ashamed using the Lord's name in vain like that."

Sharif hurriedly bent down to help Miss Jackie up, but she ignored him and leaned on the wall for support to raise herself to her feet.

"You old hag," she said as she steadied herself. "I'ma call the police on you, and don't think I won't. See if I won't tell them you're the biggest fence in Harlem. And I'ma call management and tell them you got the dogs in your apartment and make them throw your old ass outta here."

Mrs. Harris leaned heavily on her cane and fixed a stony glare at Miss Jackie. "Jackie, I'm a God-fearing woman. But as the Lord is my witness, if the police come to my door, there's gonna be another murder in this building." She stepped closer to the woman. " 'Cause the last thing my Fifi and Pinkie will do before they get hauled outta here is tear your lying throat out."

Damn! I guess Vincent got it honestly, Sharif thought as he looked at the elderly woman.

Mrs. Harris smiled and stepped back from Miss Jackie, who was looking at her with eyes wide with terror. "I'm eighty-six years old, and I don't think any judge is gonna send a little old woman like me who couldn't manage to control her dogs anywhere but home. And my Vincent will buy me a nice a little condo in Long Island and I'll be living happily ever after while you're forever burning in hell."

Miss Jackie stormed over to the security desk, careful to walk out of striking distance, and banged her fist down hard. "You saw her assault me and you ain't gonna do shit?"

The guard reopened his book. "Sorry, I must have missed it. I ain't seen a thing."

Miss Jackie's mouth dropped open, and she looked as if she was about to have a heart attack. But instead she snatched the book from the guard and flung it against the wall. "You're the one's what gonna burn in hell," she shouted, pointing at him. She swung around to face everyone in the lobby. "All y'all motherfuckers gonna burn in hell." She stormed off to the elevators without saying another word.

Sharif started off after her, but Mrs. Harris stopped him. "Leave her be, Sharif. She needs some time to herself, poor woman." She smiled down at him. "Now I want you to do me a favor and come take Pinkie and Fifi out for a walk. Lunchtime's over and I gotta get back to work."

18

Brenda stood in her robe and stared in disbelief at the letter in her hand. *This has gotta be a joke. Someone's gotta be playing a prank.* She walked from the door into the living room and sank down onto the couch. She tried to blink the sleep from her eyes, and read and reread it, hoping she had misunderstood the words.

Dear Tenant:

We must regretfully inform you that we've just been notified that the Ida B. Wells-Barnett Tower will be closed one year from now.

You'll be receiving a formal notice by certified mail within the next ten days, but we know that a lot of unfounded rumors have been swirling about the future of this building, and we wanted to let all our tenants know what is really going on.

Contained in the formal notice you'll find a hotline number which we are setting up for residents requiring more information. Please do not contact the management office because the staff is still busy carrying on the day-to-day business of maintaining the building.

Also, rest assured that the city and federal government have both pledged to provide housing relocation assistance for all residents of the Ida B. Wells-Barnett Tower.

We hope that your tenancy has been a happy one.

Management

Brenda's heart started beating rapidly. What was she going to do? She grabbed the telephone and started dialing furiously.

"Sharif? Did you—?"

"Yeah, they just slipped the letter under my door." Sharif's voice was trembling with anger.

"Can they really do this? I mean, can they really just kick us out?"

"Yeah, well I won't know anything for sure until I get over to management," Sharif paused. "We all knew this was a possibility, but I don't see how that investment group could have cut through all the red tape so fast."

"What are we going to do?" Brenda sniffed and wiped the tears running down her cheeks. "I mean, we can do something, right? I don't wanna move, Sharif."

"I know, Brenda . . . oh, crap, Brenda, I just looked at the clock. I gotta go. I'm supposed to pick up Miss Rosa to take her to Ricky's bail hearing. Look. I'll call you as soon as I get back. I gotta run."

Brenda hung up the phone in a daze. How could Sharif just run off like that when he knew she was falling apart? Who was she going to talk to now? *Damn, I'm being such a selfish bitch. Of course Sharif has to go and support Ricky and Miss Rose. But I need to talk to someone.*

She picked up the phone and called her mother, but got the answering machine. *Where the hell is she this early in the morning? Oh, hell, that's right. She did say she had an appointment with the foster care people. Why today of all days?*

She called Rosa's apartment and once again got the answering machine. Where the hell was Rosa at nine-thirty in the morning?

She gently placed the phone on the receiver and walked into the kitchen and started the coffee maker her mother had given her for Kwanzaa. What were the chances, she wondered as she watched the coffee drip into the glass pot, that she and her mother would be able to get an apartment in the same building? She'd never been away from her mother. She'd even refused to go to the two-week Fresh Air summer camp that Sharif and Rosa used to go to when they were young.

Maybe it would be good for her to finally really move away on her own, she thought as she poured a cup of coffee and sat down at the kitchen table. It was convenient having her mother right down the hall; she helped a lot with the kids, and was always there when she needed to talk. Well, almost always. Or if she needed to borrow sugar, or a couple of dollars, her mother had whatever she needed.

But she was twenty-six years old, and it was time to fully cut the apron strings. Maybe that's what she needed to really get her creative juices going. Nothing was more invigorating than true independence, or so she heard.

She knew it was going to be pretty hard finding a three or four bedroom apartment in Harlem that she could afford, or rather that welfare would be willing to pay for. She grimaced as she remembered that she needed to call her new caseworker to see if she could get an emergency check to keep her lights on. At least Miss Cabral probably wouldn't be as crabby about it as her last caseworker.

Yep, there was a real possibility she wouldn't be able to find an apartment in Harlem. And Brooklyn was getting almost as expensive. She sighed. Maybe she could find an affordable house to rent in the Bronx. The rents there were so much more affordable. Maybe one even big enough so that she could invite her father to move in. He was getting up there in age, he was almost sixty-five. He'd probably be happy to live with a real family, and he'd be such a good influence on Bootsy.

She banged her cup down on the table. *Oh, God, I'm doing it again.*

Only this time I'm substituting a father for a mother. What? Is it that I'm afraid to be on my own?

She walked into the living room and picked up the television remote. Might as well catch the last minutes of *Live with Regis and Kelly*, she thought. But when she clicked the power button, the screen displayed a bright blue nothing. *Damn, they turned off the cable.* She threw the remote up against the wall and then collapsed on the couch, crying uncontrollably.

"What's the matter, Mommy?"

Brenda looked up to find Shaniqua standing in the doorway in her Powerpuff Girls pajamas, a terrified look on her face.

"Nothing, baby," Brenda quickly wiped her face and forced a smile. "Come here," she held out her arms.

"Then, why are you crying?" Shaniqua walked over slowly, looking at her mother suspiciously.

"I had a little bit of headache. But it's gone now. Know why?" Brenda reached out and drew her daughter into a hug. " 'Cause I see my little sunshine, and I always smile when I get a little sunshine."

"I'm eight years old. I'm not little anymore," Shaniqua said as she settled herself into her mother's lap.

"That's right, you're your Mommy's big girl, and I love you every minute older you get." Brenda gave her a quick peck on the cheek. "Now go wake up your brothers and tell them to brush their teeth and get ready for breakfast."

"Hey, Vincent. Come on in." Brenda stepped back from the door to let him enter. "I'm fixing the kids corned beef hash for lunch. You want some?"

"No, I just ate." Vincent stood in the foyer and looked around. "Sharif here?"

"No. He hasn't come back from court yet. Ricky might be coming home today, you know," Brenda said as she spooned the hash into the hard red plastic plates. "I was hoping he'd call and let me know what was happening, but I haven't heard from him."

"Yeah, yeah, that's right," Vincent nodded. "I forgot that was today."

"Kids, come on and eat!"

Bootsy stuck his head out her bedroom. "Mom, can we eat in here?"

Brenda pursed her lips as she looked at her son. "I didn't know all of you were in my room. Come on out of there before you wake up Jumah from his nap."

"But Ma, we just wanna finish watching *Vampire in Brooklyn*. We can't get the channel in the living room since the cable's out. We ain't gonna wake him up."

Brenda put her hands on her hips. "What did I tell you about using that word, Bootsy?"

"We're not going to wake him up," Bootsy corrected himself. "Please, Ma?"

"All right, Bootsy. But I'm telling you, if you guys wake Jumah up . . ."

"Thanks, Ma." Bootsy ducked back in the room.

"Vince, you want something to drink?" Brenda asked after the children had taken their food into the bedroom.

"Yeah, what you got?"

"You've got your choice of grape or strawberry Kool-Aid."

"You've got to be kidding." Vincent took out a cigarette and tapped the end of it against the arm of the chair before lighting it. "Yeah, all right. I'll take strawberry. I'm thirsty as hell."

"You know what?" Vincent said after Brenda returned with his drink.

"What?" She sat down on the couch.

"You're a good little mother." Vincent gave her one of his famous half-smiles. "Always been. Which is pretty strange, considering you had your first one when you was like eleven."

"Thirteen," Brenda corrected him.

"Most of these chickenheads out here don't give a shit about their kids," Vincent continued. "But here you are with four little rugrats, and you make sure they have three square a day, clean clothes on their back, and"—he looked at Brenda and grinned—"and you ain't gonna let them get away with saying ain't. You're trying to bring them up right." He took a sip of the Kool-Aid. "You're a good woman."

Brenda grinned. "Why, Vincent, dear, are you proposing?"

She expected him to laugh, and was surprised when instead he simply shook his head. "Naw, Bren. That's not my life."

Brenda looked at Vincent curiously, realizing the conversation had suddenly taken a serious tone.

"So, then, tell me, what is your life?" she said carefully.

"Subject to change." He said with a wink. "What about you? What is your life? I mean, what would you like to do with your life? You got any dreams?"

"Well, I've always said I'd like to write a book . . ."

"Ah, yeah, that's right. You're going to be a famous author some day." Vincent grinned.

"Go ahead and laugh. But one day you're going to walk into a bookstore and see my book on the best-seller list."

"Yeah, right. I don't see that shit ever happening."

"What?" Brenda picked up a magazine and threw it at him, almost causing him to spill his Kool-Aid. "Are you trying to say you don't think I'm capable of writing a best seller?"

"I'm trying to say I don't think I'm capable of walking into a bookstore."

"You mean you wouldn't come out to hear me read my best seller," she said with a pout.

He exhaled a long stream of smoke and then stubbed his cigarette out in the ashtray. "Not if it's in a bookstore."

She'd known Vincent twenty years, and in all that time she'd never had a simple one-on-one conversation with him that lasted more than five minutes. And here he was in her living room, sipping strawberry Kool-Aid and cracking jokes. And it was rather nice.

"So," she said suddenly, "what did your grandmother say when she got the notice this morning. I know she had a fit."

"What notice?"

"About them closing Ida B." Brenda picked up the letter which was still lying on the coffee table. "Mrs. Harris didn't get one?"

Vincent took the letter and read it, then let out a whistle. "Now this is some shit. They're really going to shut it down."

"Mrs. Harris didn't get a letter?" Brenda asked again.

Vincent shook his head. "I don't know. I didn't stop in. I went straight to Sharif's apartment, and when he wasn't there I came down here. I'd better check on my grandmother. She must be having a fit." He stood up. "Make sure you tell Sharif to get in contact with me as soon as you hear from him. Tell him it's urgent."

"Is something wrong," Brenda said with alarm. "Is it anything to do with . . . you know . . . Ricky?"

He shook his head and walked toward the front door, but just before he turned the knob he turned and looked at Brenda. "You know what? This could have something to do with Ricky, after all. Make sure Sharif calls me."

19

Mitch, I gotta talk to you now!" Rosa burst through the theater door so fast the scarf tied around her neck seemed to float behind her. She looked at the cast and crew huddled around Mitch, who was sitting in his director's chair, and snapped, "And we need some privacy."

"Rosa?" Mitch peered at her over his reading glasses. "What's wrong?"

"We gotta talk." She strode over to him, and then looked at the people. "I *said* we need some privacy."

"Rosa, dear," Cissy Arlington looked around the other people, a smirk on her face. "Wouldn't it be easier for you two to go into the back room, rather than ask everybody else to leave?"

"Actually, prop girl"—Rosa threw down her shoulder bag—"I think it would be easier for me to just kick your—"

Mitch moved forward and grabbed Rosa by the arm, pulling her to him. "A few minutes, please?" he told the ensemble. Cissy's blue eyes widened, and turned ice cold, but she nodded and headed out, followed by the rest of the group.

"Now, what's wrong?" Mitch sat back down and crossed his legs.

Rosa reached down into her pocketbook and pulled out the notice she'd received earlier that morning. "This!" She thrust it into Mitch's chest, almost toppling him over. "This is what the fuck is wrong."

"What is this?" A flustered Mitch unfolded the letter, but before he could read it, Rosa snatched it from his hand.

"It's a letter saying they gonna close the Ida B.," she shouted. "But you already knew that, and shit. Right?"

"The Ida B.?" Mitch shook his head. "What's the . . . oh!" His eyes lit up with recognition. "Your building! They're closing your building. Why?"

"Don't put on an innocent act." Rosa turned and walked a few paces away. "Didn't you tell me the other night your first name is Mitchum?"

"Yes, I did."

She swung back to face him. "The same Mitchum Jeffries on the board of Chest Park Incorporated?"

"Why, yes. But how did you know—"

"How could you, Mitch? I trusted you, and shit!" Rosa's eyes brimmed with tears she willed not to fall. "I invite you into my home, introduce you to my friends, and you turn around and stab us in the back by closing down our building? What, you was just using me to get an up close and personal look at the people you were throwing out in the street? *Hipócrita! Mentiroso.*" She stamped her foot. "You hypocritical, lying bastard!"

"Rosa, what are you talking about?" Mitch stood up and tried to grab Rosa by the shoulders, but she flung his arms away.

"Why you still trying to pretend, and shit? *Piensa mi estupido?* You think I'm stupid, or something? You don't think I don't know that the city's closing the Ida B. because Chest Park wants to put up a luxury building?" Her lips curled when she saw the surprised look on his face. "Uh-huh, well, Sharif found out, okay." She paused and took a deep breath. "But when he told me that it was a Mitchum Jeffries on the board, I couldn't bring myself to believe it was you. Guess I'm stupid, huh?"

"Rosa, I'm on the board, but I—" Mitch tried to grab her arm, but Rosa pushed him back.

"Don't you put your lying fucking stupid hands on me!" she screamed at him. "And don't think I don't know the only reason you been trying to act like you're interested in my acting is so you can get some pussy!"

"Mitch?" Cissy's head peeked through the door. "Is everything okay? You want me to call the police?"

"*Puta!*" Rosa yelled in her direction. "You want me to kick your fucking ass?"

"Cissy!" Mitch commanded. "Close the door." He turned back to Rosa. "And Rosa, calm down and let me explain. I've never tried to—"

"You know what? You can explain to my pretty Puerto Rican ass as I walk out the door." Rosa picked up her pocketbook, straightened her shoulders, thrust her head up high, and headed for the door. " 'Cause if you think for one minute I would work with you, you're the one that's stupid. I got too much class."

"That fucking Mitch," Rosa said out loud as she dabbed her eyes with the worn balled-up tissue. The train slowed to a halt, and she looked out the subway car window to see which station they were pulling into. One Hundred and Third Street. Three more stops to go. She'd have been home by now if she'd taken the express train at Union Square, but with her crying, and everyone looking, she hopped on the first train that pulled in. The Number 6 Local.

She sniffed and wiped the tissue over her nose. *I must look pretty pitiful, and shit,* she thought. She looked up and saw a man across the aisle looking at her as if to confirm her thoughts. Any other time she would have made a face at him for daring to look at her, but she felt too drained to bother. Too weak, even, to will herself not to cry.

She didn't even know which she was more upset about, Ida B. getting ready to be closed down, or her no longer being in a play she had hoped would be her ticket to theater stardom. No, there was no doubt it was Mitch's betrayal that was really messing her up the most.

How could he do this shit? She crossed her arms, then crossed and uncrossed her legs, flung her shoulder bag from her side to her lap, and started chewing her lip, then stopped, not wanting to ruin her lipstick. Lipstick? She looked at the balled-up tissue streaked with pink. She didn't have to worry about that anymore. Good thing she was in such a hurry she hadn't put on any mascara or she'd be looking like a clown by now. No wonder that awful man was staring at her.

She looked up just as the doors were closing. *Oh, shit. This is my stop.* She jumped up just in time to stick her foot in between the closing doors, forcing them back open. As she walked along the platform she flashed a finger at the man who'd been gawking at her. Wouldn't you know it? He wasn't looking.

The lobby was full of people when Rosa slowly dragged herself inside. Some were arguing with the security guard, who was sweating as he alternated between yelling at them and yelling into the telephone. Even more people were gathered outside the management office, looking as if they had been there for some time.

"I know somebody better open that door and tell me something," a woman was shouting and pounding on the door. "I been living here twenty years, and you gonna just slip a note under my door and say I'm being thrown outta here."

"Ain't this some shit? Talking about don't bother management." James Murphy pounded once on the door, and then started pacing back and forth in the hallway.

Rosa felt a hand on her shoulder.

"Rosa. I suppose you got the letter, too?"

She turned around to see Mrs. Carver, jiggling Jumah in one arm and holding Yusef by the other. "Yeah. I got one."

"Umph. I had to go out early today, so I didn't even know until I got back this after—baby, are you okay? You look awful!" Mrs. Carver tried to feel Rosa's forehead, but Rosa backed off.

"I'm okay, Miss Janet. Just tired, and all. I had to be at the theater early this morning. I'm going to go upstairs and get some rest." She flashed a weak smile and made her way to the elevators.

Why did she feel guilty, she wondered as she turned the key in the door. It wasn't like there was anything she could have done. Mitch had to have had all this planned before he even met her, and there was no way she could have known. And even when Sharif found out and told her, well, there still wasn't anything she could have done. But still, when she asked Mitch his full name that night in her apartment, she should have let him have it right then and there. But no, she tried to make herself believe that it had to be another Mitchum Jeffries. She didn't want to insult him by even asking. After all, he'd seemed so sweet, and so interested in making her a better actress. And it was so nice to have someone as big as him think she had what it takes.

Yeah, it was probably too late to do anything anyway, but I shoulda said something, and shit! Rosa plopped down on the couch. *I shouldn'ta let him think he could do me and my peeps and get it away with it just 'cause he could make me a star.*

But I showed his ass, she comforted herself as she wiped her eyes with the back of her hand. *I bet he didn't think I was gonna quit the show, and shit. Yeah, I showed him.*

What would really show him, she thought, was for her to find a better, juicier role than the one she'd walked out on. She jumped up and grabbed the Yellow Pages. And it would kill him if she got in some really good acting troupe. What was the name of the repertory group she'd heard them talking about at the theater? Joe Pappy? Joe Paps? She reached for the telephone as she flipped through the Yellow Pages, and it was then that she saw all the messages flashing on the answering machine.

"Rosa. This is Mitch—"

Click. She deleted the message. That felt good, she thought with a smile.

"Er, Rosa, this is Mitch again. Please—"

Click. That felt even better.

"Rosa, I'm sorry to keep calling—"

Click. "Okay, now this is getting a little annoying, and shit," she said out loud, though she was happily grinning.

"Peace. Rosa, this is Sharif. Give me a call when you get in. I gotta talk to you about something."

Her body sagged when she heard the message. She replayed it again so that she could hear the time stamp. The call had been recorded at two-fifteen. She looked at the clock. It was three o'clock, so he was probably still home.

She sighed and stood up. There was no use in calling; she might as well face the music in person, she decided.

"It's open," Sharif's voice rang out after she knocked on his door. "Damn! You look like you just lost your mother. You okay?" he said as she entered.

"Yo, Sharif, man, I'm really sorry." She walked over and sat on the couch next to him. "You was right. It was Mitch on that board. And I fucked up 'cause I didn't come and tell you when I found out, and shit." She leaned her head on his shoulder. "I'm really sorry."

"Hey, hey." Sharif put his arm around her. "It's okay, girl. It's okay."

"But I really messed up." She nuzzled closer. "If I had just told you . . ."

"It wouldn't have mattered." Sharif kissed her on the forehead.

Rosa's head shot up. "It wouldn't?"

Sharif shook his head.

"Right," Rosa said slowly as she sat up a bit. "Yeah, right. Because by that time it woulda been too late, right?"

"Well, yes and no. If you had told me right away, there was a chance that I could have tried to talk to him and see if something could have been worked out . . ."

Rosa threw her hands out in exasperation. "So I did fuck up, then!"

"Calm down and hear me out, Rosa." Sharif chucked her under the chin. "Mitch called me about an hour ago . . ."

"Aw, man, he called you." Rosa rolled her eyes. "He's been blowing up my machine, too. How'd he get your number?"

"From that lawyer, Jonas Goldman. Now be quiet for a moment and let me finish." Sharif grabbed Rosa's hand. "He called me and told me how you went off on him this morning, and he explained a couple of things to me. He is a member of the board, but pretty much in name only. He said he hasn't gone to a board meeting in years, and had no idea what was going on. He didn't know they had designs on Ida B., and he said even if he did he wouldn't have been able to do anything about it because he's only one of twelve people on the board and he didn't know or have anything to do with the other members. He was really on the board because he was an investor. He was happy getting checks every quarter, and didn't know or care about what acquisitions Chest Park was making."

"And you believe him?"

Sharif nodded. "Yeah. Yeah, I do. So, even if you had told me right away and I talked to him, he probably wouldn't have been able to do anything. But now"—Sharif grinned—"now the way you went off on him, he's so upset he's trying to call an emergency board meeting. I don't think he'd be trying to go all like this just on my word. He's doing it 'cause of you."

Rosa brightened up. "Ya think?"

"Oh, yeah," Sharif said with a chuckle. "You lit a fire under his ass."

"Then why was he trying to hang around all the time, if he wasn't trying to spy and find out more about Ida B.? Just trying to get some leg off of me, huh?"

"Oh, yeah. He mentioned that you said something to that effect during your little tirade," Sharif chuckled. "That's my Rosa."

Rosa snatched her hand away from Sharif's. "So what you saying, Sharif? He ain't trying to get with me?"

"Has he ever cracked on you?"

Rosa shook her head. "Not even when we was up in my apartment, by ourselves. How'd you know?"

"He told me. Said he was sorry if he gave you the wrong impression. That he's very much involved with some woman, a councilwoman I think, up in Connecticut."

Rosa's eyes widened and she leaned back against the couch.

"Rosa, baby, what's wrong?" Sharif cocked his head and looked at her. "Don't tell me you liked him."

"Naw, naw." Rosa shook her head vigorously. "It's just that . . . well, it was kinda exciting to think that someone like him was, you know, smitten with me or some shit." She looked up at Sharif. "I mean look at all the time he was spending up here."

"Yeah. But you know what I think?"

"What?"

"I think your boy's a voyeur . . . You know, someone who likes to watch other people. And I think that the first time he came up here with you, his intentions really were innocent. But then, when he got a peek into your world, the world of Ida B., he couldn't get enough. I remember the excitement in his eyes when we were outside the police station, and later when we came back to my apartment. I wouldn't be surprised if we don't look in the papers some day and see a play about a building in Harlem, and the people who live there." Sharif threw back his head and laughed. "Wouldn't that be some shit?"

Rosa snorted. "Well, if so, I'd better get a lead role."

Before Sharif could respond, they heard a knock on the door.

"Come in," Rosa and Sharif said simultaneously.

"Yo, man," Vincent said as he walked in the door. "Hey, Rosa. What's happening, *mamacita*?"

"Okay, Sharif, I guess I better go before someone threatens to slit my throat," Rosa said, though she didn't make a move to get up.

"Oh, yeah, that's right. I ain't apologize for that shit, yet, huh?" Vince walked over and pulled Rosa up from the couch.

"I'm sorry, okay?" he said holding her at arms length. "I'm really really sorry. I shoulda never said some shit like that to you. You forgive me?"

"No, I don't forgive you," Rosa said, stamping her feet.

Vincent chuckled. "You're right, Sharif. She does stamp her feet a lot."

"Oh, forget you!" Rosa punched Vincent on the shoulder and walked back over to the couch. She sat down and she looked up at Vincent. "It is okay for me to sit down, right? I mean, you're not throwing me out, and shit."

Vincent waved his hand and sat down in the chair across from them. "No, I want you to stay. As a matter of fact"—he looked at Sharif—"do me a favor and call Brenda and tell her to come on up here. I got something to say, and I want all of y'all to hear it."

Vincent was silent, staring straight ahead and seemingly lost in thought, ignoring Rosa and Sharif's questions about what was going on, while they waited for Brenda to get there.

When she finally arrived, less than five minutes later, he motioned for her to sit down, then took out his cell phone.

"Hello, police? This is Vincent Harris. I live at 242 West 142nd Street." He smiled at his friends who were looking at him, mouths open. "I'm calling to confess to killing Ronald Johnson."

20

Calm down," Vincent said as Sharif, Rosa, and Brenda—who were all on their feet—started yelling at him at once. "I know what the fuck I'm doing. Okay?"

"Oh, well, yeah, you wanna let us in on it, then?" Sharif almost shouted.

"Cool out and sit down and maybe I will," Vincent demanded. "We got a little bit of time 'cause the cops don't know where I am. They probably ain't even gonna send nobody to the address I sent them to for another hour or so."

He waited until everybody had settled in before he began speaking again. "Look, y'all know I already have them two fed convictions, the gun charge and that money laundering crap a couple years back?"

Sharif nodded.

"Well, here's the thing." Vincent lit a cigarette and inhaled deeply, then let the smoke lazily drift out of his mouth, as if he had all the time in the world, while three people in the room waited anxiously for him to continue.

"Oh, good God, Vincent! The thing is what?" Brenda demanded angrily.

"The thing is, the feds've built a case against me I ain't gonna be able to beat this time. My connect on that Social Security thing got turned in by some other guy who's working the same scam with him. So he decided to cut himself a deal. Bring down everyone involved, to cut down his time. Including me. Seems like they got me dead to right."

"Oh, shit, Vince." Sharif rubbed his hand over his face. "Shit. I mean, are you sure?"

Vince nodded. "That chick Tisha, the one Aunt Pat was gonna beat up, she works in the federal prosecutor's office. Court reporter. She took the last of his, like, fifteen fucking affidavits. She managed to get her hand on a copy of the others, too. I'm all up in that mug."

"And there ain't nothing you can do, and shit?" Rosa's voice was almost hysterical, and Sharif reached over and rubbed her back. He looked at Brenda, but she sat there saying nothing, almost as if she were in shock.

"You can't, you know, convince the rat to change his testimony?" Rosa asked.

"Yeah, well, dude ain't going to be going to court. He committed suicide yesterday afternoon." Vincent leaned back, a half-smile appearing on his face. "Shot himself in the back of the head and threw himself in the river with some weights tied around his ankles. They ain't gonna find him for a while."

Sharif grimaced. "Damn, Vince."

"But the damage is already done. I took the copies to my lawyer, and he said no matter what, those affidavits are going to be admitted into evidence. And not only that, Tisha called my cell today. Said there was another guy from the Social Security office that can finger me." Vince shrugged. "I'm just fucked."

"That's why you're taking the rap for Ricky, then?" Brenda's voice was hoarse. "You figure you'll be a three-time loser and they're going to lock you up for life anyway, right?"

"But that don't make sense," Rosa said. "He could get the death penalty for killing Ronald, and he ain't even do it."

"Naw, naw, it wouldn't be a capital crime, because Ronald wasn't robbed or anything," Sharif said, shaking his head. "He'll get life without parole—same as he'd get as a three-time loser."

Vincent nodded. "My lawyer says he's sure they'll go for it. I done got away with so fucking much they're gonna be coming up at me with all guns."

"So you're just giving yourself up." Brenda sighed and stood up. "Sharif, you got any of that nasty iced tea?"

Vincent caught her hand as she tried to walk by him and into the kitchen. "Sit down," he commanded. "I ain't finished."

He waited until she sank back down, then lit another cigarette. "I'm making like a ghost."

"You are?" Brenda sat straight up.

"For real," Rosa squealed. "Yeah, that's my man."

Sharif reached over and gave Vince a pound. "What can I do to help?"

"Nothing, man. I got it handled." Vince stubbed out the cigarette after taking only three puffs. "I already took my grandmother to the condo I bought her in Long Island. And on the way out I'm going to let the people in the building know I'm leaving her door unlocked, so they can have whatever they can carry out."

"And what are you going to do?" Sharif asked.

"I'ma be fine. I set up a new identity some years back for just in case, and I'll just slip into it and move to the islands. Maybe I'll grow my hair out like Sharif, and be a Rasta man," he said with a grin. "I got quite a big stash set aside, so I ain't gonna have to worry about dough for more than a minute." He stood up. "And you know me. I'll figure out something to get into if things get tight."

He looked at his watch. "Well, I'm get outta here." He walked over and embraced Sharif. "Now, you gotta hold it down for me while I'm gone, bro. Keep the streets safe for our womenfolk." He gave Sharif a light punch on the shoulder. "And let Ricky's lawyer know to contact mine so he can get a copy of my written confession."

"When are we going to see you again?" Brenda asked as he hugged her.

"It may be a while, but you know if you need to get me a message you can always contact my grandmother. She'll always know how to get in touch with me." He lifted up her chin. "You gonna be okay?"

"Vince." Brenda sniffed. "I'm going to be okay, but I'm really going to miss you."

Rosa walked up and hugged Vincent from behind. "We're all gonna miss you, *papi*."

"Now see," Vincent grinned and reached behind him to pull her forward next to Brenda. "I'm gonna tell Tisha you're starting that *mira mira* shit again."

"I would say something, but Tisha did help you out," Rosa said sullenly.

"What do you expect? I gave her a shot a couple of years ago, and I rocked her world so good she's been trying to figure out a way to get with me ever since." Vincent wiggled his hips. "See, if y'all had given me a piece you'd understand."

"You was never serious about getting with us," Rosa said with a teary smile as she swatted him on the arm.

"Yeah, you're right, but maybe I shoulda been, huh?" he said, looking directly at Brenda as he spoke, though she avoided his eyes.

"A'ight. I'm outta here." Vincent walked to the door, but turned around and smiled as he turned the knob. "It's been real, y'all." And then he was gone.

21

"Finally," Brenda said as she taped up the last carton of dishes. "I think we made good time, Mom. It only took three days to pack up our two apartments. When the movers come tomorrow we'll be ready." She braced herself against the carton she'd just finished taping and stood up. She pulled the blue kerchief off of her head and rubbed her hand through her twists, which now almost reached her shoulders. She wiped the sweat from her forehead and pulled her loose midriff tee shirt further up her shoulder.

"How about we all go to lunch? I'll spring for some McDonald's." She turned around to face her mother, and was surprised to see the woman sitting on the towel she had placed on the couch, staring up at her with a strange look on her face. "Is something wrong, Mom?"

"No, baby. I was just sitting here looking at you," Mrs. Carver said with a little smile. "You know, you've grown up to be a beautiful woman. You look like a beautiful African queen."

Brenda chuckled. "Aw, Mom. You're always saying something sweet like that."

"Yeah, well, I've always thought of you as my little princess, but now I look at you and I see you're a queen. You look regal. Confident.

Like you're totally in charge," Mrs. Carver said. "You've really grown up over the last year. Did you know that?"

Brenda sighed. "I think we all have, Mom. It's been a helluva year." She paused as she thought of Jimmy's death, and how it had affected everyone, and also about Vincent, who'd she not seen in almost a year. "Times change and people have to change with them, right?" She sat down on the couch next to her mother. "How about that lunch?"

Mrs. Carver shook her head. "I need to take a nap. You've grown up and I've grown old."

"Oh, Mom, you're not old."

Mrs. Carver smiled and patted her daughter on the knee. "Well, I'm getting there, baby, and there ain't never been nothing wrong with that. Better than the other option, ya know." She stood up. "So are you still going out for lunch?"

Brenda shook her head. "No I'll stick around and make some calls. I want to bug the telephone people to make sure the service will be on by the time we get to the Bronx tomorrow."

"Well, at least you won't have to worry about getting your phone turned off 'cause of collect calls anymore now that your damn father's outta jail." Mrs. Carver snorted.

"Out of prison," Brenda corrected her.

"Makes no never mind, does it? The man ain't been to see you but once since he got out."

"Twice, Mom," Brenda said dismally as she thought about it. It had taken him two days after he got out before he came by. He'd played with the kids, stayed for dinner, and promised he'd come back the next morning. They didn't see him for three months, and the number he'd given her to reach him was answered by a woman who said she'd never heard of him. Then she didn't see him for another two months, when he stopped by right before Christmas to give her $500 for the kids' presents, and a leather briefcase for herself that he'd picked up hot on the street. She hadn't seen him since. *All those letters and telephone calls about how he couldn't wait to come back and be a father to me and a grandfather to my kids. What bullshit. And how foolish I was to have believed him.*

"Isn't that something about Rosa moving to the Village? I don't know how she's going to afford it. The rents down there are outrageous," Mrs. Carver said as she shook her head. "I'm glad we were both able to find something in the Bronx. We're only two train stops away from each other. We'll be able to see each other every day."

"Sure, Mom." Brenda looked up wearily.

"And it'll so much better for Bootsy, now that he's going to be going to the Bronx High School of Science. I'm so proud of that boy. He really pulled his grades up."

Brenda nodded. "He couldn't have done it without Ricky." She bit her lip as she thought about how leery she'd been was when Sharif proposed that Ricky tutor her son. Ricky was a good kid, but she didn't know what kind of influence he'd be on Bootsy, considering what he'd done, and the fact that Bootsy knew what he'd done. But Sharif was persistent, saying that it would do them both good. Ricky, because it would keep him grounded in his own academics, and his mind off his crime, and Bootsy because he could probably do better with one-on-one tutoring from someone he could actually relate to. And it had worked.

"I'm proud of Bootsy, too," she said softly.

Mrs. Carver yawned and gave an expansive stretch. "Well, let me go get my nap before I fall asleep standing here." She bent down and gave Brenda a peck on the cheek. "Now, remember, I want you and the kids to come over for a big dinner tonight. Did you remember to invite Sharif and Rosa?"

"Yep. Sharif said he might be a little late because he has to help Miss Jackie move into her new place."

"Hmph! Now see, that's why I know Sharif's a saint. Miss Jackie been trying all this time to tell the police they should lock Sharif up until he tells them where Vincent is, and then she goes and gets him to help her move 'cause won't nobody else help her." Mrs. Carver walked to the door. "And I don't know why, but I told your aunt to come to dinner, too. I hope Pat's ass don't show up drunk."

Brenda walked to the window after her mother left, and peeked through the blinds. Yep, the boys selling crack on the corner were still there. They'd probably be the last to go. *I wonder where they're going to relocate*, she thought. She turned and looked around at the apartment she would be leaving for good the next day. The majority of her life had been spent between there and her mother's apartment down the hall. Now she had to start a new life. But it seemed so hard, because there were so many memories—good and bad—attached to the Ida B. Memories that always seemed almost present reality while she was living there, but which she was afraid would become distant, and even surreal, once she moved away. She smiled. *That's deep*. She started to pull her notepad out of her pocketbook to write down the thought, but suddenly stopped and instead walked over to the briefcase lying on the couch. She pulled out the laptop computer she'd borrowed from Sharif a few days before. She sat on the floor next to an electrical socket and plugged it in. She took a deep breath and typed *Ida B., a novel by Brenda Carver*.

EPILOGUE

Brenda looked around the crowded room at the community center and experienced an extreme case of stage fright, and she wasn't even on the stage yet. She gripped the 315 pages of double-spaced type in her lap. *How the hell did I let Sharif talk me into this?* she wondered. *I must have been out of my mind.*

She'd invited Sharif and Rosa to dinner a few weeks before, and surprised them by handing them each a copy of her newly completed manuscript. Both had read it within days, and called her to tell her how wonderful it was. Sharif had called back a few days later and invited her to do a reading from her manuscript at the grand opening of the community center he was now heading in Harlem. She had declined the invitation, telling him it was premature, but told him she'd be glad to do it if and when she actually got the book published. But Sharif, being Sharif, wouldn't take no for an answer.

And here she was.

"Oh, there you go, baby."

Brenda looked up and smiled at her mother.

"I'm sorry I'm late, but at least I got here before they got started." Mrs. Carver craned her neck to get a good look around. "Where are the kids?"

"Shaniqua and Yusef went with Miss Marcie to get some cookies and punch. Miss Gracie snatched Jumah up as soon as we walked in, and Bootsy's over there"—she pointed to the corner of the room—"talking to Ricky."

"Why would you make that poor boy wear a suit?" Mrs. Carver asked.

"Don't blame me. It was his idea," Brenda said with a chuckle. "He said he wanted to look smart for my big day."

"Oh, my good Lord!" Mrs. Carver started laughing. "He's wearing sneakers?"

"Mommy, I swear I tried to talk him out of it," Brenda started laughing along with her. "But I got so aggravated I just told him to do what he wanted. And there he is."

"You know, it seems almost like a family reunion," Mrs. Carver said as she started looking around again. "Everybody from the Ida B. is here, aren't they?"

"Seems like it." A sickening nausea swept over Brenda as she thought about getting on the stage and reading from her manuscript.

Mrs. Carver seemed to notice her nervousness and placed a reassuring hand on her daughter's shoulder. "Baby, you're going to do fine. We're all so proud of you."

"But what if they don't like it?"

"There she goes with that stuff again," Sharif said as he sat down next to Brenda. "Miss Janet, would you tell her that everyone's going to love it. How can they not like something that's written about them?"

"Based on them, Sharif," Brenda said nervously. "Loosely based on them."

Sharif nodded. "And that, too."

Brenda let her head loll back on the chair. "Oh, Sharif. This is so crazy. It's not even a book yet. It's just a bunch of pieces of paper. Why couldn't we wait until I could see if I could get it published?"

"Because the victory isn't in getting it published. The victory is in you actually getting it finished. And I think everybody is going to be really inspired with your accomplishment." Sharif kissed her on the forehead. "Now get ready, 'cause there's my cue. I've got to get ready to introduce you."

Brenda gripped her mother's arm. "And you really think this is a good idea, too. Right?" she whispered.

"I think it's the best idea in the world," Mrs. Carver said tenderly. "And I think this is one of the proudest days in my life."

"Oh, Mom,"

"Shhh." Mrs. Carver put her finger to her lips. "Sharif's getting ready to speak." She motioned for Bootsy, Shaniqua, and Yusef to hurry over and take their seats. "Hurry up and go get Jumah from Miss Gracie," she whispered to Shaniqua. "I want to make sure he sees his mommy's big moment."

"Good afternoon. I want to welcome all of you to the opening of the Ida B. Wells-Barnett Community Center—a center that will provide a safe haven for our children, and will also have recreational activities for them. A center that will also provide needed social services and assistance for our senior citizens." Sharif waited until the applause died down before continuing. "Usually the politicians and government officials are thanked for their help in finding the money to open a community center, but instead of thanking them individually, I offer a blanket thank-you to all for doing what you're supposed to do."

Again Sharif waited for the applause to die down. "We have a special treat for you this afternoon, but before I introduce our special guest, I have an announcement to make. Please join me in congratulating Ricky White, who just received a letter this morning informing him that he was accepted at MIT, the Massachusetts Institute of Technology." Sharif started clapping furiously, and the crowd joined in.

"And now, without further ado, I'd like to introduce our special guest, Brenda Carver, who will be reading from her manuscript entitled 'Ida B.' "

A buzz spread through the crowd as Brenda rose from her seat. She stood there for a moment, trying to will herself to move toward the stage. She closed her eyes and took a deep breath, but still couldn't force herself forward.

"Wait a minute! Wait a minute!" Brenda swung around to see Rosa, made up like Cleopatra with heavy eye makeup and wearing a flowing white gown, running down the aisle. "Wait, she ain't got her flowers."

She grabbed Brenda, and pulled her into an embrace, crushing the bouquet between them. "I'm sorry I'm so late, but I had to come straight from the matinee." She sucked her teeth and started wiping at Brenda's face. "*Coño,* I got some of this damn makeup on you."

"Ladies and gentleman, I'd like to introduce to you a VIP who has just arrived," Sharif said from the stage. "Please join me in welcoming Rosa Rivera, who's starring in the Off-Off Broadway play, *Heart of the Nile*."

Rosa swung around to face Sharif, who gave her a wink. She broke out in a wide smile, then turned back to the crowd and performed a perfect, and obviously well practiced, bow.

"And now I'd like to once again call up to the stage," Sharif said when the applause died down, "Miss Brenda Carver, who will be reading from her novel, 'Ida B.' "

Brenda passed her smashed flowers to her mother, took a deep breath, and headed to the stage, manuscript in hand. As she embraced Sharif, she whispered in his ear, "I'm going to kill you if they boo me." Instead of answering, Sharif squeezed her arm, and led her to the chair that had been placed on the stage.

She took a deep breath and started talking. "I'd like you all to know that my book is based on my life at the Ida B. Wells-Barnett Tower, which was recently torn down—"

"Louder! We can't hear you!"

Brenda blushed and looked up to see who had shouted out. Standing against the back wall she made out a short wiry, young man with short locks, a neatly trimmed Vandyke, and dark glasses. He smiled when he realized she was looking at him, and flashed a half-smile.

Oh, my God, it's Vincent, she thought as her breath quickened. *He actually came out to hear me read.* A grin spread across her face. *But then why not? It isn't like he had to walk into a bookstore. At least not yet.*

She took a deep breath and began again. "As I was saying, my book is based on my life at the Ida B., but let me assure all of you"—she looked directly at Vincent as she spoke—"the names have been changed to protect the innocent."

Vincent grinned and flashed her a thumbs-up, and Brenda bowed her head and began to read.

"Little Belinda Carter watched as her uncles carried her mattress into the brand-new building that she had watched being built from her old bedroom window just five blocks away. . . ."